# SPINDLE of SIN

## ONCE UPON A WICKED VILLAIN

# CANDACE ROBINSON
# AMBER R. DUELL

For those who believe there is more to a villain

# AURA

O nce upon a time, the Court of Moonstone was stolen
by a dragon shifter. Aura's great-great-grandparents had
once ruled that mountainous territory, so in a sense, she
was born a princess. A princess of nothing, but she was
still a daughter of a baron, betrothed to the prince of the
Starnight Court since birth. Her family might not have a
court of their own, but being part of an original royal
bloodline was something the Starnight King wanted for
his son. It seemed she was destined to become a true
princess after all.

The only thing standing between Aura and her
birthright was the wedding ceremony. And what came
after. She smiled at the undergarments in her hands.
Inviting, enticing, *seductive*. Tomorrow night she would

wear them for Prince Pax, and finally, she would get to have him press his hard length inside her, take her maidenhead, and show her how good it would feel to be tumbled, to be *fucked*.

With a content sigh, Aura tucked the sheer fabric back into the box and rested it beside her wedding gown. She ran her fingers across the silky material of the dress, along each dip and curve, the perfect lines and seams. The material was form-fitting with a few layers of lace and a high collar. She'd been waiting her entire life for this day—her purpose—to become the prince's wife, and, eventually, his queen.

While Starnight wasn't as large as Moonstone, Aura would rule her subjects with kindness. Even if she held magic, she wouldn't have attempted to take back a court she barely knew anything about. Moonstone flourished more now, though the newest king was known to be positively sinful when it came to pleasure, and the rumors were that his partners desired it. *No one* in Grimm's twelve courts inherited magic. It was only wielded through spelled objects and potions that very few could master, generally only sorcerers, but some could shift into animals such as the Moonstone king.

Taking a breath, Aura lifted the handheld mirror beside her bed and peered at her reflection—her long blonde curls, her bright violet eyes. "This is what you've always dreamt of," she murmured, setting the mirror back down, hoping she would be enough for the Starnight Court.

A light rap came at the window and her heart thumped with glee. Aura bit her lip, knowing precisely who the late-night visitor would be. The prince she'd finally met months ago, the one she'd been dreaming about her entire life while waiting for her twenty-first birthday to arrive to prepare for the royal wedding. As soon as she was of that age, her family had traveled to a remote cottage not far from the palace grounds to begin marriage preparations.

Aura drew the velvety curtains aside, peering through the glass. She caught a glimpse of Pax's short chestnut hair, swept to the side beneath the moonlight, and pushed up the window.

"May I come inside?" he asked, his brown irises meeting hers as he pressed his callused palm to her cheek, sending butterflies thrashing within her stomach.

"I don't think it's a good idea," she whispered, her smile growing wide. "You aren't supposed to see the dress until our wedding day."

"I'm here to see what's *beneath* the dress." He grinned, his finger trailing down her collarbone, to between her breasts. "I need you, Aura."

Pax may have seen her nearly bare already, touched her to orgasm, but they still hadn't been together in the way she yearned for. He'd wanted to wait for their wedding day, for them both to give themselves to one another as their firsts, even though she'd desperately desired to have him before that.

"Do you want to go near the lake?" she asked. Pax would take her there so they could be as loud as they wanted when they brought each other pleasure. And she needed to feel him now, to have his strong arms holding her, his deft fingers skating up her flesh, along her thighs.

"We don't have time. My father wants me back soon. But"—he brought her face closer to his, his hot breath brushing her nose, smelling of grapes—"I need your mouth on me." His lips captured her own, his tongue flicking against hers, the taste of wine on him delicious.

"Then stay quiet and come in," Aura said softly, backing away from him to grab a fur blanket from her bed. She quickly covered the wedding gown just as he stepped into her small room and closed the window behind him.

Pax inched toward her, his lips catching hers once more while guiding her fingers to the laces of his trousers. "Please me like you always do."

"As you wish, Your Highness." Aura knelt before him and unlaced the ties, then drew his trousers down, freeing his large cock.

He gripped her head gently, guiding her mouth to him. Aura had been taught from an early age to remain innocent until her wedding day, but when Pax had wanted her in the same way she'd wanted him, they'd decided to experiment with other forms of pleasure. Pax was to be her husband, the man she was always meant to marry. She loved his touches, had begged to explore more with him, but he'd always stopped things before they went too far.

Aura skimmed her hands around his strong thighs, grasping his firm buttocks when he slid his throbbing length inside her mouth. Pax groaned quietly, not nearly as loud as he was when they were alone at the lake, while thrusting his hips softly. Aura pumped him, anticipating what he would do to her after, craving the pleasure he would give her before leaving.

Another groan escaped Pax as his cock twitched and he spilled himself into her mouth. She swallowed his salty arousal down, relishing it.

Aura helped pull his trousers up, then stood from the floor. Just as she was about to press her lips to his, to lead him to her bed, he lifted her chin. "I want to taste you just as badly, but I'm afraid I must leave."

Her mother had told her never to argue with the prince. Besides for the love blooming within her for Pax, being an obedient wife was her duty, for her family, her sisters. The betrothal money would ensure her siblings were taken care of, and that they could choose their own futures. "It's all right," Aura said. "Tomorrow night we can have each other fully."

"And for all the days to follow," he murmured, his thumb drifting across her lower lip, her heart accelerating.

"We'll be one another's firsts and lasts."

He pressed a chaste kiss to the back of her hand. "Goodnight," he said before slipping out the window. She closed the glass and watched as he disappeared into the night but not in the direction of the palace.

Two hands grasped Aura's shoulders, shaking her awake. "It's time to get up," her twin sister, Liana, sang. Aura peeled open her eyes to find Liana covered in specks of flour, her golden hair swept behind her in a messy braid. All five of the sisters had the same golden hair of their mother and the violet eyes of their father.

"What are you doing?" Aura asked with a yawn, tossing back the fur blankets.

"I just finished baking for the wedding."

5

Aura arched a brow. "The palace will have plenty of desserts for the occasion. You don't need to worry about that today."

Liana feigned disappointment as her hand pressed to her heart. "But they won't have *my* desserts."

"That is true," Aura agreed, her mouth practically salivating while thinking about how glorious Liana's pastries always tasted. Even before arriving at the cottage, they'd only had a few servants. Their mother genuinely enjoyed cooking and cleaning, whereas Aura hadn't inherited the gift to love either of those. For her, cooking things meant burning them to a crisp.

"I'm so relieved you were born first." Liana sighed, combing her fingers through a few knots in Aura's hair. "I don't think I could survive being royalty."

Aura rested her palm on Liana's shoulder. "You'll have your own shop soon."

"I would fight you on this if I knew you didn't love him, but because you do, I'll gladly open the bakery," Liana said, just as children's laughter erupted from another room.

"What are the little ones getting into now?" Aura pushed up from the bed, knowing when her younger sisters were giggling it meant mischief. Their parents hadn't planned on having any more children after their first set of twins and their other sister, Hana. But five years ago, a miracle happened, as their mother would say, and another set of twins had come into their lives.

"I let them bake with me. I need helpers once I open the shop, so they better get the experience now." Liana then led Aura down the narrow hallway toward the kitchen. When they'd arrived, the cottage had already been decorated with dull gray paintings that her mother never would've hung in their own home. Succulents and ivy in bright pots always filled the rooms.

Saffron and Fern sat on the counter in the kitchen, covered in flour, their tiny hands molding clumpy spheres with the dough.

Aura laughed as she scooped Saffron off the counter first, then Fern.

"Look what I made!" Saffron shouted, holding up her dough as she displayed her missing front tooth, her blonde curls tangled.

"Stop always trying to get the attention. Look at mine!" Fern cried, her simple dress too large on her tiny frame.

Aura knelt before them and inspected the balls of dough. "They are equally beautiful. Now, Liana will help you get cleaned up. We have a big day ahead of us, and you both have a very important task."

"Drop the flower petals," Saffron said.

"In a line that isn't too neat," Fern added.

The door opened just as her younger sisters scampered out of the room, arguing with one another about who would drop the first petal while Liana tailed them, telling them to hush. Aura's mother stepped over the threshold, her hand around Hana's shoulder. Hana appeared positively rumpled, her tunic and trousers torn as if she'd tumbled a shifter, which Aura was certain she had. The middle sister was eighteen, but she'd always done what she wanted, regardless of what their mother told her, and at times, Aura was maybe even a bit envious of Hana and her boldness.

"I found your sister half naked in the woods," her

mother spat. "On your wedding day, no less. You better be glad your father is already at the palace."

"Mama," Hana drawled. "I was just about to get cleaned up. I'll be ready in time for our departure—no worries about that." As she sauntered past Aura toward her bedroom, she whispered in her ear, "I saw the *precious* prince slip into your room last night."

"What did she say?" her mother asked with a huff.

"Nothing, Mama." Aura rolled her eyes. "She said she's going to help me dress for the wedding, just as you asked."

"She *is* wonderful at accentuating beauty through hair and powders. But what am I going to do with her? Especially after you're gone." Aura's mother lifted one of Liana's cookies, her shoulders dropping when she took a large bite. As always, the sugar seemed to relax her mother a fraction.

"Let Hana be Hana. That's all we can do. She's not a babe any longer."

"She didn't need to do this on your wedding day, though."

"The wedding isn't until this evening and Hana is always on time for everything, regardless of what she does. It's fine, Mama."

"Tomorrow I'll only have four daughters under this roof." Tears filled her mother's eyes.

Aura gently patted her mother's shoulder. "Father must be happy about that. Less noise and all."

"He won't know what to do with himself when all our girls are gone one day." She shook her head, taking another bite of the cookie. "Now, let's prepare you a bath fit for a princess."

Once the bath was ready and infused with rose and lavender oils, Aura slipped into the hot water. She scrubbed thoroughly, wanting the scents to absorb as deep as they could into her flesh, for her skin to be as soft as velvet for the wedding night.

When the warmth started to leave the water, Aura slid on her robe and padded into her room, the sounds of her mother telling the younger twins to stop playing around and to hurry echoing down the hall.

Aura shut the door behind her and took out the sheer undergarments, drawing them up her legs beneath the robe. The anticipation of feeling Pax's skilled fingers peeling them from her body consumed her. She bit the inside of her cheek to stop from getting aroused to the point where she itched to touch herself. Her orgasm tonight would need to be a well-awaited one. It had been over a week since Pax's fingers had stroked her clit, dipped inside her heat.

The door cracked open and Aura whirled around to find Hana, her golden hair pulled up into a high braided bun, a blue silk dress hugging her curvy form.

Aura's eyes widened in awe. "You look beautiful."

"Figured I needed to make myself presentable for the occasion." Hana chuckled. "I heard you finally come out of the bathing chambers after pampering yourself forever. I assumed I'd better get in here before Mama asks if I'm going to sneak off again."

"If you sneak off after the ceremony, I promise I won't tell." Aura pressed a finger over her lips and grinned.

Hana winked before helping Aura out of the robe and into a corset, tightening it until she could barely breathe, but it would make the wedding gown look perfect. For now, Hana buttoned a simple gown over Aura's lithe form. The royal carriage would take them to the palace later that day where they would finish preparing for the evening.

"So you believe Pax to be the one?" Hana asked, her expression growing serious.

"There's never been anyone else." Even as a child when Aura fell asleep, she would wonder about him, wonder if he would fall in love with her once they met. "He told me there's never been anyone else for him either."

Hana frowned, seeming to mull something over. "And you believe him?"

She nodded. "Even if he had been with women before, it wouldn't matter, as long as I'm the only one now. I've waited my entire life for this moment."

After a few beats of silence, Hana spoke, "Listen, I should tell you something..."

"What is it?" Aura leaned in, curious as to why her sister trailed off.

"It's nothing." Hana paused and pressed her lips together. She shook her head, waving her hand in the air. "I've just been with the hawk shifter quite a few times now is all. Though he did leave me alone last night after I fell asleep in his arms."

"You like him!" Aura gasped, then lightly shoved her sister in the arm.

"I think Father would rather like him. He's good at hunting. Mama, not so much." Her smile became sly at the last part, and Aura knew Hana took pleasure in ruffling their mother's feathers. Hana brushed her fingers over the lacy skirt of the wedding gown. "Now tell me, do you plan to have the prince peel this immaculate dress from your body or rip it right off?"

"That's my little secret." Aura laughed. Her center throbbed at the idea of Pax tearing the fabric off her, then worshiping her in the way he always promised. When he'd pleasured her before, he'd always been gentle, maybe even too gentle.

But tonight that would change.

# RUSH

*K*ing of Sin wasn't simply what the court called Rush—
it was his way of life.

*And what a fucking life it was.*

Rush gripped Mylah's hips as he pounded into her
core. She groaned around the cock in her mouth, leaning
back on her hands and knees to meet the king's thrusts.
The other man—Tanix, one of Rush's guards—gathered
her ash brown hair and guided her to take him deeper into
her throat. She made a small, shocked squeak from the
force of it and the guard eased up.

"Sorry," Tanix murmured.

Rush wasn't sorry. He'd fucked Mylah more than
once and knew first-hand how rough she liked it. She had
always swallowed him down to the hilt, an impressive

feat. All without any prompting or guidance from him. If anything, they were taking it easy on her tonight.

A knee bumped Rush's thigh and he pried his gaze away from Mylah's firm ass to the two maids beside them. Both naked. Both flushed with pleasure. Neither had participated in any of his solo or group fucks before, and he wasn't sure of their names yet. They'd only come into the room to clean, but he'd immediately offered them the chance to join. They accepted his invitation without hesitation.

The redhead smirked at the king, her legs wide open where she lay on the floor among an array of silk pillows. A blonde's face was buried in the redhead's pussy. Rush studied them as he plowed into the woman before him, the way the redhead responded so well to the tongue against her clit. He would have them both when he finished fucking Mylah. Devour them. Fuck them until they were unraveled completely and ruined for all the courts. He knew how to pleasure a woman so they begged for more.

The blonde gasped as he trailed a hand up her bare back. Rush drank in the sound before moving his hand to pinch the redhead's peaked nipple.

"Your Majesty," she groaned, her eyelids fluttering as she neared her orgasm.

"Fuck," Tanix growled.

Rush focused on Mylah again. On his own cock as it sank into her dripping pussy from behind. His body tensed with his impending finish, but he wasn't ready for the night to end. Not until he'd tasted all of the women in the room. Pulling out, he lowered himself and lapped at Mylah's sex while she sucked the guard on her hands

13

and knees. She ground her core against his face and, once again, allowed Tanix to drive his cock into her throat. Rush gripped his own hard length and squeezed until pain and pleasure stormed through him but enough to hold back from coming. His balls grew heavy, precum leaking from his tip. He was going to come all over—

"Rush!" Astor shouted. The dark-haired hawk shifter broke into the sitting room, shirtless, lithe muscles on display. He paused, his gaze drifting around the room, taking in the slick bodies grinding against one another. Finally, he settled on Mylah sucking on Tanix until she was red in the face. Astor had participated in the king's orgies once or twice. But, while he was certainly enjoying the sight, it wasn't *only* desire that filled Astor's expression.

"Care to join?" Rush asked, shifting back onto his heels to talk to his friend.

"No, I just returned from fucking Hana." Still, he adjusted his trousers. "Should I return later?"

The king smirked at Astor from over Mylah's ass. "That depends. Is it important?"

"It's not … *not* important." He rubbed a hand over the back of his neck and winced. "Fuck, Rush. If I hadn't just exhausted myself before coming here…"

"Next time." Rush rose onto his knees, wiping Mylah's arousal from his face, and lined his cock back up with her core. She squirmed with desire. He gave her ass a light smack and plunged back inside her. "Do you need to talk to me about *her*?"

"Yes," Astor confirmed, always knowing the *her* meant Aura.

His breath caught. Perhaps it was time—time to take

the prince's fiancée from him. Bring her here. Use her to get his revenge on Pax. *Finally.* It had been two years since he vowed to destroy the bastard, and he didn't want to make it to three. "Good. Give me a moment."

Slamming into Mylah harder and faster than before, Rush found his release. He grunted as he came, spilling into her, then stood. "Sorry to cut this short," he told them, his voice husky.

Moans filled the room as the others continued, unaffected by the King of Sin's impending departure. By the time Rush slipped his black trousers on, Tanix had flipped Mylah onto her back and buried his cock in her pussy.

Rush frowned. He wanted to hear her come and see what the two women would do next—with him, specifically. But some things were more important than pleasure. *Very few things.*

Wordlessly, he followed Astor into the hall. Half of the wall sconces were lit and firelight danced over the dark stone, casting the portraits of his ancestors in a ghoulish light. Rush flicked a glance up at the one of his mother and father on their wedding day. She wore a deep red gown of silk while his father's black formalwear was adorned with the ceremonial sash of a king. Black to match his father's dragon. Rush had inherited the same onyx scales from his father and his mother's silver dragon eyes. But now he had no family. No parents. No sister. The king, the queen, and Princess Constance were all dead.

"You're running out of household staff to corrupt," Astor jested, a smirk playing on his thin lips.

Rush chuckled and clapped his friend on the shoulder.

They practically grew up together, and, as the king's most trusted friend, Astor knew how things were at the palace. They'd both fucked their way through the city during their adolescence, learning all there was to learn about pleasuring women. And, eventually, Rush earned the name King of Sin. "Why do you assume I'm corrupting them?"

"Please. I've known you for too long." The hawk shifter turned down a side hallway and pushed open the door to a smaller, private sitting room. His bedchamber was on the other side of the frosted glass doors, the rooms permanently reserved for the shifter when he chose to stay in the palace. Two overstuffed chairs sat in front of a smoldering fireplace, and Astor sunk into one of the cushions with a sigh. "All humor aside, I need to talk to you."

Rush nodded, then perched in the opposite chair. "The would-be Princess of Starnight. Is it about our plan to take her, or is there something else you need?"

"There's a small issue with the timeline." Astor rubbed the back of his neck again, a nervous habit of his.

More issues? There had been enough of those already. Bargaining for a spell with a sorceress, meticulously planning his revenge until he located everything he needed... Rush lifted his brows and waited for Astor to continue. When he didn't, the king said, *"Well?"*

A flush raced up the hawk shifter's neck, filling his cheeks. "When Hana told me the wedding was next month, it didn't occur to me that it would be only days away. We were expecting to take Aura in two weeks, but the wedding is tomorrow."

"Tomorrow?" Rush boomed. He would be damned if

Pax married *anyone* that gave him the potential of happiness, but especially Aura, a rightful heir to Rush's throne. The hawk shifter hadn't been close to Pax in childhood like Rush, yet even he hated the bastard. "What the fuck, Astor? I want her *before* the wedding."

"I'm aware. That's why I left Hana in the middle of the night to tell you."

"If I didn't know any better, I'd say you're starting to have feelings for the girl," Rush drawled. "Which would be monumentally foolish."

The color drained from Astor's face. "Whether or not that's true, I have no qualms over you abducting the older sister. But it will need to be sooner than we'd thought."

Rush sat up straight and held up a hand to silence him. His pulse roared in his ears. Inside him, his dragon woke, tense and ready to fight whatever danger had presented itself. Claws sank into Rush's inner muscles as his other form inched closer to the surface. He huffed a smoky breath as the beast used Rush's eyes to take in their surroundings. *Everything is fine,* Rush soothed. *Calm the fuck down before you destroy my palace.* He hadn't lost control in years and wouldn't do so now at the thought of achieving his revenge tonight. The dragon eased back a fraction— not because of Rush's warning, but because there was no enemy here—and settled on its haunches. Waiting. For what exactly, Rush wasn't certain.

*Fucking hell.* The spoiled prince had fucked his way through the twelve courts, and Rush had always felt pity for whoever his fiancée was. But that had all changed in a single breath. Rush clenched his jaw.

"Everyone says Aura adores him," Astor scoffed. "If only she knew what a bastard the man really is."

17

*If only*. But Aura would pay for her foolishness. His plan would be less painful for her though, so she should be grateful to him for his decision.

"And Pax?" Rush asked carefully. If Pax loathed the girl, it would make things less sweet, but still worth the trouble. It also meant Astor could continue fucking Hana until he grew bored of her. If she ever discovered Aura's fate, it would ignite a hate so deep that any feelings she might have for Astor would turn to dust. That, however, was not Rush's problem. "How does the prince feel about her?"

Astor shrugged. "She fucking shines like the sun, how do you think he feels? She'll be the proper little wife to squeeze out a few Starnight heirs, but he's not about to keep his cock in his trousers."

Rush's dragon shifted beneath his skin, sending a pulse of vibrations through his body. He shook out his hands, releasing the tension he'd unknowingly built in his muscles. *Some things never change.* He leaned forward, elbows on his knees, and stared into the glowing embers. *And some things change forever.*

"I don't like that look on your face," Astor mumbled.

"No?" With a smirk, the King of Sin settled back into his chair. "When have you ever shied away from creating mayhem?"

Astor lifted a brow. "Since right now?"

"Liar." He gave a low laugh. "Now, quickly, tell me everything you know about the pending nuptials before I leave."

# AURA

The carriage jostled against the rocky ground. Aura held Saffron in her lap and glanced across from her—Hana's pale face became green tinged as she brought a fist to her mouth. With her other arm, Hana kept a firm grip on Fern while the child slept against her.

"I told you to drink the herbal tea before the journey. You never listen," their mother said, running a gloved hand down her face.

Aura smiled as Hana shot their mother a glare. To be fair, the last time Hana was given tea during one of their journeys, she'd lost her entire supper on the carriage floor, including the tops of Aura's shoes, from the constant bouncing.

"I can't wait to see you in the wedding gown." Giving

a happy sigh, their mother clasped her hands together and bumped her shoulder into Aura's. By the heavy scent of lavender striking her nose, her mother had spritzed herself one too many times with the perfume. Her mother was dressed in her finest attire—a yellow dress of silk with a fur cloak and sparkling jewelry. Something she'd been saving to wear for this special occasion.

"You already saw her in it," Hana pointed out.

"Yes, but not at a *royal* wedding at the palace." A dreamy look sparkled in her mother's deep brown eyes before settling on Liana. She leaned forward, gently pulling the recipe journal from her daughter's hands and setting it beside her lacy brown gown on the carriage seat. "Our family suffered in the past, but fate has finally seen fit to give us a different path."

Aura was thankful her family would be taken care of, that her sisters would never have to worry for anything. So many blessings. "With or without a palace, I'm pleased to marry for love. I'm grateful for everything." She thought about the night before, her lips and tongue on the prince's length, the sweet kiss he'd given to her hand before leaving.

"All hail, Princess Aura!" Saffron shouted, lifting her straw doll high into the air as Aura drew her little sister closer so she didn't slip from her lap in her excitement.

"I would choose a baking shop over a stuffy palace any day." Liana grinned, then gazed longingly at her cracked leather journal beside her. The carriage hit another rock, thrusting them all to the side, her mother practically knocking Aura and Saffron from the seat.

"I can't wait to get out of here. I would've rather walked," Hana groaned, gently placing Fern between her

20

and Liana, the younger sister not even rousing. She reclined back in her seat and gripped her stomach.

"Stop acting dramatic," her mother snapped, waving a hand in the air as if she was swatting something away.

"Me? *Dramatic?*" Hana shot back.

Aura sent a silent prayer up to the gods that they would reach the palace soon so they wouldn't have to be cooped up in this forsaken carriage together any longer. Traveling with her family always ended in bickering unless their father was there. He could always keep their mother's attention focused on him and entertain her with his calming words.

Saffron dropped her doll on the floor for the hundredth time, most likely as an excuse to get out of the seat.

Liana bent over and scooped Saffron into her lap with the doll. She then reached into her satchel and fished out a sugar cookie. "Here, Saffy."

"Oooh," Saffron said as she plucked the cookie from Liana's grip with a big smile.

Fern yawned, cracking open her eyes. Her gaze pinned to the cookie, her nose as good as a wolf's with how she could always sniff out a dessert. "What about me?"

"You already had plenty," her mother said. "I saw you sneak out a handful earlier from the case meant for the celebration. Besides, I don't want crumbs on your gowns before the wedding!"

Aura rolled her eyes and leaned forward, breaking the cookie in Saffron's hand in half, then giving the piece to Fern.

"That's mine!" Saffron whined, her rosy lips turning

into the smallest of pouts.

"Hush, you can share," Liana said as she cocked her head.

Fern stuck out her tongue at Saffron when she thought no one was looking, then smiled as she bit into the cookie. The younger twins were both dressed in pink velvet gowns with pink jewels on the front of their white shoes, their hair in loose curls.

It was only now that Aura truly realized that she wouldn't see her sisters every day, wouldn't get to hear her father tell the little ones stories, or see her mother knit blankets while humming. They would be leaving the temporary cottage and returning to their home past the mountains. The palace would be new territory for her, and the only person she was close to there was Pax. Her dream had always been to be the prince's bride, but being a princess was more than being his wife. No matter how much her mother had taught her, there would always be more to learn.

Aura stared out the small window at the emerald green foliage drifting by. She tried not to listen as her mother reminded Hana to behave herself as if she were still a babe.

"Oh, Mama, you know I *always* behave," Hana drawled.

After a few more jostles of the carriage, above the tops of pine trees, a palace with four sky-scraping towers slipped into view. Black flecked the ivory stone where it shone beneath the sun as if it were a night sky in reverse hues.

The carriage curved through an iron gate with guards on either side. They passed several statues of animals

22

holding stars toward the sky, all blessing their court, Starnight.

Aura's lips parted as they wove around the gardens. Flowers. So many bright flowers were strung together, hovering above where the ceremony would take place. Strings of garland blossoming with colorful peonies and orchids hung sporadically. Her favorites. Pax had chosen these blooms just for her and her stomach danced with butterflies at his thoughtfulness.

They went out a little farther, past the pond and ducks, to where a small rectangular cream tent awaited her—the location where the bride was to be prepared. The carriage drew to a stop and Aura and Hana kissed their sisters and mother goodbye. Her mother was to meet with Aura's father and the king to discuss a few matters while Liana watched over the little ones.

Their mother grasped Aura's wrist, her voice soft. "If you need me or anyone else, the guard can retrieve us."

"Everything will be fine," Aura soothed her.

She stepped out beside Hana, allowing the driver to shut the carriage door. Aura went to grab her luggage with her wedding things, but the driver stepped in front of her. "I'll get it for you, my lady," he said, bowing his head.

"And that brown one too," Hana started as she studied him closely. "No, not that one, the other one."

Aura turned to face the tent where a middle-aged guard with auburn hair and fine lines around his eyes stood. A silver sash draped across one shoulder of his blue uniform and a sword hung at his side.

"If there's anything else you need in there, let me know, my lady." The guard bowed his head and held up the tent's entrance.

Aura glanced over her shoulder, watching the carriage head toward the palace before slipping into the lantern-lit tent. She blinked in surprise, having expected something simple, but this was perfect. A chestnut vanity hugged a corner, two velvet chairs awaited them, more floral vines were strung across the ceiling, and fruit, pastries, and a pitcher of honey water covered a table. Beside it lingered vase after vase filled with orchids and peonies. Underneath one rested a small folded sheet of paper, her name written in cursive on it.

With a smile, she lifted the note and read the words.

*See you soon, my dazzling bride.*

Aura bit her lip and smiled wider, anxious to see her prince.

"Thank the stars I'm with you and Liana is with Mama." Hana blew out a breath, drawing the wedding gown out from the luggage and placing it on a hook hanging from one of the posts holding up the tent.

Aura poured them each a glass of water and handed one to Hana. "You truly did help me pick out the perfect gown."

Hana drank a sip from her glass, then unpacked the powders and combs once Aura sank into the plush chair. Her gaze lifted to Aura and a line formed between her brows as she studied her. "Are you sure you want to get married? I know I've asked you this several times lately, but I want to make certain."

"Of course I do." She placed her hand on top of Hana's, halting her from setting down a brush. "And I'm proud that you're the one to help me prepare for the wedding. A servant wouldn't have felt the same."

Hana's face softened. "I'll do anything to always see

you happy, Aura. Regardless of what Mama thinks. I know I'm not supposed to have one, and even though I love you all, you're my favorite sister."

Aura winked. "I won't tell anyone."

"All right, so you're not my favorite anymore," Hana huffed as she brought a comb through Aura's tangled lock. Her sister had been at it a while, complaining that she should've ran a brush through it right after Aura's bath. "Your hair is akin to a nest of hawks."

"I think you just wanted to bring up the word hawk." Aura laughed. "When are you planning to see him again?"

"Hopefully soon." She grinned, the comb slicing through the knot. "There!"

"You'll have to introduce me to him."

"He's shy, but I will."

Hana braided the top half of Aura's hair into a crown, then mirrored her weaving with a few single plaits across her locks. Aura looked from the dress to the basket of flowers. "Perhaps we should put the gown on before putting the flowers in my hair."

"Powders first. We wouldn't want you ruining your gown." Hana then added rosy powders to Aura's cheeks and eyes, followed by a pale shade to her lips that held a scent of strawberries.

Hana loosened the buttons of Aura's dress until she was in nothing but her corset and sheer undergarments. Her sister lowered the light fabric of the wedding gown for Aura to step into it, then laced the back of it up. The silk hugged her lithe form just right and the collar was high, hiding her cleavage but not the shape of her breasts. As lovely as the dress was, she couldn't wait for Pax to peel it away from her body after speaking their vows to one another.

Farther away, flutes and stringed instruments played. "People are arriving," her sister said, sliding tiny blue and pink flowers into Aura's hair. Once she pressed the last small bud between two plaits, Hana turned her to face the mirror on the vanity. "Even though you looked like a princess before, you do even more now."

Aura gazed into the glass, tears pricking her eyes. "Hana, you truly work wonders."

"Your palette isn't a hard one to work with when you're naturally beautiful." She placed her hands on her hips. "Now, no more tears—I don't want the powders ruined before the wedding."

"How much time do we have left?"

"Someone should've been here already," Hana said, scowling. She stepped out of the tent, and Aura could hear her talking to the guard. "Why hasn't my father come yet? Are you supposed to take her there instead?"

"Your father is coming to collect Aura once Prince Pax is ready. His Highness was delayed and is running late."

"Late?" Hana snapped. "What better things does he have to do on his wedding day?"

"I wouldn't say such things of the prince," the guard reprimanded.

"Hmph." Hanna slipped back inside. "I'm going to see what's going on. Father should've at least come

26

already."

"Unless he was told not to." Aura shrugged. "*His Highness* better have a good excuse. I'll return shortly."

Aura watched her sister storm from the tent, unsure what had gotten into her. She'd never been like this when anyone was late. It was Aura's wedding day, but if a problem had arisen, throwing a tantrum wouldn't make the situation better. The prince had promised a wedding to unite not only their families, but their love. And she believed in that.

Tapping her fingers against the table, she read over Pax's words several times, then brushed her digits along each of the flowers as she waited for the nervousness brewing within her to subside. She continued to linger, to wait, to pace, but Hana never returned, and more than enough time had passed.

A scuffing sound followed by a grunt echoed outside and Aura froze. She glanced around to find any sort of weapon. Only a fork rested beside the fruit on the table. Even though she knew it was a poor choice, she grabbed the utensil. Better than nothing.

Heart pounding, Aura clenched the fork and pulled back the fabric of the tent to the night. Torches blazed, lighting the area, the blossoming trees, but the guard was gone.

She took a hesitant step outside into the cool air. In the distance, the instruments continued to play, the area lit with lanterns. It wouldn't take her long to walk to the garden where everyone would be gathered. But then a shadow slipped out from behind a tree, becoming clearer as he sauntered toward her. He raked a hand through silky black hair that brushed his shoulders. Beneath the bright torches, eyes of molten silver, with a thin black line circling the irises, met hers, and she blinked. She ignored the man's strong jaw and his lovely features on a ruggedly handsome face. A handsome face that was part of a man who was most likely up to no good.

Aura held the fork out in front of her, feeling like a fool, but it could draw blood if necessary. "Who are you?"

"A guard," he purred, seductive, alluring, as he inched closer. "I think it's time I escort you to the garden."

She narrowed her eyes. This man was a liar, and a terrible one at that. He wasn't even disguising himself in guard attire—instead, he wore a rumpled black tunic and wrinkled trousers as if he'd just tumbled someone.

"Where's Hana?" she asked between clenched teeth.

"The last I saw of your sister, she was trying to find out why the prince is so *busy* on his wedding day." He smirked. "And she was about to stumble upon something rather interesting."

Aura's heart dropped, dread filling her as she clenched the utensil tighter. "What have you done to Prince Pax?" There wasn't a sword at the stranger's waist for him to wield, so she darted forward while aiming her fork at his chest.

He moved fast, knocking the utensil from her hand and pulling her tightly against his firm chest, an alluring smoky scent enveloping her. Just as she parted her mouth to scream, his hand clamped over her lips and he backed her against a tree. "I'll tell you a little secret, Aura," he cooed. "The wedding's off."

# 4

# RUSH

Rush leaned in so the tip of his nose grazed Aura's ear, inhaling her scent, something that he could only describe as starlight. But this woman was nothing like starlight— she had cast a shadow upon him, even if she didn't know it. A woman who could've been the Princess of Moonstone. "You're mine," he whispered to her. Her purpose would now be to return what was ripped from his territory. From him.

Aura drew in a sharp breath and clawed at his forearm, her fingernails digging in, tearing flesh. Her pitiful attempts did nothing to loosen his grip. The effort brought a soft chuckle from his throat and he wondered what she would've managed to do with the fork. "Now, now, kitten. Play nice."

She thrashed and shrieked like a banshee into his palm. Not from anger, though she was clearly full of it. Her thin slipper fell from her foot as she kicked his shin, eliciting a small, pained whine from her. Rush straightened to stare down at her. She *was* a gorgeous little thing. Soft hair haloed her head and her violet eyes glimmered with an intense emotion. Oh, anger was not the correct word for what she was feeling. Fury shone back at him. And fear. *Good.*

A grin spread across Rush's face. He hadn't expected her to be so feisty, so … tempting. It would be fun to toy with her. "You *should* be afraid," he said.

The music coming from the garden cut off just in time for trumpets to blare. Either Pax had finished fucking the curvy wedding guest behind the stable, or the king had arrived to witness the ceremony. Regardless, Rush was out of time. Aura's father could come for her at any moment, given that he was meant to escort her to the ceremony. Everyone would see his dragon eventually, but he wanted to avoid the hassle of a fight.

He tugged Aura away from the tree to give himself space to shift. Aura twisted and turned in his grip, more muffled screams pouring into his palm.

Rush held her effortlessly as his dragon unfurled inside him, a great power anxious to unleash itself. Pressure built beneath his muscles until the dragon broke the surface. The pain that began as an ache quickly became a sharp sting. Rush's skin cracked and peeled. A flash of agony followed when the onyx scaled beast burst free, something Rush had grown used to. The discomfort only lasted a moment, then power, deep and raw, raged through his veins.

The tent crunched beneath his taloned foot, the ground trembling, while the other wrapped tighter around Aura. Glimmering black scales covered his massive body, and fire brimmed in his gut, his mouth tasting of ash, begging him to release it and burn the entire palace down. But that would only create an unnecessary war, one he didn't need at the moment when he had a single goal. Rush blinked to adjust to the heightened vision. His long tail swept out, ripping two large shrubs from the ground near the garden pathway. Stretching his dark wings, Rush cast Aura in shadow, and her body went unnaturally still.

Shouts rang through the air, but that was no surprise. It wasn't every day a dragon shifted in the middle of the Starnight Court. The wedding guests were already racing toward them from afar. A smirk formed on his scaly lips, baring his sharp teeth, and he narrowed his reptilian eyes at Aura.

*Such chaos,* he thought to himself. *Let's go now, shall we?*

Tightening his scaled foot around Aura's body, careful not to prick her with his talons or squeeze too hard—he *needed* her—Rush beat his iridescent obsidian wings. Once. Twice. He leaned onto his haunches and leapt into the sky as Aura remained still. The clamor of armor filled the ground below. Arrows would follow shortly, he was certain. While the tips wouldn't do much damage to him in this form, Aura's body was soft and vulnerable. He pulled her closer to his chest and flew straight up into the night sky.

The darkness swallowed them, his onyx scales camouflaging their escape. Aura's entire body was tucked into his foot, and as though coming out of a frozen spell,

31

she finally released a bloodcurdling scream. The sound like music to his ears, and he grinned as her body writhed. There was no one below to hear her or anywhere to go except to plummet to her death. As if realizing that possibility, her sounds and movements ceased.

He hated to admit it, shouldn't be thinking it, but she was more beautiful than he'd expected. If he were in Pax's position, he would've been more than satisfied to have her in his bed. Undo her hair so it spilled down her back, strip the white gown from her lithe body, and make her come hard.

But, whether or not the prince was happy with the idea of having a wife, he wasn't about to change his habits. Just before finding Aura alone and frightened outside her tent, Rush had seen the prince. His bare ass, to be exact. It had clenched with each thrust into the woman's cunt as she filled the air with moans.

"Please." Aura's voice was barely audible above the wind cutting across his ears. "You don't have to do this."

*But I do.*

If it wasn't for her, Rush might not have needed to seek revenge at all. No one else would give the same hint of sweetness to his vengeance. He sailed higher, beneath the stars, his body becoming one with the night. There weren't many dragons in the courts, but enough that Rush could feign innocence. His council, his skilled liars, could deal with any ambassadors sent to Moonstone. The Starnight King had been friends with Rush's late father, so that could be an advantage.

Rush beat his wings, the cool breeze brushing his skin as he reveled in the sense of freedom flying gave him. *He needed this.* The growing ache in his wings after being in the air for so long was nothing at the moment. Not compared to the lightness in his chest. Running the court took up most of his time in the years since his father passed and he hadn't taken to the sky nearly enough. Something he would need to remedy.

The moon followed them the entire journey, only falling behind a mountain when his palace came into view. Rush glanced down at Aura as he descended and his body jerked with surprise. Her lips were blue, teeth chattering.

*Fuck.*

He'd forgotten how cold it could get at high altitudes. At least her body was cocooned in his foot—he needed her alive for his plan to work. He released a huff of warm air, keeping his fire trapped in his belly. Aura's violet eyes widened as smoke curled around her. Rush enjoyed her gaze on him, the loathing she held. He snorted, smoke puffing from his nostrils, and she paled.

Rush dove toward the ground, his sights set on the waist-high hedges. The low vines had been forced to grow in winding designs so it was as enticing from above as it was on the ground. They curled around the red stone walkways, circling a pond where black swans swam, flowering trees, sweet-scented bushes, and a gazebo with billowing curtains.

And, at the very center, an open clearing, awaiting him.

Cracking his wings, lifting his upper body, Rush landed on his back feet. He set Aura unceremoniously on the ground and dug his talons into the pebbles. She gasped and wobbled as she stood, clinging to the long skirts of her ivory wedding gown.

Rush called his dragon back. His scales withdrew, sinking into his skin, and bones shifted. The fire in his gut was wholly contained, not a whisp of smoke remaining in his lungs. Another quick flicker of pain and the dragon was curled up inside him once more. The King of Sin stood before Aura in all his glory, without a stitch of clothing to cover his taut and muscular form. Aura released a shriek, her eyes saucering as she turned to run, as if she believed she could return to Starnight so easily. Rush grabbed her upper arm before she made it a single step.

"I can't imagine I'm the first man you've seen bare," he drawled. "Though, I imagine the size of my cock is rather shocking compared to your *precious* betrothed."

Aura whirled around and raised her hand to slap him. He circled her wrist, halting her chance. "You're wicked!" she screamed. "Take me back to the palace right fucking now."

"Or what? You'll attempt to use a fork on me again?" A slow grin spread across his face as her nostrils flared. "I told you, kitten. The wedding is off. You should be thanking me, don't you think? Marrying that prick would've been a mistake."

Her eyes narrowed. "You don't know anything about him. Or me. Or *us.*"

Rush knew exactly what Aura's life would've been like as the prince's wife. *Tragic.* "That's where you're wrong. I know more than you do about the prince, and I know he wouldn't have satisfied you. Not when he couldn't keep his trousers on when he was supposed to be at the altar with you. Humor me: why do you think he was late?" A thrill coursed through him as he awaited her response.

Aura sucked in a breath and studied his face. A blush crept up her cheeks—from anger, he suspected, but perhaps embarrassment. "He was..."

Rush's grin grew. She had no idea. Of course she didn't... "He was fucking a wedding guest behind the stable. I'm certain you would've tasted cunt on his lips if you'd had your ceremonial kiss."

"You're a liar!" Aura ripped herself from his grip and he released her. She stumbled but caught her balance. "Take me back. Why did you bring me here?"

He shrugged. If she wanted to delude herself with the image of a perfect prince, so be it. It wouldn't matter to her much longer that Pax was a skillful liar, to women especially. There was no sense in convincing her of it. "There's no going back to Starnight. You won't be leaving Moonstone again, kitten."

"You can't—"

He grabbed her by the throat, his fingers wrapping around it, digging in enough to get her attention. To let her know she was *his*. "You belong to me now. You want to tell me I can't do something?" He gave a mirthless laugh. "I can do anything I want in my court."

Aura clenched her fists into her skirts, not the least bit frightened his fingers could easily snap her neck if he wished. "Take. Me. Home."

*So you want to be difficult.* That was fine. There were ways of forcing someone to submit. "*This* is your home. You'll live in this palace until I have no further need of you."

"*Need of me?*" Her voice rose in disbelief. "What could you possibly need from *me* of all people?"

35

Rush lifted his chin and looked down his nose at her. "For now, I need you not to make a nuisance of yourself."

"You do realize this court originally belonged to my family, don't you? I should be a princess here and I demand you take me home."

"What *should be* and what *is* are two different things. Your family nearly brought this court to ruin and look at it now, *thriving*. Because of dragons. Because of *me*. If you tell anyone who you are and where you're from, I'll bring your sisters here and lock them up in cages. Understand?"

Aura inhaled sharply but nodded.

A pair of guards—Tanix and Laird—rounded the curve of the garden. Rush flicked his gaze toward them, the guards accustomed to seeing him bare after a shift, and signaled them over with a nod. Tanix, the higher ranking of the two, was twice as wide as Laird, but what the younger man lacked in muscle, he had in height.

"Meet my new pet." Rush purred, his stare pinned on Aura. Her mouth parted, her chest rising and falling with rapid breaths. While the guards were loyal to Rush, feared the dragon fire he would use on them if they betrayed their king, servants talked amongst themselves. It was best for everyone that they think she was his latest fuck. Just until he and Astor completed the spell needed for his revenge. "She'll be entertaining me for now, doing a bit of *damsel in distress* roleplay. Show the little kitten to the room adjacent to mine and make sure she doesn't escape. If she tries, strap her to the bed."

"Yes, Your Majesty," Laird said, and Tanix reached for Aura's arm.

"Don't touch me," she snarled, stepping back to avoid him.

"There she goes, getting into character." Rush chuckled. "If she doesn't follow you willingly, you have my permission to use the rope. She likes to play rough."

Aura threw him a scathing look. "If any of you lay a hand on me—"

"You'll what?" Rush cooed. He waved a dismissive hand at the two guards and they each grabbed her by an arm. No one in the palace would ask Aura her name unless she or the king gave it—the staff knew better. He turned his back on them, walking away, as Aura shouted obscenities more colorful than he expected. He wasn't sure which of them she thought was a *rutting bastard*, but Rush suspected it was him. Loathing one another would make things easier.

Rush entered the palace and two of the servants eyed his naked form with lustful gazes. But he ignored them before navigating the halls while his mind was focused entirely on his plan. The most important element to creating his spell was now under control. A finishing touch was all that stood between him and casting it.

His feet were quiet against the dark stone steps leading to the cellar once he passed a door left ajar for him. A chill ran up his spine the farther he descended, pebbling his skin. *Fuck.* He should've spared a minute to grab trousers, but, instead, he knocked on the wooden door.

Astor opened it and a fireplace held a crackling flame, greeting Rush with a wall of heat. "You look rather smug. The mission was a success, I take it?" the shifter said as he walked to a long work table covered in various glass vials filled with potions of reds, greens, or blues. A few bubbled and fizzed while others stood still. He then ground a mortar and pestle together, prepping a concoction.

Rush lifted a stained apron from a hook on the wall and wrapped it around his waist. "Of course it was." Sauntering across the room, he trailed his fingertips along a row of spell books on the wide shelves. He glanced toward the red velvet curtain hanging in the corner of the room, shielding his masterpiece from view.

"You can grab a princess from her wedding, but not a pair of trousers?" Astor grumbled.

Rush chuckled. "If you don't like my ass, don't look at it."

"How did Aura react to you bringing her here?" Astor tapped the heavy stone pestle against the side of the mortar.

"Screamed at first." If she was plotting an escape, Rush trusted his guards to thwart her plans and strap her to the bed.

Opening the lower doors of the cabinet, Rush pulled out a large, teardrop-shaped hookah. He gave the black glass a shake, the slight slosh of water still inside echoing. *Fuck.* It hadn't been cleaned out after his last use. The flavor would be terrible now, but given the long day he'd had, Rush couldn't bring himself to care.

"Already got a clean one packed and ready to go," Astor told him with a smirk. "Figured you'd need it after the long travel."

*Flying for so long after fucking the night before.* The trip back to Moonstone tested all of his physical limits, his joints aching, muscles humming from exertion, but it was worth it to fuck with Pax on his wedding day. Rush flopped down on the worn leather chaise where he slept on nights when his research went on too late.

"It's right next to you." Astor nodded toward the side table as he tapped grounded powder into a tin.

Rush groaned, leaning over to grab the blue glass. While his whole body ached, his mind raced with anticipation. There was so little left to do, to prepare, and for the first time in two years, it felt as if everything were within reach now that Aura was his. Settling back into the cushions, Rush released a long breath, a smile curling his lips.

"It's ready," Astor announced after an hour of brewing the potion.

The King of Sin allowed the hookah to fall from his hand as he pushed off the chaise. The hawk shifter held up a small tin container with a clear paste inside and Rush smiled. In two strides, he yanked the curtain back to expose the spinning wheel. He unfastened the spindle from the back and twirled it between his fingers.

"Hand me the potion to make her sleep," he told Astor.

"Why? Once you cast the spell she'll fall asleep anyway."

"Because I'm not going to risk pricking myself when she fights me." Rush took the tin from Astor and dipped the tip of the spindle into the concoction. "The kitten has claws."

# 5

# AURA

The two guards tightened their grip on Aura's arms as they carried her down a dim hallway. She thrashed the entire way, attempting to loosen even the slightest. "Release me!" she seethed. Though she'd never tell them that the king had captured her—after his threat—she wouldn't go easy on them either.

Due to the king's lies about a sick roleplaying game, neither of the guards paid her any mind as they halted in front of a door. The taller one pulled it open before they tossed her into a candle-lit bedroom that wreaked of sex. She crashed to a dark stone floor, a sharp pain running across her hip.

With a grunt, she pushed herself up, just as the door slammed shut. Aura darted toward it anyway—the sound of a lock clicking echoed. She gripped the knob, wishing she had a spell to open it, but sorcerers preferred to keep their secrets.

"Let me out of here, you beasts!" Aura screamed, kicking at the door and pounding against it with her fists to no avail. She wanted to break the wood into pieces and find the blasted king, then claw at his precious face. Her nostrils flared and her heart thudded furiously in her chest as she threw her one remaining shoe at the door. She rarely found herself angry or riled. Usually she drifted in those emotions like a calm lake, but not this evening, on what was to be her damn wedding night! The King of Sin had ruined everything. She didn't know much about the dragon shifter king, except that he wasn't sinful just in pleasure, but in stealing women on their *wedding day*. Now that she'd met him, she loathed him with every fiber thumping inside her. Perhaps he had a vendetta against her family from when they'd ruled, even though neither he nor she had been alive during that time. So then why her? Why bring her here when she'd never met him?

The obsidian room was empty, save for a bed cloaked in dark sheets and too many lacy pillows. No wardrobe, no desk, no chairs. She peered at the bed, its slightly rumpled silk blankets, knowing the scent of pleasure filling the air came from those sheets.

Aura's gaze fell to dark curtains, the thin slit in the middle exposing a glass window. She rushed toward it, throwing the thick fabric back, only to find iron bars lining the glass. Making a tight fist, she struck the pane with it as hard as she could. Not a single crack ran up its length or spiderwebbed across. Even if she would've shattered the glass, she never would've been able to squeeze through the bars.

Night still blanketed the court, the sky darker here, the stars brighter. Aura didn't know how long Rush wanted to keep her in Moonstone. If he planned to kill her, he most likely would've done that already. Unless he wanted to toy with her first... Perhaps he planned on requesting something in exchange for her though. Her family didn't have anything worthy to trade—what he wanted would have to come from the royal family of Starnight, from Pax.

Someone would come for her though. Pax would fight his way through dragon fire to save her if necessary. Rush had spewed lies about her beloved to get her to turn against him. The King of Sin was a deceiver, and she wouldn't believe anything that spilled from his filthy mouth. But despite knowing the lies weren't true, Rush's words slithered within her, making her stomach churn.

Hana had never come back to the tent, and Rush had never given a clear answer about her whereabouts. What if she was hurt somewhere? The thought terrified her, but she had to believe she was safe for now.

Aura stayed staring out the window, at the stars, waiting for the door to open, for someone to walk in and tell her anything. But no one came. She stood there until the muscles in her legs ached, her eyes heavy, and she sank to the floor, praying to wake from this nightmare.

The door creaked inward and Aura peeled open her eyes

to the world around her. She blinked, clearing the drowsiness from her gaze, before the horrors of the night came back in a rush. Aura stared at the king and another man standing beside him from her spot on the floor where she'd fallen asleep. The man was as tall as Rush, only more muscular, his dark hair short, his features sharper and full of angles, a rugged sort of handsome. She wondered if his heart was as black as the King of Sin's. Rush was now dressed, wearing a black button-up shirt with the sleeves rolled to his elbows, trousers hugging his strong legs, and boots that reflected the light as if they'd just been shined.

Aura couldn't push away the image that slipped into her mind of Rush's bare form, how he'd spoken to her about his length in a taunting manner. He wasn't wrong about the size of it. Even though it had been soft, it was large, and that only made her blood boil—she would have relished spewing at him how tiny his cock was.

No one spoke as they stopped in front of her, so she chose to break the silence, her voice raspy from lack of drink. "Oh my stars, you found trousers and a shirt. Now I won't have to go blind." Her gaze pinned on Rush's silver irises without shying away from his heavy stare.

The king smirked. "In my court, most prefer my clothing off, kitten."

Aura narrowed her eyes, wanting to throttle him, but she decided to play nice to see if he would release her. "I want to go home. Will you please take me back and we can discuss things there?"

"I want a lot of things." Rush shrugged, then turned to the man beside him. "And I always get what I want, isn't that so?"

Aura shoved up from the floor, an ache crawling up her spine from a night sleeping on the hard surface. Her back pressed against the bars of the window, reminding her that she was trapped inside this room. Heart pounding, she stepped forward. "No one's touching me."

Rush shifted between her and the window swiftly, and before she knew what he was doing, he drew her arms behind her back. "Astor, you see what I have to deal with?"

Aura froze. *That name.* She'd heard it at some point…

"You!" she spat, glaring daggers at Astor. "You're the hawk shifter, the one who's been seeing my sister! What trick did you pull on her? Where do you have her?"

Astor pursed his lips, and she wasn't certain whether he was going to ignore her or speak before he released a heavy sigh. "She's safe in Starnight, not here. No one's touched her. And no tricks—only omissions."

"That's the same thing!" She lunged toward Astor, but Rush pressed her against his firm chest. His smoky scent crawled across her senses, and she wanted to stop breathing any part of him in.

"Go to the cellar," Rush said to the hawk shifter.

As soon as the door shut behind Astor, Rush released her and she ran for her escape. A hand slammed against the door, preventing her from opening it.

"You're fast, but I'm faster," Rush taunted, his foreboding presence at her back making the hair along her arms stand up. "Anyone, besides apparently you, would at least *pretend* to be complacent."

"That bastard skulked around my sister without telling her who he truly was!" Hana needed to know. Aura backed away from the door as if she could find another

44

way out to get to her sister.

"Oh, he did a lot more than skulk. She practically begged him to fuck her. What did you want? Him to deny her?" Rush arched a brow, his face smug.

"Fuck. You," she spat, pointing her finger at him.

Rush edged toward her like a predator until he stood mere inches away. He leaned in close, whispering in her ear, his breath hot on her neck. "If you'd like, I can take you on the bed. I'll let your sweet cunt ride my tongue before I fuck you so hard you forget how to breathe, or perhaps you want to use the window bars? Grip them as I thrust inside you from behind, bringing you to the utmost sinful bliss. Has the pretty prince done those things to you? Has he fucked you the way he did the wedding guest?"

Aura slapped him across the face, the sound like thunder booming off the walls. "Stop telling lies! And I would never let you, your filthy tongue, or your disgusting cock, ever touch me. The prince and I have saved ourselves for one another all our lives, you savage bastard!" she shouted, her chest heaving. Aura waited for him to slap her back, to press a blade to her throat, to threaten her about her family, to do something in retaliation for striking the king. But he didn't even lift a hand to his reddening cheek. She'd never slapped anyone before—there'd only ever been a few small scuffles and hair pulling when she, Liana, and Hana were younger.

A heavy silence filled the air as Rush studied her with a neutral expression. For a moment she thought he now understood how she felt, that he was going to give in and send her back home. But then a laugh, deep and mocking, poured out from his throat. "I think that was the most pathetic thing I've heard from your mouth yet. Do you honestly believe that? Are you so naïve?" He pushed her hair behind her shoulder as though she were a child. "And you're telling me you haven't let dear Prince Pax fuck you?"

Warmth flooded up her neck, and Rush chuckled again when she didn't answer. "Oh, I see now. *He* wanted you to wait for the wedding day, isn't that right? Wanted to give you the illusion that he was a gentleman. But every night that you lay in your bed, staring up at the ceiling, touching yourself, you pretended it was that fucker making you moan. You would've let him slide that cock of his deep into your warm cunt the first day you met, wouldn't you have? And there's nothing wrong with that. We just met, and I wouldn't mind fucking you one bit. To feel you clench around me, lick your arousal like sweet nectar, hear how loud or soft you gasp. You could even slap me again during sex. I like it *rough*."

Aura's cheeks blazed, growing hotter. No one had used such foul language toward her, but deep down, she wished Pax would've talked to her like that every time they'd kissed, touched. However, she wasn't going to dignify his words with a response.

"Why do you hate Pax so much?"

"Does it matter?" Rush lifted a finger, running it across his lower lip. "Would you like privileges in my palace? Your room unlocked, to be able to walk around my gardens?" He waited a moment as if he truly wanted an answer before speaking again. "Then I suggest keeping that pretty mouth of yours shut and do as you're told, kitten."

"Stop calling me that!" she hissed.

46

"I'm sorry, do you prefer Princess Aura? As you said, this should've been your court. Take it back then. Kill me. Kill everyone here. Cast it back into darkness," he challenged. "You heard the tales, I'm sure, and can't deny that my family made it *better*."

Aura tightened her fists and clenched her teeth, knowing that part *was* true. People had basked in filth, disease, and barely held money for food. "I've *also* heard that your focus is having orgies here every night!"

"Not *every* night, but before coming to get you, indeed I did." He smirked and lifted his fingers toward her face.

A shimmer of oil caught Aura's attention just before she shut her eyes to avoid his touch. His fingertips were cool as they slid down her eyelids. She jerked back from him and rubbed at her lashes. What disgusting things had he been touching? A sudden tug of exhaustion flowed through Aura, like a warm blanket caressing her. "Take me home. I'll do anything you wish." She yawned, her eyelids becoming heavy.

Rush watched her closely, a smile growing wide across his face. "It's too late. I could've taken one of your sisters, or even a girl from Moonstone, but I chose *you*. You see, I *relish* toying with the prince."

"You're not half the man he is," she slurred as though drunk on wine. What was *happening*? What had he done to her?

Rush's smile fell away into a harsh sneer. "Ask Astor. He saw the prince with another woman while out with Hana."

"Lies." Aura collapsed against his chest as she yawned once more. Her muscles and bones were too heavy to gather the strength to push up from him, to claw at his

47

face.

Rush's sturdy arms looped beneath her knees and he lifted her, then carried her to the bed as her eyes drifted shut. She couldn't care less that the blankets smelled of pleasure as their softness cocooned her.

"Sleep, Aura," he whispered as something sharp pressed to her finger.

She opened her mouth to curse him, to ask what he was doing, but her tongue was too heavy to lift. The darkness hidden beneath her eyelids turned lighter, weaving colors together until a forest of lush trees brimming with plump fruit and bright flowers appeared.

Aura was in a dream—she knew it as one sometimes does. She was no longer in her wedding gown but a simple lavender dress embroidered in white beads. A woodsy scent drifted with the wind as it blew past her.

Behind her, a rustling stirred and she whirled around. Aura expected the king to be standing there, prepared to talk about his cock once more … even in her dreams. But her gaze landed on a slender woman with wild black hair, her pale blue dress sopping wet. She stood near a tree, her back facing Aura as she reached to grab an orange from a limb.

The woman couldn't stretch far enough, so she jumped, snagging the fruit from the branch. She slowly turned to face Aura—eyes as blue as sapphires met hers, and a glowing smile shone on her heart-shaped face. She wasn't a woman, after all, but a girl of around sixteen, just a couple of years younger than Hana.

"I'm waiting for him," the girl said with her radiant smile. "He meets me here in secret. Always. I have something to confess to him, but I trust you won't tell anyone." She rubbed her stomach, and beneath the dress, barely noticeable, Aura saw a hint of a bump there. "He's going to be so happy. He told me he's always wanted a family."

"Who are you?" Aura asked, attempting to recall if she'd ever seen her before.

"Um." The girl furrowed her brow, concentrating. "I can't remember." And before Aura's eyes, the girl vanished as if she hadn't been there at all, leaving Aura alone in the forest, in this strange dream.

Aura pinched her arm as hard as she could, trying to pull herself out of slumber. "Wake up!" she screamed.

Flames crawled from the ground, licking their way up the trunks, engulfing them. Aura's heart thundered as she looked for an escape, but the crackling fire faded. The forest was now completely gray ash. The only color came from her, making her a beacon in this dead forest. One by one the trees collapsed, bits of ash drifting up toward the gray sky. And then droplets of water rose from the ground, inching toward her and sliding across her skin. She attempted to wipe them away, but it was as though they were a part of her.

Aura screamed again, demanding to rouse herself from this pit of ash by thrashing, jumping, slapping her cheeks, yet she remained. A light brush tickled the inside of her chest, akin to a hand skimming across the muscle. Then a deep pain struck her index finger, the same sensation she'd felt earlier.

Her body jerked forward with a start, and she gripped her hand, but the brief pain in her digit had already subsided. She was awake, back in the bed inside Rush's palace, and a small red spot marked her finger as though it had been pricked by something sharp.

# RUSH

Rush watched Aura as she slept. Still. Peaceful. Beautiful. He gripped the spindle, held his breath. But she didn't stir once in the handful of minutes he stood in the shadows near her bedside. He'd lied to her about giving her privileges, being able to leave her room—he wasn't above lying to keep her quiet. The spell was cast which meant she would *never* wake again. A victorious smirk played on his lips.

Now he just needed to get to the cellar and—

Aura lurched up with a gasp, clutching her hand to her chest, and the blood drained from Rush's face. She looked around the room, scowled, then glanced at her finger where he'd pricked her. Her gaze rose again, landing almost instinctually on him.

"What the *fuck*?" he roared.

"That should be my line," she snarled. "What did you do to me?"

*No. No, no, no!* He'd worked on his revenge for *two years* after his bargain with a sorceress. Meticulously planned every minute detail. Searched the twelve courts for ingredients, killing and imprisoning others in the process. And Aura was fucking *awake.*

*I'm going to murder the sorceress*, he growled inside his head. She guaranteed it would work! He'd given her an entire mountain range in exchange for the information. And bargaining with a sorceress was no simple task.

Rush stormed from Aura's bedroom, his vision blurred with rage, and made his way to the cellar. When he tore into the room, Astor startled behind the worktable where he was cleaning equipment.

"She fell asleep but now is awake again," he barked.

Astor's brows rose. "Maybe you need to put the spindle back on the wheel first?"

Chest heaving, Rush approached the wheel and slipped the spindle into place. He stepped back. Waited to see if something happened. Nothing did. He reached for the spindle again, to make certain it was secure, but his fingers hit an invisible barrier.

Rush paused and used both hands to explore the smooth surface. What seemed to be a thick protective coating encased the entire machine. Hard and cold— except for the barrier around the spindle itself which was warm. "I can't fucking touch it." If he couldn't touch it, how could he try again? "Astor—"

The hawk shifter unsuccessfully attempted to touch the wood. He pursed his lips and seemed to consider for a moment. "Perhaps it's activated now."

"You bastards!" Aura's faint, muffled voice echoed through the halls of the palace, originating from a level above. "Let me go!"

Rush's hands balled into fists and he swung one at the wall. His knuckles burst open with the impact. If it had worked, she wouldn't be screaming at his guards. Wouldn't be roaming the halls, likely trying to escape because he hadn't thought to lock her door.

"There's got to be another way," Astor said quietly. "Another object we can spell…"

"No." It had to be the wheel—it was already linked to the spell. At least *that* part had succeeded. "I'll have my men track down the sorceress so I can get answers. Until then…" He wiped the blood from his knuckles onto his trousers. "Until then, I'm going to enjoy fucking with her."

Rush paced through the dew-coated gardens. Gravel crunched beneath his boots and bugs chirped in the bushes. All was quiet, but extra guards stood at every exit. For a change, he'd left Aura's door unlocked today, knowing she would likely try to escape again, but that was part of the entertainment.

The chase.

Letting her find a flicker of hope, only to rip it away. Just like his hope was torn from him when she didn't fall into a permanent sleep.

He cast a glance up at her barred window. No light glowed within. She had still been asleep, making small pained sounds, when he'd exited the palace that morning. Astor had gone back to Starnight to listen for gossip about Aura being stolen away. After spending all day reading over the spell to ensure he hadn't made mistakes, meeting with advisors, and attending to his official duties, he found himself alone with too much on his mind.

This was usually when he got a few people together for a bit of pleasure, but he wasn't in the mood. Not tonight. Tonight, he was restless. He had Pax's bride and *still* justice evaded him.

"Your Majesty," a guard called, exiting the palace into the gardens. Rush made his way back toward him, eager to hear the news. "She's awake and wandering the palace."

Rush grinned. "Keep me informed if she tries anything. We're enjoying our little game."

The guard bowed and backed away from the king.

Rush looked up at the window again. Where was she now? What was she doing? The dragon quivered inside him, anxious to come out and hunt, but he had more patience than the beast.

A window slid open on the third floor and a blonde head peeked out. Rush smirked, waiting for what would happen next. He almost laughed when a line of tied sheets dropped over the sill. Two guards below moved forward with a start, but Rush held up a hand to stop them.

"Leave," he told them quietly so his voice didn't travel to Aura's ears.

They disappeared into the palace, allowing Rush to watch Aura's feet slip out of the window. He crossed his arms and tilted his chin up. Aura's body slid outside slowly, feet planted on the exterior wall, as she held onto the sheets. With stiff movements, she walked down the bricks toward the gardens, muttering softly to herself.

Her skirts tangled around her shapely legs, making her efforts twice as difficult. It was hard to believe Pax hadn't fucked her yet. If he were to bet, the prince would say it was Aura's decision to wait until the wedding night. Rush's grin grew. If he *really* wanted to piss off the Prince of Starnight, Rush would fuck her while he waited to see if the spell would work. Not only that—but he would make her *want* to fuck him. Make her *beg* for his cock. And then he'd send the stained sheets to Pax, letting him stew and wonder if it was or wasn't Rush who took his betrothed's maidenhead.

Aura's foot slipped and she released a small yelp. Her body swung around, hands gripping the sheets, and her back hit the wall. She drew in a deep breath and, just as she was about to adjust her grip, she looked down. At Rush. Her eyes widened, lips parting on a gasp.

"Hello, kitten," he purred. "I'd say I'm surprised to see you here, but that wouldn't be entirely truthful."

"I... I..." she sputtered.

"It's a little disappointing that you chose such an unimaginative way to escape," he continued.

"Stop talking," she growled.

Rush arched a brow. "Let go. I'll catch you."

"As if I would ever trust you." She managed to flip herself around and brace her feet again.

"A broken leg might make you more obedient. Regardless, trying to leave the palace grounds won't be as easy as you think."

She paused and glared down at him. "Another threat?"

He shrugged. Astor had a backup plan to keep Aura in Rush's possession, that would link to the original spell, while they sorted the rest out. All it had taken was collecting a few of her breaths as she slept and ingredients stocked in the cellar. "Do it again and see."

Her foot hit the lip of the second story window and her grip slipped. She screamed when she fell, her hair whipping in her face.

Rush extended his arms and caught her, as he'd promised. She was light when he'd carried her in his dragon form, but he'd expected her to be heavier. "Don't they feed you in Starnight?"

She squirmed frantically in his hold and he dropped her. "I'm going to kill you," she snarled.

"Sure, kitten. Maybe next week." He chuckled and motioned one of the guards forward. "Lock her back in her room."

"Mix oil with the valerian root," Rush murmured to himself. "Add powdered chamomile." He studied the labeled jars spread out before him, then lifted them to confirm the contents were as desired. They were. "Heat over a low flame until a layer of foam forms on top."

If the flame had been any lower, it would've extinguished itself. And the foam had been perfectly even across the surface of the mixture before he'd added the dash of bergamot and the ingredients he'd collected from the different courts. *Fuck.*

Astor had done all of that correctly. It had congealed when he added a pinch of powder the sorceress had supplied along with the spell. Had Rush written something down incorrectly? Shifted a line on the diagrams just a *little*, making everything worthless? The sorceress disappeared from Moonstone after their last meeting and he was unable to locate her again to verify his parchment. He thought she would've taken up residence in the mountains since she'd been so adamant about wanting the land in exchange for the spell. Perhaps his *pinch* hadn't been enough. Or had been too much.

With a sigh, he rolled the parchment up and tucked it safely back into a metal box on his bookshelf. He peeled off his black jacket, now covered in yellow dust from inventorying powders, and pulled back the velvet curtain. Sorcha's old spinning wheel sat in the corner—waiting. Waiting for what though? He couldn't even touch the damn thing anymore.

Rush's blood simmered beneath his skin, his rage begging to be unleashed. He drew the curtain back in place, shielding the wheel from sight, and stormed from the room. Aura would pay for Pax's mistakes, even if her suffering here wouldn't make a difference to the bastard prince.

"Where is she?" Rush asked Laird at the top of the staircase. He'd told the guards they could escort her through the palace after three days had passed.

"The kitchens, last I heard, Your Majesty," he answered.

*The kitchens.* Hopefully that meant she was eating her

fill of whatever the chef made. He needed her alive and well when he corrected the issue.

Rush navigated the stone hallways. It had been a long while since he'd visited the corridors where the servants worked. He and his sister, Princess Constance, used to play down there—running through hallways, sneaking desserts, while the servants went about their day. Some laughed at their antics, others scoffed—even dared to yell on occasion.

His boots thudded against the floor as he made his way to the kitchens and the scent of warm bread floated up to greet him. Men and women called to each other, asking for ingredients, giving warnings that they were behind while metal clanked together.

"Slice those thinner," Marion instructed.

After a short pause, Aura asked, "Like this? I've always been awful at preparing food."

"Precisely. Wonderful."

Rush strode faster down the hallway leading to the kitchens where Tanix stood, guarding Aura as instructed. She wasn't here to make friends or to be ... *mothered*. And that was the very tone Marion used. Aura had a purpose here and the less people that cared, the better. One day, she would vanish, as far as everyone else was concerned.

Most people would disapprove of the extreme measures Rush was taking to get revenge on Pax, so the less she mattered to anyone here, the easier things would be later. He would lie if anyone asked, tell them he'd tired of his latest fuck, but ultimately he was the king. Kings did not owe anyone an explanation.

"Pet!" he snapped, stepping into the kitchens. Aura flinched at the sound of his voice and shifted closer to

Marion. A table with a variety of savory meat pies stretched between them as five other servants worked around the space. Aura stood just out of the way, slicing an apple. "Who the fuck let you have a knife?"

"Marion's teaching me how to make apple crumble. Since you so *graciously* decided to finally allow me out of my room this morning," she said, narrowing her eyes.

"Put down the knife," he ordered. While she was the least dangerous person in the room, Rush wanted her feeling defenseless. Helpless.

Marion patted Aura's shoulder. "It's all right, dear. We can make another one later."

Aura continued to glower at Rush, and he couldn't help but consider it a delicacy. Those pouty rose-red lips of hers pressed into a tight line as she lifted the knife and slammed the tip into the wooden cutting board. The sound echoed, the blade wobbling from the force of it. "There. Good enough for you, dear King of Sin?" she drawled.

*Feisty little vixen.* The dragon within him lifted his head. Stared. Parted his mouth and dragged in a smokey breath. Lust stirred, raw and needy, but he couldn't blame the beast either—she *was* beautiful.

"Elated," he said sarcastically. "Now come."

Aura crossed her arms. "Where?"

"Does it matter?" He quirked a brow and waited for her to move. Seconds ticked by, his muscles tensing more and more. Kings did not wait—not for anyone. "*Now,* kitten."

"Keep calling me that and I'll scratch your face off," she muttered under her breath.

Marion blinked when she glanced at Rush. She gave

him a quick bow and plucked the knife from the cutting board. He turned on his heel and strode from the kitchens with Aura, surprisingly, following him.

"You could've just *asked* me to come with you instead of ordering me around," she said as they turned down a corridor.

"If I asked, you would've said no," he said in a low voice.

"True," she mused.

Rush spun to face her and grabbed her upper arm. "You're not allowed to handle weapons while you're here."

She wrinkled her nose, her violet gaze latched onto him. "Excuse me? Are you talking about the *knife*? That I was using to slice apples."

"Slicing apples today, stabbing my guards tomorrow," he growled. She was brave enough to try killing her way to freedom—not that she would succeed based on her poor attempt with a *fork*.

Aura huffed. "Not all of us lust for the sight of blood. You did something to me, and I know you pricked my finger with an object. I can *feel* something is not right with me at times."

Rush narrowed his eyes and his dragon shifted slightly in annoyance, although pleased that he could confirm the spell was doing something. He'd killed before, of course. Enemy raiders obliterated by his dragon fire, his hands snapping the necks of assassins, a letter opener to the eye of a spy. But it wasn't as if he went around killing for the thrill of it. There had to be a *reason*. On occasion, the reason was that someone chewed too loudly, yet that was hardly the point.

"Believe what you want, but my lips are sealed. However, I murder when it's required," he said, tightening his grip on her arm.

"And abducting women? Is that also when you *have* to?"

"Hmm." He smirked. "Would that make you jealous? To know of all the other damsels I've locked away in my palace? *Ravaged* them when I haven't given you the same pleasure?"

"If you so much as touch beneath my dress, *I'll* be the murderer," she spat.

"Ah, right. You're saving yourself for the wedding night with Pax. Are you still refusing to believe he didn't do the same?" He lifted her hand to his mouth and licked the apple juices from a finger just to fuck with her. His tongue wrapped around the digit, sucking as if he were licking another part of her. Inside him, his dragon purred at the thought of her legs hooked over his shoulders while he feasted.

Aura let out a horrified screech and ripped her hand free. She raised her palm as if she were about to slap him and he tilted his cheek to welcome it.

"You taste sweet."

"It's the apples!" Aura blurted, her cheeks burning red with embarrassment. She furiously wiped her finger with her skirt.

"I wonder what other parts of you taste like. My dragon is *especially* curious to find out." His eyes flicked down past her breasts to where her core hid beneath her skirts, then back up to meet her gaze. "Tell me, sweet Aura, does Pax like how your cunt tastes? Did he ever bother to lick you to bliss?"

61

"He'll come for me, you know." Her voice was even and calm, as if she had no doubt her prince would save her. "I would prefer it if you would lock me back in my room now."

"Starnight might come searching, but not Pax himself. Even if he does, he won't find you here," Rush added, lifting his chin to stare down at her. No one who worked for him would betray the secret if they discovered the woman inside his palace was the same one missing from Starnight, and, when Starnight came looking—because, eventually, they would—she would be well-hidden, deep in his palace, where none of his staff knew she would be.

She jerked out of his touch. "How are you going to get your ransom if he doesn't know I'm here?"

Ransom? Where had she gotten that idea from? Rush chuckled mirthlessly. "Is that the reasoning you settled on, kitten?"

"That's the reason you took me, isn't it?" she demanded.

He grinned. She wasn't going to pry the information from him, no matter how hard she tried. It was more intriguing this way. Letting her wonder and worry.

"Fine, keep your secrets."

"If you behave, you won't be locked in your room anymore. You can go anywhere you want as long as it's within the palace grounds. The gardens, the stables, I don't give a fuck. You want to suck my valet's cock? Go right ahead. Perhaps I'll watch."

*And then I'll claw out his heart for touching you.*

Rush drew in a sharp breath. Her soft golden hair, plump breasts, curved waist. She could release every ounce of rage while riding him hard and fast, raking her nails down his chest until he bled.

And the best part?

Pax would be fucking livid if gossip spread to Starnight that the King of Sin had claimed his bride-to-be, made her quake with pleasure. Rush would relish that moment, that he would be the one holding the answer while the prince seethed, not ever knowing the truth since Aura would never be found. Maybe the spell's delay wasn't so bad—as long as it was corrected soon.

Aura stormed around Rush in the hallway and pounded up the nearest staircase. "What a fucking bastard who—" She gasped and mumbled a soft *sorry*.

A moment later a maid exited the staircase, her red hair drawn back into a low bun. One of the two women from last week that he never got to fuck because Astor had walked in. She smiled and gave him a small curtsy.

"I never caught your name," Rush purred, smiling back.

"Janee."

Rush eyed the staircase behind her where Aura had just disappeared. His dragon unfurled as if he were about to run after her. To show her precisely what she was missing with Pax, but Rush wasn't a complete monster— he wouldn't touch her until she begged him to. And when that day came, he would revel in bringing his enemy's fiancée ecstasy with *his* name on her lips.

"Janee." He tore his eyes from the stairs and reached out to trail a finger down the column of her neck. "Would you like to finish what we started the other night?"

She shivered at his touch. "I'd like that very much, Your Majesty."

# AURA

"Fuck, you feel so good," Rush growled.

Aura sat on the floor beneath the window, staring up at the ceiling with clenched teeth as she listened to the King of Sin pleasuring someone just outside her door. She wanted to crawl into the new wardrobe filled with dresses that had been brought into her room. Couldn't he have at least escorted the woman to anywhere else in the palace? But she believed he was doing the deed on purpose, so she could hear every moan of ecstasy.

Even though Aura had been held a prisoner in Moonstone for a week, that morning was actually quite lovely when she'd gone to the kitchens. The sweet smell of pastries and pies had reminded her of Liana, how she would start preparing something as soon as she woke.

Marion had taught her how to make an apple crumble after she'd asked, in hopes that she would one day get to pass on the recipe to Liana. Thankfully, this was the first time she hadn't burned something.

"My king," the woman shouted. "Oh, my *king*." A final moan passed through the rattling walls before Rush released a deep and guttural groan that sent a lick of heat low in Aura's belly. She shook the feeling away and pretended it was Pax she'd heard, but her chest tightened as she wondered if that was what he'd sounded like when he'd pleasured another. *No, Rush is a liar.*

Rustling of fabric stirred, followed by footsteps fading away. Before today, she hadn't seen Rush's cocky face since attempting to escape out the window of another room with poorly tied sheets. Rush should've expected her to not *behave* while being allowed to roam the hallways.

Each day, a tugging, like a pinch, fluttered against her heart. Not the painful sensation that had drawn her out of her last dream but still something. Since that strange dream where she'd conjured up a pregnant girl who vanished into thin air, there hadn't been another.

However, when the guards escorted her to bathe with a servant or brought her food, no one answered her questions, seeming to believe she was genuinely playing a sinful and pleasurable roleplaying game. She hated them all besides Marion. The king had pricked Aura's finger with something that had to be a mystery spell, and she needed to find a way out of the palace.

As she shoved up from the floor to stand, a hard knock came at the door. "Go away!" she shouted, not wanting to see the king or another moody guard.

It didn't matter what she'd said, the door slowly opened to reveal another bastard. Astor. She scowled at him, and at that moment, she couldn't decide if she wanted to throttle him more than his king. This shifter had lied to her sister, tumbled her, then worked with Rush to keep her in the Moonstone palace.

"Are you here to apologize for what you did to Hana?" she said through gritted teeth.

"Would I be forgiven?" He cocked his head, pinning her with his neutral stare.

"No." She took a step toward him.

Astor drew the dagger from his hip. "I need a lock of your hair." Did he always seem so stiff and emotionless around her sister? For the life of her, she couldn't believe Hana, who was full of smiles, would fall for someone who didn't seem to know how to laugh.

"For what?" She frowned. "I'm not a fool. I know you and the King of Sin are doing something to me. I can feel it each day."

"I'm going to take it regardless of your feelings, but if you give it willingly, I'll tell you about Hana."

Even though it could be lies, she had to risk it, no matter what it was. "Is she safe?" she whispered, her voice pleading.

He closed the distance between them and lifted a few strands of her hair, then sliced through them with his dagger. "She's fine, but she's been different since you came here. Distant. Doesn't talk as much."

*She knows.* If Hana trusted him, she would've confessed what was going on inside her head, even if she was worried or melancholic that Aura had been taken. It wouldn't have mattered. "How else would she act

66

knowing her sister was stolen away on her wedding day without so much as a goodbye?" Aura said, smoothing out her tone so it didn't sound like a lie. "And why are you still seeing her?" He didn't answer, so she continued, "She'll find out when I go home. I'll tell her the truth."

Astor remained silent as he tucked the dagger back into its sheath. "I never meant to deceive Hana for so long."

"I'm certain all will be forgiven when she hears that *gracious* news." If anything, that would only infuriate Hana more.

He released a sigh before leaving the room, and the sound of the lock turning never clicked. Aura blinked, her heart racing, not knowing if he'd meant to keep it unlocked. When she'd first come into her room not long ago, the guard had locked it immediately. But the king had mentioned to her if she behaved...

This time it might be simpler since she could attempt an escape straight from the gardens instead of inside the palace. Shoes would be nice at the moment, but not a necessity. Each day Aura had been here, she'd been given a new dress to wear but no shoes. As if only having one shoe would halt her from trying to escape. She wasn't going to behave for the king when she needed to return to Hana and Pax.

As she pushed open the door, she glanced down the hallway and spotted one of the guards who'd first brought her to her room as she writhed. Laird.

Aura slowly walked down the hall, the pads of her feet cool from the onyx floor.

"My lady," Laird said and bowed his head.

She arched a brow—he hadn't said a word to her

67

every time he'd escorted her to the bathing chambers. "Do you need to accompany me?"

"Per the king, as long as you stay on the palace grounds, venture wherever you like, save for the cellar and the king's quarters when he's not there."

No escort? This might be simpler than she thought. Guards would most likely be outside the palace doors, but perhaps she could reach the gate without them following. She didn't have a shifter ability as Rush had, but she could run like the wind and hide like the moon during daylight.

Aura cast a hesitant glance over her shoulder, not truly believing him as she started down the hallway. But he didn't come after her, so she descended the black staircase when two female voices drifted through the air.

"The king's quite the lover, isn't he?" a woman asked.

"Quite." The other giggled. "Perhaps tonight we can have a gathering of eight. It's been over a week since he's had an orgy."

"I miss it being nightly."

Orgies were truly every day? Did the king even perform any royal duties?

The servants glanced her way as she hit the bottom step. Neither were women that she'd seen before, but they were both pretty with curvy bodies and delicate features.

"We'll see if she can join us," the redheaded servant whispered.

Aura's eyes widened and she increased her pace. She didn't care who wanted to tumble who, but she would not be participating in any of that.

Her feet padded across the black floor. The décor mainly consisted of the same dark shade—walls, sculpted art pieces, and a set of velvet chaises. Black was everywhere besides for a few splashes of red here and there. Paintings of Rush's ancestors lined the walls, yet she wasn't certain who was who. She knew Rush's parents and sister had died within a handful of years. There wasn't pity for him, but for the ones who'd lost their lives.

Aura opened the door to the front gardens, finding two guards standing on either side. They bowed their heads as she wandered away from them out into the bright daylight. The air was calm and a few spotted butterflies fluttered above the red roses. Besides those flowers, the gardens mostly held green bushes that were as tall as her waist and formed a labyrinth of swirling designs. Farther out, steam wafted up from a small pond. The only guards she could see were the two at the door.

Up ahead, she caught sight of a man tending to a white horse outside the barn. Blond hair fell to the young man's shoulders on one side, the other was shorn to the scalp. Rush's words came to her about not caring who she tumbled.

"Good afternoon, my lady," the man said as he glanced up, the sun's light catching on his handsome bone structure.

"Hello," she said. "And you are?"

"I'm the stable hand, Brix."

"That's a lovely name." As she thought about Rush's threat to keep silent on who she was, she hoped he wouldn't ask for her name, but if he did she would make one up.

"This is Cersa." He ran a hand through the horse's ivory mane. "Do you know how to ride?"

"I do. Very well actually." Her father had taught Aura,

Liana, and Hana when they were younger. The two little ones had yet to show any interest in learning.

His lips tilted up at the edges. "Feel free to ride her through the gardens. I can help you mount if you need it."

If the palace wasn't surrounded by closed gates, and she could get a guard to open one of them, she would've taken the horse and fled. "Perhaps another time. Thank you, I'll ... see you around." Or never, since she hoped to escape in the next few moments. If not, there was the chance she could befriend him so he would want to help her.

Aura walked through the gardens at a casual pace, as to not be too noticeable. She stopped to smell a red rose when she approached the fence. Birds chirped, and a nervous feeling washed over her as she realized something. Astor could shift and easily spy. Some of these animals might be shifters too.

But it didn't matter—she would try anyway. Aura gripped the iron bars and didn't pause as she climbed up the fence, careful to not impale herself or catch the fabric of her dress on the sharp finials at the top, then dropped on the other side to the grass.

Aura glanced back, her heart roaring inside her chest. Not a single guard ran after her. *Strange.*

Exhaustion swarmed through her then, her muscles heavy. *No, not now, damn it.* This wasn't the tugging sensation to her heart—it was the same draining feeling she'd suffered a week ago. Rush had given her no answer about it.

Gathering what strength she had, Aura forced herself to dart toward the trees. But she stumbled, her bones aching. *Keep going. Don't stop.* She needed to get as far away from the palace as possible before someone came for her.

An invisible prick struck Aura's finger—her knees buckled and she collapsed to the ground. A moment later, a shadow slid above her. His face pulled into view and she gazed into those deep silver irises rimmed in obsidian.

"Didn't I tell you not to leave the gardens, kitten?" Rush purred.

"A shame I don't take orders from bastards," she yawned, her eyes too heavy to keep open any longer.

Aura sat on what must have been a bed in a pitch-black room that held a sweet berry scent. She was dreaming again. But she preferred a dream over seeing Rush. If she could, she would claw off all his skin.

A flickering flame ignited atop a candle, bathing the area in a soft orange glow. Aura was in a tiny room she didn't recognize. A single portrait hung on the wall of an obsidian dragon wearing a crown. She couldn't get away from the pretentious ass, even in her sleep.

The rustle of papers stirred, and Aura was no longer alone. At a long wooden desk with a vase of red roses sat the girl from Aura's last dream, her dark curls wilder than before. Water droplets fell to the floor from the fabric of her still-wet dress. The girl didn't seem to notice Aura studying her as she dipped her quill in black ink and scrawled across a page. Who was she?

As if hearing her thought, the girl peered up at Aura,

the same warm smile forming on her lips.

"We meet again," the girl said. "What a pleasant surprise."

"What are you doing?" Aura asked, pushing up from the bed. She approached the desk and saw only a blank page in the girl's hands.

"Writing my beloved a letter. It's been too long since he last visited. I still haven't gotten a chance to tell him about our child." She set the quill down and rubbed at her temples. "I seem to remember things and then forget. I still can't remember my name, but I remember him, his face. He promised that one day we would live together. But we must keep our love a secret for now."

Was she talking about living together in Moonstone or a different court? "Which court do you reside in?" But when the question left her lips, she believed it to be a foolish thing to ask when a portrait of Rush's royal dragon hung on the wall.

The girl furrowed her brow, her eyes closing in what must have been concentration. "Moonstone," she finally whispered. "Yes, I live in Moonstone."

"Where are you now? I can find you when I wake." She couldn't right away since she was unable to leave the palace grounds, but once she could...

"I-I don't know." The girl inhaled a sharp breath and gripped her chest as she sobbed. "It's coming back. The pain, the hurt, his words. He lied to me and never wanted me at all. Death was the only way, my fate..."

"You're dead?" Aura gasped, reaching for the girl's arm, but it passed straight through. *A spirit.*

"Rush!" the girl screamed as water poured from the ceiling. More rose from the wooden floor and seeped

72

through the walls.

Aura couldn't wonder why the girl was shouting for the King of Sin now—she needed to get them out of the room before they drowned. It was only a dream, but what if they could still get hurt here?

Aura waded through the water to the door. "Come on!" she called, glancing over her shoulder, her hand stilling on the doorknob. The girl's lips turned a deep shade of blue as water spilled from her mouth and her body bloated.

The door wouldn't budge, so Aura banged on it. The girl vanished into thin air just as she had before, leaving Aura alone with the water rising higher. Cool water licked up her torso, weighing down her dress. Her heart pounded when it seeped up to her chin, and she hurried to climb onto the mattress. The water filled the room faster and faster, snuffing out the candle on the desk before casting her into complete darkness.

Her body shook as panic coursed through her. "Let me out of here!" she screeched, sputtering water when it brushed her lips. The water lifted higher until it covered her completely, and she held her breath, unable to see anything within the dark liquid. A crushing sensation struck her finger.

Aura jolted forward, her eyes flying open as the pain ceased. "What is *happening*?" she whispered, her chest heaving. Aura was back in this damn bed that she'd been avoiding since she was placed in it last. She knew precisely who'd put her here and she was sick of it, sick of this palace, sick of the daily tugging sensation, and now these dreams. The girl ... who she wasn't certain was even real. But if she was, Aura couldn't admit she was seeing her, not if the dream could somehow get answers. What did Rush have to do with her? The girl was writing a letter to a beloved then called out his name. She wouldn't put it past him to murder someone, but a pregnant girl? Perhaps so. It sounded like madness, yet maybe not. Or maybe it was only a dream.

Aura darted for the door and she jerked on the knob to find it locked. She beat against the wood while screaming, "Get the king, now!"

The door opened to Tanix, the other guard who'd first brought her to this awful room, then had silently followed her through the palace the most. She lifted her chin in defiance. "I need to speak with the king."

"Certainly, my lady. He's been waiting to see you." His muscles bulged through his tight uniform as he motioned her to follow him.

Aura narrowed her eyes but pressed her lips into a tight line before she spewed words that would make him toss her back into her room. He led her down several hallways with hanging banners, stained-glass windows, and high archways until they reached an open door. Inside, the space held walls of books, and flames crackled in the fireplace. Two black leather chairs faced each other and, slumped lazily in one with his legs wide open, was Rush, poring over a book. She couldn't help but notice how the dark trousers hugged his powerful thighs, and the black shirt he'd left unfastened halfway down to reveal his taut and muscular chest. *Arrogant bastard.*

"She's awakened, Your Majesty. I brought her here just as you asked," Tanix said.

"Good. Leave us." He didn't look up from his book while motioning the guard away.

Tanix nodded, and as soon as the door closed, Rush snapped his book shut. "Finally awake, kitten? Took you long enough." A vengeful smile spread across his face.

Aura snatched the book from his hand and tossed it into the fire.

"What did that novel ever do to you?" He watched, unbothered, as the flames licked away the pages.

"What have *you* done to *me*?" Aura hissed. "Why did I faint for a second time when I shouldn't be tired at all?"

"I warned you not to leave the palace grounds, didn't I?"

"You didn't tell me I would fall asleep, you ass!" she spat.

Rush slowly stood from the chair and sauntered to her. He hovered above her, his smoky scent brushing her senses. "A king commands and others obey."

Aura scoffed. "You are not my king."

He gently pushed her hair over her shoulder. "You're in Moonstone, so that makes you my subject."

Aura tightened her fists, ignoring his asinine comment for a more important matter. "Tell me what's happening to me? Why does my heart feel a tug each day? What spell did you put on me? Why did Astor need my hair? I will not run again, so remove it."

Rush backed her into a wall of books, caging her in. "Ah, that's not particularly believable now, is it? I won't remove it. Be satisfied knowing that the spell won't kill you."

Horror churned within her. "Satisfied indeed. Break it."

Rush's lips formed a tight line. "No."

Her fists trembled when he wouldn't tell her anything

more. "At least bring Pax to me so I can explain everything to him."

Rush growled. "Don't mention that fucker right now."

An unintelligible sound came out of her throat as she shoved his chest, but he didn't budge. "I'll mention him a thousand times if I want. Again, you are *not* my king."

Rush drew in a deep breath, his eyes narrowed. "If you promise to behave," he purred, "I'll allow you to speak to someone else. You had a guest arrive a few days ago after your spell outside the gardens."

"A few days?" Her voice rose an octave. "I slept for *days?*"

"Don't go past the gardens if you don't want it to happen again."

It didn't matter because she knew better now. Hope and curiosity bloomed within her—someone had come for her. To save her? "Who's here?"

"A sister with a dirtier mouth than you."

"Hana," Aura whispered as her chest tightened with fear. "What did you do to her?" If he'd hurt a single hair on her sister's head, she would rip him apart. "Take me to her."

"You still haven't promised to behave."

"I promise," she said between clenched teeth.

"Liar." He chuckled. Still, he led her to a door on the opposite side of the room. A set of stone stairs trailed downward while torches lit the way, the flames' shadows dancing on the walls.

Below, a woman's shouts echoed toward them as they descended the steps. "You fucked me to get information on my sister!" Hana screamed.

76

"Only at first." Astor sighed. "But things changed, Hana. I don't know how to make you understand."

"I'm going to put an arrow in your heart, then rip off your wings."

"Rip off his wings first," Rush cooed as they reached a dimly-lit area. "If you put an arrow in his heart first, he won't feel it."

Astor stepped aside to scowl at Rush while Aura gasped. An iron manacle circled one of Hana's raw ankles, trapping her only feet from the wall by a chain. Her blonde hair hung in tangles and dark circles ringed her eyes.

"Hana!" Aura rushed to her sister's side and threw her arms around her.

"Aura!" Hana exhaled heavily.

"Why do you have her chained?" Aura hissed at Rush. "I've kept my identity quiet. You asked me to do nothing else to protect my sisters."

"Your sister entered *my* palace grounds and threw a dagger at Astor. I think that's reason enough," Rush said.

"You took my sister prisoner!" Hana shouted, lunging forward, but the chain yanked her back before she could reach Rush. "I wouldn't have known except I traveled to Moonstone in search of the dragon who stole my sister and saw you with that prick." She looked out the corners of her eyes toward Astor. "I then followed him back to your palace, but I should've fucking told all of Starnight first."

Ignoring Hana, Rush focused on Aura. "Ask Hana about your fiancé. Ask her what she saw him doing when he was supposed to be at the altar with you."

The room turned silent—not even the sound of

breaths echoed. Aura met Hana's gaze and sympathy reflected back at her. That expression was what caused Aura to falter, for her words to stutter instead of coming out confident. "What did you see at the wedding? Is it true Pax was late because he was bedding another?"

"I'm sorry, Aura," Hana murmured. "I wanted to tell you, but I didn't want to hurt you. It's true. He was, and I hate him. I've seen him on more than one occasion, yet I thought he would stop after the wedding. I never expected he would be so fucking brazen to do it before the ceremony. This marriage was what you'd always dreamt of. You relished your birthright the way Liana loves baking."

Aura stood still, unable to move a muscle. She waited for her sister to give a secret signal that she'd been forced to say these awful things. But there were no indications that everything she'd spoken was a lie. When Hana's eyes brimmed with tears, Aura *knew* she spoke the truth.

"I see," Aura finally said without a hint of emotion. She turned to Rush. "Congratulations, I now know I've been a fool all along. Let my sister go home."

"I can't allow that. She'll tell everyone where you are," Rush said.

"What about the forgetting potion?" Astor pointed out.

Rush studied the shifter for a long while, the vein along his jaw feathering. "For you, I suppose." He drew a small glass vile with blue powder from his pocket and handed it to Astor.

"No!" Aura shouted while Rush ripped her away from Hana.

Her sister backed away as Astor uncorked the vial. He

blew the contents toward Hana and whispered words she couldn't hear.

Aura thrashed in Rush's grip and he held her tighter. "She'll be fine. She'll only forget ever meeting Astor and me. The caster chooses what they want the person to forget."

Aura stopped bucking—she didn't like the idea of her sister forgetting, but if it wasn't taking away all her memories... She would be safer at home not remembering who Astor was or how he'd tricked her. Aura hated thinking it, but this was for the best.

Hana fainted and Astor caught her in his arms. A line furrowed between his brows as he studied her. "I'll take her home." He removed a key from his pocket and unlocked the manacle around her ankle.

"Don't take long," Rush commanded and Astor nodded.

As Astor carried Hana up the steps, Rush drew Aura back, preventing her from following. "Now," he growled in her ear. "When I give you a warning, listen. When I ask something of you, do it."

"Yes, *Master*," Aura mocked as she glared at him. "May I go to the gardens now?"

"Go to the kitchens and eat first."

"Fine." As she took a step forward, a strange feeling erupted within her and she glanced back at him. "Why did you already have that vial on you if you didn't intend to use it on Hana?"

"In case I ever decided to forget." He scowled. "Now go."

Aura spent longer in the kitchens than she would've thought, watching as Marion baked. Besides not having eaten in days, she supposed she stayed because it reminded her so much of Liana. Marion knew so many secret recipes that Liana would've given up her life for them.

After she had a second helping of potato soup, Aura left the palace walls and ventured out into the gardens. The wind ruffled her hair, and the blue of the sky became darker. She hoped Hana was safe now, that Astor would keep his word and take her home. But as long as Aura stayed within the gates like a tamed animal and kept her identity a secret, she believed her family wouldn't be bothered.

Now that she was alone, the gate inside her mind burst open, releasing a flood of memories about Pax. She'd tried not to think of him, and it had worked until this very moment. Her entire life had been built around becoming the Prince of Starnight's bride. She hadn't cared if he'd had lovers in the past, but once she met him, once they started pleasuring one another, it was meant to be them only. For him to lie about everything was far worse than just simply telling Aura that she wasn't enough for him, that he wanted to spread anyone's legs when she wasn't looking.

Blood stormed in her veins and she wanted more than to slap him—she wanted to *murder* him.

"My lady, I haven't seen you in days. What a pleasant

surprise." A man's voice drew her out of her raging thoughts.

It was the stable hand—Brix. She hadn't realized she'd approached the stables. "Sorry, I was held up in my room. You know, sometimes one has to get their beauty rest," she sniffed, wiping a few angry tears from her eyes.

"Is everything all right?" he asked.

Aura peered at this stranger's handsome face. Since she'd been in the palace, he'd been the only man kind to her, even if it was only for two brief moments. She was exhausted, hurt, and lonely. Most of all, she didn't want to think about Pax. "Perfect now. You don't have a lover, do you?"

His brows lifted and the edges of his lips tilted upward. "Not a permanent one."

"That's good enough." Aura grasped his face and brought her mouth to his. There was no hesitation as he kissed her back. Sparks didn't ignite as they had with Pax, but it still felt good, the way his lips caressed hers, how he tasted of mint.

Brix backed her against the stables and his hardness pressed through her skirt. She wanted to rid herself of Pax. Let another touch her, allow herself to touch them, just so that Pax didn't have to be the last person who'd pleasured her.

Aura unlaced Brix's trousers and dipped her hand inside to grasp his length. She stroked him while he groaned. Brix rubbed her mound through the fabric of her dress and she moaned for more. He didn't leave her begging as he lifted her dress, but before he could dip his hand into her undergarments to touch her heat, a deep voice boomed from behind them, "Touch her cunt and you'll lose that hand."

# RUSH

*B*urn him.

The dragon roared inside Rush. *Raged.* Coarse hands on her silky skin. Touching. Kissing. Exploring.

*Burn him now.*

Rush prowled closer to where Aura stood, brushing her skirts down. Heat colored her cheeks. Lips swollen. Chest heaving. If he'd been even a moment later, Brix's fingers would've caressed her silky center. Heard her moan. Made her come.

*Incinerate.*

Balling his hands into fists, the King of Sin positioned himself between the pair. The scent of smoke filled his nostrils as he towered over Brix. "Off. Limits," he warned, his voice a mixture of his own and the gravelly snarl of his dragon.

"Forgive me, Your Majesty," he quaked.

Rush didn't have it in him to *forgive* anything at the moment. If Aura wasn't at his back, and if he wasn't in a hurry to take care of court duties, the stable hand would be a pile of fucking ash. "Retrieve my horse."

Brix darted away the moment the last syllable left Rush's mouth. Then he spun on Aura. She peeked up at him, part fear, part insolence. She crossed her arms in a silent dare for him to speak.

"No," was all he could muster without losing his temper.

"No? *No!*" she shrieked. "You're the one who told me I could fuck anyone I wanted!"

Rush's lips curled into a sneer. "And now I'm telling you *no.*"

She released a wordless, outraged cry, and Rush left her standing there alone. If she spoke another word, she would find herself locked in her room until the spell completed. And right now, he didn't have time to properly punish her for letting someone else touch what was *his.*

Bright orange flames crackled in Rush's bedroom fireplace the next morning. He studied the burning logs as he stood in front of them, soaking up their warmth. His dragon stirred inside him, relishing it just as much. In one swallow, Rush threw back a glass of ale. The golden liquid slid smoothly down his throat, drowning out the image of Aura and the stable hand.

"Don't pack my cloak," he ordered his valet, Joff. "I'll wear it when I leave."

"Yes, Your Majesty," he replied. The middle-aged man was new to his position, but decent enough to keep around. Joff moved from Rush's wardrobe and packed a change of clothing into a small leather sack.

The door to the bedchamber slammed open and Astor strode in wearing a frown on his face. Taking Hana home seemed to have only made him drearier. The shifter paused as he took in Joff packing, then rose a brow at Rush.

"You really need to work on knocking," Rush said in a flat voice. Anyone else would've already received a bloody smile across their throat if they'd barged in.

"I've seen your ass before." Astor filled himself a glass of Rush's ale and downed it. "Where are you going?"

"Rusmire." The king pulled a letter from his pocket and held it out for Astor to read. "This came an hour ago from one of the guards I sent to locate the sorceress." Aura had woken from every slumber she fell into. Even when she didn't immediately wake, he checked the cellar and confirmed the spell wasn't completed.

"Rusmire is half a day's walk." Astor unfolded the paper and skimmed it over. "And she was seen there three days ago. Do you think she's still there?"

"That's what I'm going to find out." Rush set his glass on the mantle and snapped his fingers at Joff. "Cloak."

The man snatched it from where it hung in the wardrobe and practically sprinted across the room. He draped it over Rush's shoulders and fastened the silver clasp. A moment later, the valet held the cinched bag out to him.

Rush slung it over one shoulder and looked at the shifter. "Are you coming with me?"

Astor snorted a laugh. "With the alternative being that I have to listen to Aura bicker and inquire about *everything*? Fuck yes, I'm coming."

"Good. I want to arrive by midday and stay at the inn, so gather what you need. We're leaving shortly."

Astor spun on his heel and left the room, well aware that Rush *would* leave without him. He'd done it on the last journey when the hawk spent too long gathering his belongings. Rush moved quicker without him, but it was beneficial to have someone watch his back on occasion.

Rush waved Joff from the room and plucked a small sack of gold from one of the ornate boxes on the fireplace mantel. He tucked it into his black tunic alongside the parchment with his spell. He'd find the bitch sorceress in Rusmire and get an explanation as to why the spell wasn't working properly.

Rush took a deep breath and strode out of his room. Tanix stood in the hall, dressed in his black uniform. "You," Rush growled. "Keep a close eye on the girl while I'm gone. Two guards—no, three—on her tail at all times, understood? No one touches her unless she's wounded. If they do, my dragon will burn them to ash."

"Yes, Your Majesty," he agreed with a small bow, his face tight with worry.

Rush stormed through the palace, eager to get his answers from the sorceress. Aura couldn't escape the palace grounds, but he didn't need her attempting it either. Falling asleep wouldn't harm her, but doing it in the wrong place could. Falling too far, tumbling into the pond ... it was better to have her watched every moment he was away.

"Ready," Astor said, panting as he caught up with Rush near the entrance to the palace.

"Keep up," Rush said, flicking his hood over his head as they approached the stables.

Brix met him just outside with two brown mares. A rush of blistering anger flowed through him at the sight of the handsome stable hand. Yes, he *had* told Aura she was free to fuck anyone but seeing it was another thing. It didn't matter they'd fucked the same women at a few of his orgies—Aura didn't belong to Brix.

"Your Majesty," he practically squeaked. Rush sneered in response, squaring his shoulders to make himself larger.

"Two?" Astor asked. "How did you know I'd be back in time to join you?"

"I didn't." Rush ripped the reins of the younger horse from Brix's hand. "I asked him to saddle two so I could choose which I preferred."

Astor laughed and swung himself onto the second horse. "Wouldn't it be easier to fly?"

"For you," Rush snarled. A hawk was inconspicuous. He would blend in and go unnoticed, while Rush's dragon could cast an entire farm in shadow. If the sorceress was evading him, he wouldn't announce himself so boldly. He mounted his mare and nudged her with his heels.

Astor rode beside him down the wooded path leading south. Astor whistled a somber tune as they journeyed. Whistled and whistled until, halfway to Rusmire, Rush wasn't able to ignore it for another moment.

"What the fuck is wrong?" he growled.

Astor sighed, head thrown back. "Hana doesn't remember me..."

Rush rolled his eyes. "What did you think would happen? You're the one who wanted to use the potion on her."

"I know." Astor groaned and rubbed the back of his neck. "It was the only option. I didn't want to keep her prisoner."

"Find someone else's cunt to fuck. She was probably tiring of you anyway."

He grinned. "Trust me. She was *not* tiring of me."

Rush tightened his grip on the reins and sighed. He wasn't one for courting advice. Or courting at all. If Hana didn't remember him anymore, good riddance. "There are plenty of women in Moonstone who will ride your cock. Take your pick of anyone at the palace." Except for one. Aura. Whether asleep or awake, she was *his*.

"I can't," Astor said softly. "I like her."

Rush peered at him, incredulous. "Then woo her all over again and fuck her out of your system. She won't linger in your head forever," he muttered.

Astor was quiet for a long moment, then resumed his somber whistling. Rush groaned and urged his horse to go faster, leaving the hawk a few yards behind. Perhaps it made him a bastard, but Rush had no tolerance for matters of the heart. The best way to deal with emotional turmoil was to slide his cock in someone. That wasn't on the schedule today, however, so Astor was on his own.

Seeming to understand, Astor kept his distance until they reached the edge of Rusmire. Rush stiffened as they silently entered the city, scanning the area for threats.

Weather-worn siding and mossy roofs covered the buildings, and the streets were freshly cobbled. People bustled about without paying Rush and Astor any mind. They were too busy pushing carts of bread and baskets of flowers toward the city center. Most of the stalls were already set up for market day—trinkets and jewelry and pastries. With any luck, the sorceress had come for the market, or at least decided to stay long enough to shop it.

"Stop here." Rush pulled his mare to a halt and dismounted, his boots thudding against the cobbles. "Find a stable for the horses while I get us a room."

Astor took the reins from him and tossed his small sack to the king. "I'll meet you in the market after."

Rush pushed his hood down and approached the closest inn. The scent of warm bread wafted from the bakery on one side of the whitewashed building and an apothecary sign hung on the other neighboring structure. The door creaked open to a smoke-filled lobby smelling of spices and musk. "Welcome, sir," called a portly man. "What can I help you with?"

Rush crossed the red carpeted room and produced a gold coin from his pouch. "I need a room for tonight. Two beds."

"Of course." The man ran a soot-stained finger down a ledger and tapped it. "Room four is just what you're looking for." Rush slid a coin across the desk toward him and the worker handed over a heavy key. "Will you need anything during your stay? Supper? Company?"

"Supper, perhaps, but I don't pay to fuck." He wanted his women willing and eager for his cock—not eager for his coin.

With his business settled, Rush climbed a wide

staircase to room four, finding it already unlocked. Everything was clean and orderly inside. The frilled bedspreads weren't to his taste, but it wasn't important for a single night. He tossed his and Astor's bags on the floor before venturing back outside.

Rush followed the flow of the crowd to the bustling market. Astor had somehow beaten him there and was purchasing a powdered pastry drizzled with chocolate from one of the first stands. Rush approached and shook his head the moment the young woman opened her mouth to ask what he'd like to buy.

"You don't know what you're missing," Astor mumbled around his first bite.

"That's what you said when you tricked me into eating one of those lemon squares." Rush walked away from the stand, searching for a familiar face. One with gray streaking her long dark hair, a wide nose, and piercing brown eyes.

"I forgot your dragon hates citrus," Astor said. "But he likes sugar, doesn't he?"

Rush shot him a glare from the corner of his eyes. "He likes birds of prey. Fresh and bloody, preferably."

"Hmph." Astor stopped at a second stall and chatted up the woman selling flower crowns. Rush let him without complaint. It gave him an excuse to linger, to watch. He was just the bored companion of an overly friendly spendthrift.

Rush observed every person that passed by. Man, woman, and child. The sorceress could be disguised, though she rarely bothered. Unless she'd spotted Rush and cast a spell to conceal herself from him. His dragon was just as observant inside him, eyes narrowed, pulling in deep breaths in hope of scenting magic.

Rush dragged his gaze to Astor, holding up a necklace. A teardrop ruby hung from a gold chain, catching the sun. His dragon practically salivated, though the gemstone was nothing out of the ordinary. But it was *pretty* and *sparkled*. Everything that his dragon enjoyed hoarding—as evident by his collection hidden away in the dungeons of his palace.

"Don't tell me that's for Hana. You can't bribe her into remembering you," he said, forcing his gaze away.

Astor huffed. "I'll take it," he told the seller.

A glimmer in Rush's peripheral drew his attention back to the table. *Jewels.* So many. Large, small. Oval, square, pear-shaped. Rings and necklaces, bracelets and earrings. His dragon pressed forward with a surge of raw *need* and Rush's pupils shifted into slits.

"Fuck." He was going to need to buy *something* just to shut the beast up so he could focus on his task. His gaze ran hungrily over the selection and caught on a pair of amethyst earrings. A large stone was backed by three long silver chains, each with alternating amethysts and diamonds woven in. "Those," he practically growled to the jeweler.

"Wonderful choice, my lord." The man took the coin from Rush and moved to place the earrings into a box.

"No." Rush snatched them off the table and tucked them into his coin pouch. His dragon vibrated with pleasure.

Astor chuckled. "A gift for Aura?"

Rush scowled. They were his—for *his* horde. Unlike his father, he would never share it with his wife. When he *did* marry, it would be for political gain and she would have no access to his precious gemstones.

"Why don't you make yourself useful and grab an aerial view of the city?" he snapped.

Astor clasped the necklace he bought for Hana around his neck and hid it beneath his shirt for safe keeping. "Fine, but after that, I want stew."

Rush blew out a harsh breath and walked into the crowd. *Bottomless fucking pit of a shifter.* But by the time Astor finished looking down every alleyway, they would both be starving. Rush meandered through the market until he'd completed two full rounds without any sign of the sorceress.

This meant he was going to have to communicate. *Play nice* with them so he could extract information. Torture was usually more effective, but that could cause a scene. He ran a hand over his face and made his way to the fortune teller's shop he'd seen on the fringes of the market.

The room was dark, only a single candle lit in the center of a round table. Other than the table and candle, the room was bare. "Hello?" he called out.

"My king," came an airy, feminine voice. "I've been expecting you."

Rush tensed. He could sense the woman's presence, but saw no one. "Come into the light."

A rustle of skirts preceded a figure in a black, lacy dress with sleeves that flared at the wrists. Her white hair was tied back, and her face free of wrinkles. Milky blue coated her eyes, yet they seemed to stare straight into his soul.

"You are not here to have your cards read," she said knowingly. "Nor do you want to ask of your future."

"No." Though, now that he was here, he couldn't help but desire what she would tell him. Would his plan be successful? Would he get his revenge on Pax?

She cocked her head, her milky eyes latched onto his. "You seek the sorceress who was in Rusmire days ago."

"Where is she now?" he demanded.

"Gone." The fortune teller stepped up to the table and ran her hand over the flame. "She came to purchase a few things. Was in and out of the city within hours."

*Fuck!* "Where did she—"

"She's hidden to my sight. I only know she was here because she bought from me. A few herbs, crystals. Nothing of importance."

"I need to find her," he said through gritted teeth.

She smiled, her front tooth chipped. "I can't help with that, but I can tell you that your spell is accurate."

Rush froze. "How do you know about that?"

"How?" The woman laughed. "Do you think of me as a fraud, Your Majesty? Your spell is *accurate*."

"But it's not—"

"Not working?" She shrugged. "I assure you that it was properly cast and will do what it was always meant to do. It will just take time. How much? That is to be determined. I have nothing else of importance for you."

Couldn't she be more specific? A week? A month? "I'm finished here." Rush spun on his heel and slipped back into the market. He needed the sorceress to confirm what the fortune teller spoke was true and he'd continue searching for her. For now, he would take it as the spell was slowly doing what it was meant to. A hawk cried overhead and Rush looked up to find Astor circling, his wings beating against the wind. Then he dove into a

93

nearby alleyway where he must've hidden his clothing.

Astor, fully clothed in his human form, met with Rush a few moments later at the alleyway's entrance. "Anything?"

"Nothing that will help you," he answered, brushing himself off.

Astor shifted between his feet. "What now?"

What else *was* there to do? "Get some fucking stew."

"Now that's something I've been waiting to hear," Astor said.

Rush wasn't feeling particularly hungry, but eating was better than laying in that frilly inn bed, overthinking the entire fucking trip. The sorceress? Gone. The fortune teller? Unsettling. His dragon? Still humming with joy over his new gemstones. Astor? Lovesick, apparently. And Brix? Touching what belonged to him. *Aura.* His head was a spiral of vexing emotions. Ones he wished he could fuck away.

"Shall we plan an orgy soon?" Astor asked.

Rush looked over at him with a raised brow.

He shrugged. "I can read you like a book."

Pausing as they passed a booth selling sheer, scanty clothing for just such an occasion, Rush observed the fabrics. Hanging in the corner was a long, sheer crimson dress that drew his gaze. A silver shine was woven into the fabric, concealing the important parts beneath while also allowing a hint of skin to tease the eye. Before his dragon could make his opinion known on the glimmering garment, he reached for his coins.

"You plan everything," Rush informed Astor. "And make it fucking extravagant."

Rush followed the sound of a piano that drifted out from the ballroom, the melody swift and chaotic. The doors were wide open and, inside, one of the guards sat behind the instrument, fingers flying over the keys. Aura spun around the center of the room with a young boy, barely ten—the son of the guard on the piano, if he remembered correctly. She guided the dance, counting steps while he giggled. Two other guards stood just inside the door, watching.

"Hello, kitten," Rush called from the doorway.

The song came to an abrupt halt and the boy lurched away from Aura to bow. Rush had demanded that no one touch her, but his dragon wouldn't burn a mere child to ash.

"Did you miss me?" he asked, prowling toward her.

"Miss you?" she scoffed. "I wasn't even aware you'd left until the guards were swarming around me like gnats."

His lips curled into a smirk. "Leave us," he ordered. When Aura moved to follow the others, he grasped her wrist. "Not you."

"We have nothing to discuss unless it's you mentioning how Hana is faring," she hissed, trying in vain to pull away.

The moment the door shut behind the guards and little boy, Rush tugged her closer so her chest was pressed against his. "Your sister is back home and in one piece. But I'm having a ... gathering next week. Astor is arranging it as we speak."

Aura wrinkled her nose. "Do your pleasuring away from my room this time." She pushed at him and he allowed her to step back so he could reach into his cloak. He pulled out a paper-wrapped package and held it out for her. "What's this?"

"A gift."

"A gift?" She arched a brow and flipped the package over. "Why?"

Rush crossed his arms. "Open it."

Aura looked from the present to him and back to the gift with a crease between her brows. Slowly, she tore into the paper until it fell to the floor. Left in her hands was a pool of crimson fabric. Her eyes narrowed as she held it up by the shoulders, letting the skirt fall.

"What is *this*?" she hissed.

"Your dress." He grinned. "For the party."

Aura's lips parted as his words sunk in and a soft blush rose in her cheeks. "I'm not going to your *orgy* and I'm certainly never wearing *this*!"

"Oh, you'll wear it, kitten."

A harsh laugh fell from her lips. "I certainly will *not*."

"You're forgetting I know where your family is." He lifted one of the curls that hung over her shoulder and pulled gently, letting it spring back up. "How easy would it be for Astor to drag Hana here and chain her to that wall again, eh? So you'll wear what I tell you to wear and come to the party with a smile on that pretty face. Won't you?"

Her breasts rose and fell with each heavy breath. Defiance shone in her eyes, but so did fear. "I *will* kill you," she promised.

"Hmm, perhaps." He chuckled. "But not before I see

96

you in that dress."

# 9

# AURA

Aura studied the scarlet dress in her hands as they shook with fury. The King of Sin had given her a sheer garment to wear to his party. And by party, from his reputation, she knew it meant *orgy*. The only thing that was keeping her from shredding the fabric to pieces, then throttling him, was Rush's threats and his warning about her sister. If he chained Hana to the wall again, she didn't know if he would hurt her sister. She wouldn't let that happen.

"And what are you planning to have me do at this *party*?" she asked, narrowing her eyes at him.

He stepped forward, his muscles flexing beneath his tight tunic, and a knowing smile spread across his shapely lips. His molten silver eyes seemed to ignite with a hidden secret while studying her. "You'll behave and act as though I'm your king, that you bow down to me, that you *want* me."

Aura scoffed. "No one will believe that lie."

"Then make them believe it," he cooed. "The staff in the palace believe we are fucking anyway. That you're enjoying our little game." His smoky scent caressed her senses as he drew even nearer, his chest only a hair's breadth from touching her breasts.

"I'm not going to fuck you," she spat, shifting away from him.

"What a dirty little mind you have." Rush chuckled. "You couldn't handle my cock, kitten, but what you *will* do is pretend. Hang on to my every word, stay by my side, and most importantly—look *pleased* while doing it." He traced a fingertip down the side of her neck. "You'll also write a letter to your fiancé to officially end things once you leave the ballroom. Be sure to tell him why and don't mention where you are. You can also write one to your family members. Short and sweet or it won't be delivered."

She gripped the garment tighter and pressed her lips into a tight line to keep from cursing him until she was blue in the face.

"I take your silence as agreement." He tilted his head and shifted backward, still wearing that infuriating smirk of his.

Releasing an ugly sound between her clenched jaw, she stormed past him and out of the ballroom. Why couldn't he have been pierced through the heart while out on his short journey? Or if anything, he should've stayed away longer.

Before the king returned to the palace, Aura hated to

admit it, but the day hadn't been quite as bad as others. The guards weren't uptight as usual even though they hadn't spoken with her when they'd followed her into the ballroom. She'd heard a piano melody drifting through the air and had found a guard playing the music for his little boy. The young boy, Radley, had been spinning a wooden top as if it would somehow teach him to dance before asking her to show him how, to which she'd politely refused. However, when he'd appeared crestfallen, she couldn't help but oblige for a few songs.

As Aura stomped into her bedroom, she slung the garment into the back of the wardrobe filled with clothing that guards had brought into the room for her. Beside the bed rested a new night table with blank paper, ink, and a quill. The bastard just knew she would write Pax his damn letter. After sending word to Pax, she hoped the party would be canceled or that Rush would forget she existed.

As Aura thought about the prince, anger reared its ugly head, and she snatched the quill while sitting on the bed. She ripped straight through the first sheet of paper by pressing too hard. Easing up, she gritted her teeth as she wrote the letter to the deceiver of a prince.

*Prince Pax,*

*If you are searching for me, don't any longer. The wedding will not take place. I would've loved you until my last breath, but I know your filthy secrets, how you tumbled women behind my back. I won't be returning home, nor do I want to, and I am living a new life with someone else.*

*Aura*

And then for the brightness in this moment, she took the quill to another sheet of paper and wrote one to her family.

*Dear Father and Mother,*

*I'm sorry to have hurt you all, but I can't marry the prince. I have my reasons and I'm better off here than with him. Hug my sisters for me and tell them I'm sorry.*

*Love,*

*Aura*

With a steadying breath, she folded both letters and went to peer out the barred window. In the middle of the gardens, Brix walked a chocolate mare toward the stables. Since their moment of pleasure that ended with Rush threatening Brix, she hadn't seen him, too embarrassed by what had happened. Because of her boldness, he'd almost lost his hand, or worse, been killed. She at least owed him an apology.

Aura left her room and handed the letters to Tanix to give to Rush before venturing outside. The sky was already darkening so she lifted her skirts and hurried through the garden's labyrinth until she caught up with Brix.

His blond hair was draped over one shoulder, the shorn side facing her as he kept his head down and his gaze averted from her.

"I wanted to apologize for yesterday," Aura said hurriedly. "I shouldn't have thrown myself at you like that when we only just met. I'm sorry that I did it for all the wrong reasons. But I would like to be your friend."

Brix lifted his head and glanced toward the palace, a nervous tick in his jaw thrumming. "We usually share one another here. The king doesn't generally care who pleasures who. It's my fault for not knowing you were his, my lady."

"I'm not *his*." Aura scowled.

"His Majesty would say otherwise. I think it's best we keep our distance unless you need a horse. I will always help you with that. And, for what it's worth, I've never seen the king react that way about a woman." Brix pulled the reins of the horse and walked away from her.

It wasn't as though she was in love with this man. She'd practically used him to forget about Pax, to make her stop thinking about the prince pleasuring other women. But because of her recklessness, she'd lost one of the only people here who might've been a friend.

Aura turned toward the palace and stilled. Standing on the balcony with his arms dangling over the ledge as if he were watching a fool's performance was Rush, smirking.

If she could flee the gardens without a spell putting her to sleep, she would do it just to irk him, even if he could catch her. But if she did it now and passed out, it would only give him the pleasure of reminding her that she couldn't leave.

Balling her hands into fists, she trekked back through the shrubbery and inside the palace, not looking at any of the servants' or guards' faces. She slammed her bedroom door behind her and found her usual spot on the floor where she rested at night. Tears stung her eyes as she curled up on the stone. The only thing keeping her from sobbing uncontrollably was that Hana was safe in Starnight.

A prick pierced the pad of her finger and she yawned. However, like before, nothing was there. Even though she was tired, the motion had come from somewhere deep within her chest. Her eyelids fluttered shut, lulling her into sleep as it had the other instances. She didn't fight the spell this time. Instead, she allowed it to simply take her away where she wouldn't have to remember she was a prisoner in Moonstone.

The darkness of her dream pulled back like a curtain, the world gaining color. She stood in front of a lake, surrounded by white and pink flowering trees.

The warm breeze ruffled her hair, and she stared at the shimmering blue water.

"You still haven't told me your name," a familiar voice said from behind her.

Aura startled and whirled around to find the same girl from her past dreams holding a basket of red roses. Her dress was wet and clung to her, the same way it had in that first dream. The girl smiled, her sapphire eyes sparkling, and Aura took a moment to answer. "I'm Aura. Do you remember yours yet?"

The girl's face fell as she shook her head. "No. My memories drift in and out of my head. That's what it feels like anyway. As soon as I pluck one, it vanishes. I remember dying, the water swallowing me whole." She pressed her hand to her stomach, tears beading her lashes. "The both of us."

Aura's chest tightened at the thought of this young, sweet girl and her child dying together. "So you drowned? I suppose that explains why your dress is wet. Do you remember how?" Aura thought about her last dream, the water filling the room, but she didn't think it could've happened that way. Not without a sorcerer's spell...

"I don't, but it was this lake. I don't know where you could find it when you wake though." The girl pointed toward the water, her expression serene.

Besides the small pond on the palace grounds, she couldn't leave to search for it anyhow. "Before, you were

103

writing a letter to a beloved, then later you said Rush's name. Is he the one you were writing to?"

"Rush," the girl whispered, her brow furrowing as if the name was both familiar and not. "There is pain when I think of that name. There is pain when I died. Too much pain. I don't want you to have this pain either." Tears filled the girl's eyes and before Aura could ask anything else, the girl vanished into thin air.

Above Aura, the blue sky darkened to slate and lightning cracked. Her breathing increased, and she took a hesitant step back as the lake turned obsidian. A sound like a heartbeat thrummed, coming from the sky in between the cracks of lightning. Behind her, a bright flash of light struck the ground and she jumped.

"Wake up, Aura," she hissed at herself. "Wake up *now!*"

The lake rippled and a shadow rose from the water. Her eyes widened when she realized it was the water itself. Long fingers curled on a massive hand as an arm reached toward her.

Aura spun, darting toward the trees, but not fast enough. Velvety digits grasped her ankle and yanked her backward as she screamed. The hand pulled her across the grass while she dug her fingers into the dirt. But nothing prevented her from being pulled into the lake's freezing depths.

The crushing pain struck her finger and Aura jolted forward, drinking in the air. She kicked her legs to get the watery hand off her, but she was no longer beneath the lake. The obsidian ceiling of her room stared down at her, welcoming her back to this nightmare.

What was the reason for these dreams? The girl there?

Rush had already told her she wasn't going to die from the spell, but he was certainly doing *something*. Aura couldn't ask just anyone about the girl since they all aligned with Rush. She was supposed to meet Marion in the kitchen to help make another pie, so maybe she could get some sort of answer from her if she asked the right questions.

Morning light spilled through the window, so she tossed on one of the simple, clean dresses in the wardrobe before padding toward the kitchens. Since Rush was back at the palace, the guards no longer trailed her from room to room. Marion stood behind the granite counter, specks of white flour dotting her face and hands.

"You two take these into town," Marion said, handing two female servants each a basket filled with pastries.

"Of course," they both chirped and left the kitchens.

"You're late. I didn't think you'd make it in time before I started on the pie crust," Marion chimed. "Add the flour, sugar, and butter to the bowl."

Even though she didn't like cooking any more than she had before coming to the palace, Aura wiped her palms on her dress and did as instructed while Marion explained the necessary steps. As she mixed the ingredients for the crust, Aura's gaze flicked to the woman in indecision. She didn't know how long Marion had worked at the palace or if she would even know anything about the dream girl. But this was the moment to try anyhow. "You've been here a long time, I'm assuming. What were the other royals like before they passed away?"

Marion smiled sadly. "They were lovely. King Rufus was jovial, Queen Muriel full of laughs, and Princess

Constance was incredibly kind." She pinched her lips together, wiping away a few tears. "Anyway, the king and queen only took pleasure in one another and ensured the court didn't fall back into darkness."

"What about Rush? Has he ever had a beloved? Someone meant to be his queen?"

Marion giggled, eyeing her as though she wished Aura might stand a chance. "One could only hope. Oh! Let's get the fruit ready for the pie."

Aura knew asking anything else would be suspicious since she'd never shown interest in Rush before, so she focused on the pie. When Marion turned the other way to place the dessert in the oven, Aura snatched a smaller knife and slid it up her sleeve.

"I better go, but I'll come back tomorrow morning." Aura kept her tone even as she backed out of the kitchens so she could hide the knife in her room. Marion might be nice enough, but she would still tell the king that Aura had snuck a knife up her sleeve.

Marion furrowed her brow. "Are you not going to try your own baking?"

"Save me a slice for tomorrow," Aura said, keeping her tone even. She then walked at a brisk pace through the hallways.

As she reached the stairs, Rush stepped down from the last one. *Damn it.* She twitched, grasping the sleeve of her dress so the knife didn't slip out.

Aura forced a smile. "Hello, Your Majesty."

Rush studied her for a long time, his muscular body taking up the entire width of the stairs because of the angle he was standing. "If you're going to sneak a weapon into your possession, at least steal something better than

106

a dulled kitchen knife."

"I didn't steal anything," Aura bit back as beads of perspiration dotted her brow.

Rush grabbed her arm and rolled up her sleeve, then took out the knife, his callused fingers brushing her flesh. "I don't recall gifting this to you, kitten. But I do recall instructing you that you're not allowed to handle weapons while you're here."

Aura sighed. "Fine, I took it, but I wasn't going to *kill* you—that's a task I'll leave to one of your countless enemies. It was protection for the party … if you—"

Rush cut her off with a bitter laugh. "When we fuck, kitten, it's going to be because you're begging for it, not because I'm forcing myself on you. Have your measly weapon." He placed the knife back into her palm and sauntered away from her.

"What do you mean *when*? There won't be any *when*— it's *never*," she yelled at his back, but he only arched a brow over his shoulder before he disappeared around the corner. *Bastard.*

Aura ascended the steps, then slipped into her bedroom. She placed the knife in the back of her wardrobe and spent the rest of the day out in the gardens, sitting alone near the roses. The red ones reminded her of the dream—the girl's basket filled with them. She frowned and thought about the girl … what if she wasn't even real, but someone Aura was conjuring up?

Every so often she glanced back at Rush's balcony, wondering if he'd watched her at all, yet it remained empty.

One of the servants brought her out a sandwich and a glass of water, to which she downed them both. If Liana were here she would've been appalled by how dry the bread had been. And that made her think about the rest of her family, how she missed them. Aura wondered if the little ones were sneaking desserts, if Hana was riling up her mother. Was her father searching for her? She bit the inside of her cheek to hold back tears.

Defeated and tired, she decided to go back to her room. Perhaps she might visit the ballroom later and see if someone would play the piano for her.

As she opened the door to her room, her gaze caught on a penned letter resting on the bed beside two glistening objects. A pair of amethyst stud earrings, their backing long silver chains with alternative amethysts and diamonds. On the sheet of paper, elegant cursive script read: *These will go with your dress for the* orgy.

Her blood boiled in her veins at the taunting last word that she'd used the day before. And although the earrings were beautiful, she wanted to hurl them at Rush's face. Tightening her grip around them, she bounded down the hall toward the king's bed chambers.

Aura marched past Tanix and barged inside the king's room to toss them somewhere whether he was there or not. But as her gaze fell to the bed, she halted in place. Rush lay on black silken sheets, his muscular body bare, as he stroked his hard cock. The second one she'd ever seen, its girth and length even larger than Pax's…

The earrings fell from her hand, clacking to the floor. Heat crept up her neck, then spilled into her cheeks. "What are you doing?" she hissed.

Rush's gaze latched onto hers, but he didn't stop pleasuring himself. A lazy smile spread across his face. "What am *I* doing? That's rather obvious, kitten, but I should be the one asking that question." His head fell back against the headboard, eyes glazed with lust, and he released a small, pleasured groan. "Make sure to shut the door behind you when you run off."

That was what the King of Sin expected her to do. Did he think she feared watching a man stroke his length, regardless if she'd only touched Pax's? In truth, she might have if anger wasn't muddling all rational thought. She wasn't going to prove him right though, so she inched toward his bed and pressed her fists to his silken sheets. "I think I'll stay and watch, Your Majesty."

Rush's lips parted for only a moment before curling into a wicked grin. Her heart pounded at how the expression made his face more handsome, alluring. A handsome face with a bastard heart.

He pumped his cock, circling the tip with his thumb before his pace grew faster. A groan escaped him as his hooded eyes held hers, and she felt that sound down to her bones. "You want to know what I'm imagining?" he asked, his voice gruff.

Aura bit the inside of her cheek to hold back the temptation to answer him.

"You peeling off that dress, crawling up my body ever so slowly until you're sitting on my face. I'd fuck that sweet cunt of yours with my tongue until you begged for my cock instead," the King of Sin rasped.

She took a deep swallow as warmth dipped low in her belly. Although she wouldn't admit it aloud, she imagined it too, his wicked tongue on her slit, swirling over her clit. Aura's eyes narrowed at her own deceitful thoughts and she crawled up the bed beside him to let him know precisely how she felt. He drew in a breath, all the while continuing his meticulous rhythm. She leaned in toward him, inhaling his smoky scent as she whispered in his ear, "I wouldn't touch your filthy cock if you told me I could be the queen of every court in Grimm."

He grabbed her wrist with his free hand, squeezing gently. His nose skimmed her cheek as he turned his head toward her. "You're not running though, are you?"

They stared at one another, battling a rich tension she couldn't explain. He stroked faster, the mattress vibrating when his body jerked and his seed spilled over his hand. As she stared at the glistening liquid trailing down his flesh, a foolish part of her wanted to lick it up, to find out how he tasted.

Aura shook the horrified thought away, locking her gaze with his when she pushed up from the bed. "Don't bring me jewelry again, or next time I'll throw it off the balcony," she said, managing to keep her voice cool. But as she left his room, the apex of her thighs throbbed, needing to be touched, satisfied, *desperately*.

Slamming the door to her bedroom behind her, she hiked up her dress and shoved her hand inside her undergarments to feel her pooled arousal. As she circled her clit, she hated him for making her do this too.

Over the days leading up to the party, Aura had avoided the King of Sin as much as possible, but his slitted eyes always drifted to hers. As if he'd known that she'd touched herself to bliss in her bedroom after he'd spilled himself. But even if she'd been thinking of him while doing it, that didn't mean she liked the bastard. She still had every intention of uncovering what he was doing with her.

Each day the slight drain to her body had come, only for a moment, the brief tug. However, there were no more dreams with the nameless girl. Perhaps she would attempt to escape the gardens again to see if that would return the girl to her dreams.

Aura peeled off her robe after being pampered by servants with a bath of lavender and herbs. Her hair was nearly dry, hanging in loose waves down her back for the servant to return and style soon. She decided to forgo bringing the knife with her—if Rush wanted to take her against her will, he could've on numerous occasions by now. Besides, he would easily see the knife through the garment she was meant to wear.

Wrinkling her nose, she studied the sheer dress and held her breath as she put it on. The hem brushed her ankles while the sleeves came to her wrists. The back dipped to where her buttocks was and the front neckline sat low. It wasn't disgust she felt, but awe—the fabric was lush against her skin. The way it showed off the curves that were normally hidden beneath her simple dresses. It barely covered her breasts, mound, and backside with the sewn-in silver sheen. This would've been perfect to wear on her wedding night, and she shoved that thought away. Even though she loved it, she didn't know if she could wear the garment in front of Rush and an entire party of people.

Closing her eyes for a moment, she called upon her courage. She could do it for her family. And for another reason, a darker one. If Pax somehow heard of her *affection* toward the King of Sin after receiving her letter, it would be satisfying. She would pretend her damned hardest to show that she wanted the king.

# RUSH

Sultry music floated through the halls of the palace, the violin dragging out each note. The party Astor organized had begun an hour ago, but Rush was always deliberately late. All the build-up to the real entertainment, *conversing* with people, wasn't the point of these gatherings. If they wanted to ask how each other's lives were going, they could talk on their own time. The King of Sin wanted the dancing, the *fucking*.

But tonight he was later than usual for an entirely different reason. Tonight, he needed to make a grand entrance with the runaway Starnight bride—not that anyone would be aware of her identity. The maid was finally escorting her now. Black trousers hung low on his hips, his silver shirt untucked and halfway buttoned. He worked his jaw as he waited.

"My lady," the servant urged in an exasperated voice. "*Please*, hurry."

"I don't think I will," Aura said slowly.

"If you could only walk a bit faster. We're already late and the king—"

"Can wait for me," she finished for the maid.

Rush scowled. Aura was just asking for trouble—if she wanted to play games, he would play them better.

"My king," the maid chirped when she rounded the corner and dipped into a curtsy. "I apologize for our tardiness."

"It seems someone else should be saying that." He flicked a hand at the maid, dismissing her. She scurried past him just as Aura stepped around the corner.

Rush sucked in a breath at the sight of her. Silky hair lifted off her neck into a low chignon with small curls framing her heart-shaped face. Eyes rimmed with kohl, shapely lips the same shade of her crimson dress. The sheer scarlet fabric clung to her body in all the right places and whispered around her slippered feet. Her breasts and mound were shaded by shimmering silver that swirled and spread over the dress. It showed just enough skin to stiffen Rush's cock. His mind flooded with lustful memories of how she watched him fuck his hand, and he swallowed the low growl that built in his throat.

"Spin," he demanded, his eyes hooded.

She crossed her arms. "Good evening to you too."

"I said *spin*." When she stood still, he added a sarcastic, "Please."

Aura huffed and turned around quickly. The silver swirls caressed her ass, tempting him to ask her to spin for him once more.

Rush approached her and lifted her chin. "If your betrothed could see you now…" He smirked. "On display. On *my* arm."

"He's not my betrothed anymore." She yanked her chin from his fingers. "He's likely received the letter by now and is cursing my name."

Rush released a dark chuckle. Yes, Pax must've received her missive. Cursed her. Torn through his precious palace like a man possessed by dark magic. She had rejected him. Embarrassed him. It wasn't enough to quell Rush's thirst for revenge, but it was a start.

"Remember, do as you're told and smile," he drawled, brushing a finger against the closed door. "No one bites. Unless you ask them to."

Rush could see how Aura fought back against narrowing her eyes, the rage swirling within those violet depths. But she put on a false smile and nodded, even when a laugh burst on the other side of the door, brassier than the sensual music.

"Then let's not keep them waiting," Aura said, lifting a brow.

Rush arched his in return and looped her hand into the crease of his arm. Instead of her lips curling into a snarl as he'd expected, she held her tight smile and took the first step toward the door.

"I don't normally make a grand entrance for these parties." He looked her up and down, taking in the swell of her breasts, the curve of her hips, and his dragon stirred in awareness. "But tonight, I have something to show off."

He caught her scowl, and he couldn't help but smirk.

Rush rapped on the door once, a signal to be announced. The music screeched to a stop and the door swung open. He squared his shoulders and lifted his chin while Aura didn't even bristle.

The loud voice of a male guard boomed, "His Royal Highness, King Rush of Moonstone."

The crowd of nearly three dozen turned toward them inside the dim room, their faces cloaked by shadows but bright enough to see the sea of various fabrics. Light caught on colored glass that decorated their faces, shimmering along their brows and cheekbones. Aura was the only one swathed in crimson after he'd forbidden the color be worn by anyone else. Goblets of wine were lifted into the air as a wordless cheer rang out, welcoming the king and his unnamed guest to the festivities.

Rush led Aura through the doorway, squeezing her hand that rested on his arm, forcing her not to pull away. He didn't glance at her. Didn't offer any encouraging words as they approached his throne. He had none to give. She *should* be worried because this evening would be an offense to her morals. An awakening of sorts. Rush turned, spinning her to face the crowd when they reached the dais. The back of the obsidian throne framed him from behind with sharp, jagged edges. A massive pair of dragon wings made of obsidian glass stretched toward the ceiling on either side.

"Welcome." Rush's voice echoed through the silent room as he lowered himself into his throne.

The guests needed no other encouragement. The violins and piano started again, low and sensual, and the guests began swaying against one another in languid movements. Aura stood rigid at his side where he left her standing beside the throne, absorbing the dancers. He smirked and leaned back into the chair, ignoring her. Since the spell wasn't putting her to sleep just yet and the sorceress still couldn't be located, he wanted her to see what pleasures life had to offer. Soon, someone would approach him and ask about the beauty at his side. He *never* came with anyone—he always found a willing woman at the party to wet his cock—so walking in with her was a statement.

As the dancing continued, Rush tilted his head toward Aura. To the curve of her ass, delectable, exquisite, and just beside the arm of his throne. His fingers flexed where they rested on his knee, straining to touch her, but he wouldn't. Not until she begged him to. She shifted slightly, drawing his eyes upward to her flushed cheeks.

"What's on their faces?" she asked, her violet irises pinned to his.

Rush admired the flashes of color that caught the dim lighting. "Glass." He shrugged. They wore them, sculpted to look like dragon scales, around their eyes, across their brows, along their cheekbones. Different shades, a variety of intricate designs. All of them to worship the King of Sin.

Aura chewed her bottom lip as she watched the people brush their hands seductively along one another's flesh. It wasn't disgust that shone in her gaze but curiosity. Rush could practically hear her thinking. He'd purposely left her free of the glass so he could decorate her himself.

"Your Majesty," Vikram, the lord of Uleis—a territory in Moonstone—greeted as he approached the dais from the left. He was an older man with thinning hair

117

and a scraggly beard, the only one in the room besides Aura without any glass. Why the *fuck* did Astor invite him? "My nephew and chosen heir was invited to join you tonight."

"And?" Rush drawled, watching a young redheaded male run his tongue up a woman's swanlike neck instead.

"You haven't been formally introduced yet, so I'm here to make introductions. Then, I'll leave you to your amusements," he said with a knowing chuckle.

Rush sighed. "Fine. Where is the welp?"

The lord turned and waved a man with dark brown hair, close in age to Rush, forward. Dark blue scales decorated his tanned brow and flared out across his temples. He bowed, his white tunic standing out against his gray trousers. "Your Majesty."

"This is Dzmitry, future Lord of Uleis," Vikram said.

Dzmitry straightened his spine and peered first at Rush, then at Aura. Expected, of course. She was new, she stood at the king's side, and she was alluring. But his gaze *lingered*. He raked her up and down, spending extra attention to the swell of her breasts.

Rush glowered at him. "Do you like my kitten, Dzmitry?"

The man jerked, his gaze lowering to the ground. "Forgive me, Majesty."

"She is quite fetching," the lord admitted. "Might we ask her name?"

"You may not." Rush skimmed the back of his fingers over Aura's hip. The heat of her body soaked into his skin.

"You look familiar, my lady," Dzmitry blurted.

Rush lifted a brow. Could this young man recognize

Aura? Uleis was a Moonstone town that bordered Starnight, and Pax's soldiers were likely nosing about. A *dragon* had made off with their future princess, after all. It was only a matter of time before they petitioned to enter Moonstone to search for Aura.

"I hear that often," she said in a flat voice. Her gaze drifted to Rush and she put on a smile.

"Go," Rush growled at the two men. They gave each other a knowing look before backing away from the dais. Vikram headed toward the door almost immediately while Dzmitry cast another longing glance at Aura over his shoulder. Rush's dragon snarled inside him, his fire coursing through his veins.

"Did I give you permission to speak?" he asked, his voice a low hum as he shifted forward in his seat.

"Do I *need* permission?" Aura hissed.

"You need my permission for everything, kitten." His fingers circled her wrist and he drew her in front of him. After motioning to a servant who stood along the wall, Rush sat forward and turned Aura to face him.

"Rush," she breathed, shifting nervously.

His vision wavered for a flicker of a moment, zeroing in on her with his dragon's sharp eyesight before he shoved the beast back down. "Kneel, kitten."

"What? I'm not—"

"It isn't *that*." His lips tilted up at the edges. "Now do as you're told and *kneel*." He took her second wrist and she went down on her knees.

A table appeared beside the throne, the servant placing a small golden chest upon it before fleeing.

"You can ask for things nicely," Aura mumbled, eyeing the table.

Rush grabbed the chignon at the base of her neck and tilted her face up toward him. "If you insist on sassing me all night, I can lock you back up in your room."

Her jaw clenched, her eyes not wavering from his. "Fuck you."

"Now, now." He leaned in to whisper in her ear. "Is this what you call behaving?"

Dzmitry was speaking to a group of men and women in the far back of the room, their eyes darting over to Rush and Aura, then away again. A surge of protectiveness raced through his veins. If the bastard truly had recognized Aura, Rush would have to act before word spread. He lifted a piece of hair that framed her face and tried to imagine what he might be forced to do to protect her.

When she remained silent for a few moments, Rush released her hair and leaned back in his throne. "Good girl."

She let out a breath and murmured, "What am I doing down here?" The last word came out shaky, nervous, and for a moment, a brief one, Rush's heart pounded too fast. But he had to remember he wasn't the person he used to be. He wasn't *kind*. Wasn't *soft*. Those things were too dangerous for him.

"Unfortunately, not sucking my cock." He gave a throaty chuckle as crimson seeped into her cheeks. "So scandalous, I know." She opened her mouth to speak and he placed a finger over her shapely lips. "Hush now."

She slowly blinked but remained quiet. Rush removed his finger and leaned to the side to open the chest. A collection of silver glass scales shone inside, sparkling like jewels. They were spelled to adhere to skin for half a

120

day—a simple, well-known trick that young sorcerers used to practice their skills and earn coin. Rush lifted the thin metal tool and selected one of the larger scales.

"What are you doing now?" Aura sighed.

"Do you know why everyone is wearing these?" Rush held the glass in front of her, tilting the scale so it caught the firelight.

"Is that a glass *scale*?"

"It is." He met her eyes and felt a pang in his chest, an eagerness to see her wear them. "You didn't answer my question."

Aura pursed her lips. "Because you're a narcissist?"

"Because I'm their *king* and they choose to honor me." He brought the scale to the space between her brows and pressed it in place. His dragon sat up with a purr that vibrated through him. The sight of silver gleaming back at him, the exact shade as his beast's eyes, made him want more. More of her, more of *him* on her. Staking his claim. He hid a wince at the idea of it, and covered it with a grin. "I missed the portion of the party where the guests applied theirs because you took longer than expected."

"Beauty can't be rushed," she told him with the arch of a brow.

"Mmm," he agreed. His dragon gave a small trill of excitement as Rush added a second scale to the outer edge of her eye. The primal urge to cover her in glimmering scales tore through him, to take her to his hoard and keep her there. But she wasn't a possession—she was a means to an end. "When you allow someone to apply your scales, it's a sign that you're interested in ending the evening with them."

"By escorting them home?"

"Perhaps." Rush grinned as he gently pressed two more to her warm flesh. "And then tucking them into bed." He swept a lock of hair from Aura's forehead and created an upward swirl with the scales. "Right after they fuck themselves into exhaustion."

Aura's mouth parted, her red lips begging to be kissed, licked, nipped, but she didn't use that alluring tongue of hers to speak. She only simply drew in shuddering breaths.

Rush's hands brushed across the soft skin of her face as he finished one side. The scales followed her brow line, then splintered at her temple. One rising toward her hair, the other snaking down the edge of her face and onto her neck. The sensation of her gentle exhales against his fingers as he worked sent hot blood into his cock. What would it feel like if her breath skated over that part of him as he sat in his throne? As everyone watched her lick his shaft? Simply having her watch as he stroked himself was enough to make him come when she barged into his room.

Rush's dragon unfurled at the thought, but Rush tamped it away. If she didn't fall into a permanent sleep soon, he *would* fuck her as part of his revenge on Pax, but she would *want* him to. He completed the second half of Aura's face and placed the tweezers onto the tray.

Aura ran her delicate digits across the line of glass decorating her brow. "Does the King of Sin not wear scales to his own party? Wouldn't his dragon want him to?"

One side of his lips curled. "Do you miss him, kitten? Do you *like* my dragon?"

122

She rolled her eyes and moved to stand, but Rush was faster. He gripped her throat gently, running his thumb up and down the curve of her neck. Drawing a deep breath, he called upon the *smallest* bit of his dragon. Just enough that the beast wouldn't take over. Scales pressed through the skin of his face, and what he knew to be a spattering of glossy black along his cheekbones. A tease of a shift that took immense concentration to accomplish.

"Is this better, kitten?" he asked, his voice sharp as his dragon prowled inside him, asking to be set free. Later, he would make amends by going for a flight.

Aura bit her lip, lifting her fingers and skimming over them. "They're warm."

The gentle touch ignited his blood, his groin straining harder against his trousers, and he jolted back. "Go dance."

She blinked. "What?"

"*Dance.*" He drew in a ragged breath. "Go. And don't mention your name to anyone." What was he *doing*? He needed to hold onto the past, to loathe Aura and get his revenge. Unfortunately, the damn sorceress was still evading him.

Aura climbed carefully to her feet and turned. She paused for a moment before stepping off the dais and into the crowd. Guests didn't hesitate to allow her into their midst. Dancing. Swaying. Touching her appropriately with the unspoken knowledge that she belonged to *him*. He leaned back in his throne and watched her through slitted eyes.

"Your Majesty?" a soft feminine voice asked.

He snapped his gaze to a raven-haired woman with black scales trailing up the bridge of her nose. A golden dress barely contained her large breasts. "Do I know you?" he asked, his eyes seeking out Aura again.

"Not intimately," she said coyly. "Not *yet* anyway. I'm Emilia."

Rush shifted, his cock painfully hard as he watched Aura smile. *A true smile.* Her body moved side-to-side, swaying slowly, arm movements expressive. Her rhythm was different, captivating, and he just knew she would be glorious while riding him. He imagined her head thrown back, squeezing her own breasts as he rubbed her clit, moaning his name.

"Shall I?" the woman asked, now kneeling where Aura had only moments ago.

Rush's hands curled over the ends of his arm rests. He didn't want her mouth on his cock—he wanted Aura's. And even though he needed it, desperately, he would show Aura just how good he could make her feel. "No. Hike up your gown and sit in my lap."

The woman smiled and eagerly lifted the silk fabric, her wet cunt free of undergarments. His gaze was pinned to Aura as he pulled the woman into his lap, her back pressed to his chest.

Rush trailed his fingers to the woman's mound, spreading her curls to dip his fingers into her heat. The woman arched into him and moaned, but all he could focus on was Aura, begging her to turn and watch him. Others took notice and they slowly abandoned the center of the room to find a more intimate location. The music soon coupled with moans of ecstasy, but Aura continued dancing without a single glance at the throne as he meticulously worked this woman. With his other hand he gripped her hip, urging her to grind her ass against his stiff cock.

He *wanted* Aura to fucking look. To want—

Dzmitry stepped up behind Aura and snaked his arm around her waist as if she were *his*. Pressing his palm against her stomach, he whispered into her ear. Aura's gaze snapped up to Rush and her lips parted as she watched with wide eyes.

*Yes, kitten. This* could *be you*, he thought while rubbing the woman faster, her moan spilling through the room.

But instead of storming up to the dais, instead of ripping his hands from the woman's cunt to place on hers, she turned her back on him to dance with Dzmitry.

And Rush's vision went red.

# AURA

Aura's heart roared in her chest, embarrassment swarming through her at the sight she'd beheld of the king and the dazzling woman. She grasped Dzmitry's shoulders, perhaps a bit too tightly, as they danced. However, she didn't press her body too close to his, unlike the other guests who left no space between their partners.

Dzmitry leaned in and murmured in her ear, "You're quite good at this. And might I add the most beautiful woman in the room." He then stared past her, annoyance swirling in his gaze. Without looking behind her, she knew his emotion was at the king because he believed the situation upset her.

Aura took a deep swallow, growing uncomfortable in

this room—it didn't matter that Dzmitry was kind enough. She kept her back turned to the king, even though the urge swelled within her to glance over her shoulder. When she could fight the impulse no longer, Aura peeked through a slit of people, finding the king scanning the guests, his hand no longer on the woman's mound. The woman turned in Rush's lap to face him, blocking Aura from seeing his expression. As the woman arched her back and rolled her hips, the ballroom seemed to spin and close in on her.

Needing an escape, Aura stood on her tiptoes and spoke to Dzmitry over the music, "I'm sorry, I think I need fresh air."

"I'll escort you outside, my lady," Dzmitry said while glowering toward the king, his arm still draped around her waist.

The pianist continued to finger his way across the ivory keys as the cello's lovely and seductive melody reverberated off the candlelit walls. Their sounds were perfectly in tune with the blood pulsing through Aura, mirroring the beating of her thunderous heart.

Around her, a few more guests slipped out from the dancing crowd, finding places to grope and pleasure one another against the walls, the furniture, somewhere in the halls, or perhaps the many rooms. A few of the candle flames were snuffed, making the room dimmer. To a visitor, it could be considered either enticing or beguiling.

It wasn't the fact that the King of Sin's orgy was beginning that vexed her, but how he continued to keep her there. What was the purpose of remaining in this ballroom if Rush no longer needed her as a statue at his side? However, Rush had been true to his word—he hadn't forced her to give him pleasure or brought her to bliss during his conceited little party. And yet, she couldn't get the way he touched the female from her thoughts, how instead of infuriating Aura, it only made her blood grow hotter.

As she and Dzmitry weaved through the crowd, she didn't glance back at Rush. But now the heat of Dzmitry's arm against her bare back was too close for comfort. Her pace picked up and she shifted from his hold. He was pristine and attractive, but she also remembered how Rush had threatened Brix. This was another man she didn't know, only that he lived on the border of Moonstone and seemed concerned when Rush pleasured another woman.

Aura remained quiet beside him while they walked past a man drawing the top of a woman's dress down to expose her perky breasts. She wasn't certain why she needed the reprieve and couldn't just stay in the ballroom regardless of what the king was doing. It was strange seeing Rush pleasuring someone. But why did it matter? She'd heard him bring another woman to orgasm just outside her room and watched him pleasure himself, yet this was *different*. The way he'd watched Aura as if he was taunting her, touching *her*...

The King of Sin was a narcissist, but for a few brief moments, he'd been gentle when he'd applied the glass dragon scales to her face. The callused pads of his fingertips softly brushing her skin. Yet that wouldn't take away any of what he'd done. Making her his prisoner. Chaining her sister to a wall. The unknown spell. But Rush hadn't lied to her, the way Pax had. She reached up to touch the warm glass on her brow. Somehow, despite everything the king had done, she'd rather be in Moonstone instead of with Pax where he could whisper more deceitful lies into her ear.

Throughout the hallways, couples fondled one another, some with three or four people touching and tasting exposed flesh. She spotted Brix with his head tilted back as a woman knelt before him. Aura's eyes remained wide. She'd heard about acts of pleasure, had experienced several of them with Pax, but this was something she might have only witnessed if she'd gone into a brothel in Starnight.

Near the front door of the sitting room, two guards remained alert, seeming unfazed at what was occurring around them. Tanix lay on the chaise and groaned when a shirtless younger man took his cock into his mouth.

Aura grasped Dzmitry by the arm, tamping down the bit of lust swirling within her. "I need to go alone. Thank you for accompanying me here."

Dzmitry bit his lip and nodded as she walked toward her escape. It most likely came across as rude, but her thoughts were spinning in so many directions. Even wondering what she would've done if she'd discovered Pax had been bedding women after they were married.

Neither of the guards followed Aura into the warm night air. Surprisingly, the gardens were empty of couples, the temporary lust inside her fading. Her gaze caught sight of one lone figure standing in the shadows near a tree. Astor leaned against the trunk, his arms folded across his chest as he kept watch of the area.

She'd noticed him absent in the ballroom, but now she wondered why he would voluntarily guard out here away from most of the pleasureful acts. Deep down she knew it was because of Hana, yet he didn't deserve her sister. As if hearing her thoughts, Astor glanced back over his shoulder, frowning at her.

With a scowl in return, she hurried through the labyrinth of bushes until she reached the secluded rose garden where she hoped to find a few moments of peace. The moon cast its silvery glow over the manicured bushes, highlighting the bright petals. Even though there hadn't been more dreams of the girl, the scarlet flowers reminded Aura once again of her.

She took a seat on the bench and stared up at the starlit sky, counting each bright fleck as a distraction. The number hadn't gotten too high when footsteps echoed behind her. She turned to find Dzmitry carrying two glasses of wine.

"I know you wanted to come alone, and I can leave, but you looked as though you needed something to drink," he said with a boyish smile and handed her a glass.

"It's fine. Perhaps I could use a bit of company after all." Aura scooted over, making room for him. She caught a whiff of apple cider as he sat closer to her than she desired.

Dzmitry ran a hand through his thick brown hair and drank the entirety of his glass while she watched the liquid swirl in hers.

He leaned back against the bench, then let out a puff of air. "I've never been to one of the king's parties. I didn't realize they were so—"

"Sinful?" She laughed softly. "This is my first too." When she was dancing, she'd secretly hoped it wouldn't be her last. The guests were kind and it was more freeing than she would've expected until she'd seen Rush watching her intently while touching another woman's mound.

"You might say that I'm a little confused, *Aura*," Dzmitry said slowly, his deep brown eyes studying her intently. "You broke the engagement to Prince Pax by letter after fleeing Starnight because he was having sex with other women, yet you are in Moonstone with the King of Sin who doesn't give his heart to anyone. Not only that, but he was just pleasuring another woman in front of you."

Aura tensed. Dzmitry knew her true identity. How? Had she seen him before in Starnight? Perhaps at one of the dinners she'd attended at the palace? She couldn't let him know that she feared his discovery, feared what would happen to her family if Rush knew, so she forced a smile. "Mmm, but who says that I'm *with* the king just because I'm here in his palace? I'm only visiting. He can do whatever he wishes."

"My uncle told me the king never brings a woman to his parties, and yet you were by his side after being stolen away on your wedding day by a dragon. I think we both know who that dragon is."

Aura needed to be careful of how she worded things since she was trapped here. But even if she confessed everything to this stranger, what could he do? Start a war between the two courts? For now, her family was safe and that was what mattered most. If she were rescued and returned to Starnight, she might be in a worse prison. One where she was shackled in marriage to Prince Pax if his father demanded it.

"You must keep quiet that you've seen me. My heart is freer here than it would be in Starnight," Aura finally

131

said. "The king helped me realize things I should've already known." She stilled at her own words, realizing they were true. Rush may have taken her against her will, but he saved her in a sense.

Inching closer, Dzmitry's arm came around her shoulders and a shiver crawled up her spine. "What about you? Can you do anything you wish?"

"I did come out here, did I not?" She tried to move over, but her thigh met the edge of the stone bench. Aura's heart pounded nervously against her sternum when his other hand grazed her collarbone.

His too-hot breath brushed her neck as he spoke, "I can't wait to fuck you while you're wearing this dress. But first, you will kneel before me like you did the king and suck my cock."

Fury stormed through Aura. She jerked up from the bench and tossed the wine from her glass in his face. "If you wanted me to tumble you here, you should've said so earlier and I would've saved you the effort," she spat. "I think I've had enough fresh air for this evening, you ass."

As she spun on her heel and started to walk away, Dzmitry's hand clamped around her mouth like a vise, the glass falling from her grasp, the soft dirt preventing it from shattering loudly. He hauled her to his chest while she writhed and ground out in her ear, "You shouldn't have done that. Now you'll lick every drop of the wine from my face, or I'll gut you and claim the Moonstone King did it when I return you to Starnight for the reward."

Both terror and absurdity coursed through her. Did this foolish man truly believe she cared if he blamed the king for her death? It didn't matter though—she didn't want to die or find out what else he would do to her before he murdered her.

Another form pushed out from behind a tree near the edge of the rose garden. She recognized his thinning hair and peppered beard from earlier at the party. The Lord of Uleis. Dzmitry's uncle, Vikram.

Her eyes bulged as she attempted to urge him with garbled words that were trapped by Dzmitry's hand to get his nephew to release her. Yet when he spoke, hope dissipated.

"The carriage is waiting for us." Vikram adjusted the cuff of his shirt sleeve. "We'll fuck her as soon as we clear the gates. You can have a go at the little whore first, but we need to leave now. The hawk shifter is slinking around the gardens."

Aura kicked her foot into Dzmitry's shin and bit down on his hand. "Bitch," he cursed, but didn't relinquish his grip on her.

Even with her squirming, he easily hauled her through the shadows of the gardens. She didn't see Astor anywhere, and for the first time, she wished he would've been there.

As they approached a large chestnut carriage, true fear coursed through her. It wasn't only what Dzmitry's uncle had said about them taking her unwillingly, but that she would fall into a deep slumber once the carriage left the palace grounds. Would they still slide their cocks into her sleeping form? Why hadn't she brought the knife she'd taken from the kitchens? Why hadn't she smashed the glass of wine against the bench, then stabbed the bastard with it instead of walking away?

"Where's the coachman?" Dzmitry whisper-shouted

at Vikram.

A tall form rounded the carriage, wiping a bloody dagger on his silver tunic, and Aura relaxed at the sight of him. "Oh, he's dead," Rush purred.

Both men stilled and Aura's gaze fell to a burly man on the other side of the carriage, resting in a pool of blood seeping from his slit throat.

The lantern light illuminated Rush's blazing, molten silver eyes as he stepped toward them. "And just where are you planning to take my property?"

Aura was too relieved to curse him for calling her his property.

"Your Majesty," Vikram stuttered. "She belongs to the Prince of Starnight. Our duty is to bring her to him."

"No, she belongs to *me*," Rush seethed. With quick reflexes, he lunged forward and sliced with his dagger clean across Vikram's throat, making a wound that mirrored the fallen coachman's.

A gurgled sound escaped Vikram as he slumped to the ground. He grasped at his throat with desperate motions until his body grew still.

Dzmitry didn't attempt to press a blade to Aura's throat. Instead, he relinquished his grip on her and shoved her toward the king, to which Rush caught her. "It was my uncle's plan. He made me do it."

"Is that so?" Rush drawled, then looked at Aura after letting go of her arm. "Do I take his word for it, kitten?"

Aura's hands balled into fists and she shifted closer to Rush. She shook her head as she trembled. "No, they were both a part of it."

Rush's lips drew into a wicked grin while studying Dzmitry. "One chance. Try and make it out of my gardens. Now run, rabbit."

Dzmitry blinked, but then whirled around and took off sprinting through the garden's labyrinth. Still grinning, Rush watched, not doing a single thing.

"He's going to tell Starnight lies," Aura hissed.

Rush held out the dagger toward her, beads of crimson dripping to the ground from its blade. "Aim for him then."

Aura pursed her lips. "No one ever trained me on how to use weapons. I was trained to be *married*."

"Oh yes, I remember your skill with the fork." He chuckled.

"I wish you had no tongue, or better yet, no voice at all." But just as Aura contemplated ripping the dagger from his hand and going after Dzmitry herself, Rush started counting backward.

"Three. Two. One." And then, in the distance, Astor slipped out from a tree and thrust a sword straight into Dzmitry's chest.

"Betraying me normally results in death by dragon fire," Rush told her when Astor approached. "It's a shame to ruin the party though, so let's keep this to ourselves, hmm? I don't want anyone thinking I've gone soft."

Before she could reply, Astor whispered something to Rush and they began talking quietly. Aura silently left them alone, wanting to get away from what had almost happened. If Rush and Astor hadn't been there...

As she ascended the stairs and padded past rooms filled with moans, she refused to think about it. Aura pressed her palm to the doorknob leading to her room when a hand closed around hers. She jumped back, colliding with a familiar strong chest, his arm circling her waist to hold her to him. But this touch didn't make her recoil the way it should have...

"You slipped away again without saying a word?" Rush ground out.

She sighed, wiggling out from his warm arm. "I was only going to my room. I did as you asked, came to your party, and almost *died*. I'm tired."

Rush grasped the handle and pushed open the door. "We can speak inside then."

"What do you want to talk about?" she asked while crossing the room to lower herself on the floor beneath the window.

With an arched brow, Rush sauntered toward her until his tall frame hovered above her. "Why are you sitting on the floor?"

"There's no other furniture in here besides the bed that reeks of stale sex, so I've been using the floor, *Your Majesty.*"

"You've been sleeping down there like a pauper?" he asked, incredulous.

Aura rolled her eyes. "No... Like a prisoner. Isn't that what I am? I might as well act like one."

"Don't be dramatic, kitten. Your door has been unlocked for a while now," Rush mocked.

"Me?" Aura snorted. "You're the one making people kneel before you at the party as if you're a god."

"I made *you* kneel. No one else." Rush smirked, making her want nothing but to slap it away.

"You're unbearable!" she snapped.

He motioned at the air as if what she'd said was nonsense. "I do enjoy your insolence, but we have something else to discuss. What precisely happened with Dzmitry and Vikram?"

Aura blew out an exasperated breath at how he could be so flippant, but she told him all that had happened between her and the two of them, how they'd recognized her. In truth, it wasn't much, but with each sentence she spoke, his jaw grew tighter.

"You should know that I would've killed Dzmitry for following you outside, regardless."

Aura gritted her teeth. "So you'll kill any man I talk to?"

"I'll kill any man I wish, but the guards heard you wanted to be left alone. He should have respected your wishes."

She scoffed. "As if you've respected all my wishes. But what if I'd *wanted* to fuck him? Then what? Would you have threatened to cut off his hands or kill him?"

He narrowed his eyes, his lips pinched into a tight line. "While you're here, there will be no more parties."

Aura sucked in a sharp breath. While she was here? Would he decide that she could go home soon if she *behaved?* "And how long is that precisely?"

"Forever." He shrugged.

The blood inside her veins ignited with fury. She shoved up from the floor and poked him against his hard chest. "I'm getting so sick of these antics. Are you going to be vague *forever?* Are you not going to tell me what this spell you cast on me is *forever?* Am I going to have to watch you pleasure others *forever?*

Rush's lips curled up at the edges, his eyes becoming hooded as he studied her. "Did it bother you watching me bring another to bliss on my throne?"

Her nostrils flared.

He lifted a lock of her hair and twirled it around his finger. "It must have if you mentioned it." His smoky scent enveloped her as he drew closer, and she swore she could taste his flavor on her tongue. "You want to know what I was thinking as I stroked her clit, while I pressed my fingers into her soaked cunt? I was thinking of *you*. Wondering how wet you would feel. What kind of sounds you would make if you were the one I was pleasuring." He backed her into the bars of the window, and unlike when Dzmitry had been near, she didn't feel nervous. She might be the King of Sin's prisoner, but she knew he wouldn't force himself on her.

Aura's gaze fastened to his, her chest heaving while his words played like a repetitious melody inside her mind. Another question nagged at her, "Why do you hate me so much?"

His lips parted a fraction, seeming surprised by her question before his smirk returned. "I don't hate you, kitten. I simply enjoy taunting you."

"But why?" she murmured.

Rush's gaze stayed pinned to hers, and she wasn't certain if he would answer her when he finally did. "For one, you were going to marry Pax. Through you, a once-rightful heir to Moonstone, he could have had access to my throne."

"I wouldn't have wanted your throne." Aura furrowed her brow, not understanding. "Why do you loathe him though? What did he do to make you feel this way?"

"He takes things that aren't his," Rush growled.

"But isn't that what you're doing to me?" Her pulse sped as she awaited his response.

"Pax doesn't give a damn about anyone but himself."

"And you do?" She arched a brow. "If you think you're a better man than Pax, you'll break the spell, let me go free."

"It's too late for that."

"Nothing's ever too late." It was something she always believed, what her mother had instilled in her ever since she'd been a child.

"I'm mending what was broken in my past, so you're right, kitten." He lifted from the wall, stepping away from her. "Meet me in the gardens in three days."

She wrinkled her nose. "You never have me meet you anywhere." Besides the party, there hadn't been one other instance.

He cocked his head. "I do now."

As Rush opened the door to leave, she called, "You forget that Pax took everything from me too."

He slowly turned around, and an emotion she couldn't name brewed in the depths of his eyes. "Not everything, Aura. Your heart still beats, no matter how shattered you may believe it to be."

# RUSH

"Your Majesty," Joff said, approaching the massive ornate desk in the royal study.

Rush dipped his phoenix quill in the inkwell without looking up at his valet. There were only a handful of decrees left that needed his attention before he met Aura in the garden as planned. His dragon demanded he seek Aura out, protect her, touch her, but that was impossible. Rush needed Aura for his revenge, no matter how attractive the dragon found her, and the beast would just have to come to terms with that.

So why had he asked her to meet him? Ever since he murdered for her during the party three days ago, the beast had become unbearable. Snarling and pacing. Unable to sleep. And when his dragon did manage to settle into a slumber, her starlight scent was enough to wake him with a list of vicious demands.

To put it mildly, Rush was *fucked.*

So the past few days he'd gone on horseback, seeking out the sorceress and coming up empty. He refused to throw away two years of hard work to complete the spell. To right all the wrongs in his life. Aura had a purpose and he wouldn't be thwarted by a pretty face. If she hadn't walked out of the party with Dzmitry, if she had returned to him on his throne, he could've pleasured her and gotten the need for her behind him.

"What?" Rush snapped when Joff continued to stand silently across the desk.

He held out a silver tray with a letter bearing the Starnight seal, and Rush froze at the sight of it. "An urgent letter arrived for you."

Rush dropped the quill, splattering ink all over the parchment, to snatch it from Joff. He ripped into it and scanned the harsh, slanted writing of the King of Starnight.

*As I'm sure you've heard, the future Princess of Starnight was taken by a dragon.*

"As I fucking know," Rush muttered under his breath. He mumbled lines from the letter, his eyes narrowing further with each word. "Terrible news, etcetera, etcetera. How long ago did this come?" he asked Joff without looking up. He'd expected it when Aura was first taken, not after all this time had passed.

"Just now, Your Majesty."

There was no chance the king only sent this to inform Rush of his misfortune, so he skipped down a bit, past the sob story to Starnight's *real* purpose.

*The captor is a dragon shifter witnessed by the entire wedding party. With how few black dragons there are and the animosity between yourself and my son, it's safe to say we know who the offender is. I've spoken at length with my advisors and there is only one solution to be had. Return the lady before we're forced into a war neither of us want.*

Rush snorted. "Neither of us? I wouldn't mind burning your court to the ground." If the King of Starnight knew what had happened between him and his son, he might understand how much Rush desired to set their palace on fire.

But there was one issue with the threat. As little as Rush feared a conflict with Starnight, he couldn't have Pax arriving at his doorstep just yet. No—when the bastard came to Moonstone, it needed to fit the plan. The moment *precise*. If Starnight showed up to claim Aura before the spell was complete, everything would be ruined. *He* would be ruined. More than he already was.

What if that fucker Dzmitry had told someone at the party who Aura was before his death? Was that the reason the king had reached out after all this time? Pax could be on his way to the Moonstone Palace at this very moment.

The dragon snarled inside him. His mouth tasted of ash and smoke, heat filling his belly. Aura wouldn't be going anywhere. If he had to hide her deep in his palace and find someone who resembled her to present to whichever diplomat arrived, he'd do it and slaughter them if he had to.

"On second thought," he mused aloud and met Joff's gaze. The valet raised his brows in confusion. "Postpone my meeting with the lords."

Rush didn't wait for him to respond before storming

through the palace. "You," he snapped at Tanix who stood guard near the front entrance. Rush might not be back in time to meet Aura in the gardens, but she could be left to wonder. She needed to remain safe, though—now more than ever if Starnight thought to threaten his court. "Three guards on her at all times while I'm gone."

"Your Majesty." It was half acknowledgment, half question, but the guard would get no further information.

The moment Rush was outside in the gardens, he shucked his clothing. He released a breath and his dragon rose to the surface, the beast begging to be freed. Obsidian scales pressed through his skin. Bones shifted. Eyesight sharpened.

Then, finally, massive iridescent wings burst from his back. His dragon let out a relieved, piercing screech. It *did* feel good to stretch those muscles, but there would be plenty of time for that on their flight across the border. He cracked his wings and leapt toward the sky. Wind hissed over his scales as he sped into the clouds with thoughts of snapping Pax in half.

Gravel crunched beneath Rush when he landed in the center of the Starnight palace courtyard. Guards wearing bright blue uniforms shouted for him to halt while they nocked arrows in his direction, and courtiers raced from the open square with terrified shrieks. He blew a harmless spark of fire from his mouth just to fuck with them as they scurried through arched doorways before shifting back into his other form.

Horrified gasps came from every direction. Rush wasn't sure if that was because of the shift or that he now stood in front of dozens of nobility with his bare form on display. He smirked and strode straight for the main palace entrance.

Inside, gold glittered across the walls, embedded between floor length mirrors. A large scrolling chandelier hung from a ceiling, painted to look like a starry night with its dark sky and glistening white orbs.

"Goodness!" an older woman exclaimed while clasping her mouth, scandalized.

The man beside the woman shielded her eyes. "Sir, what are—"

"Your Majesty," Rush corrected. He gave the man a once over, taking in his size and shape. Though he was old enough to be Rush's father, they were roughly the same size. "Not *sir*."

The man sputtered wordlessly.

"Now, give me your trousers."

Red burst into the man's cheeks, his lips pursed tight. "I most certainly will not! How dare you—"

Rush was in his face a moment later. "The King of Moonstone dares to do anything he pleases. Now give me your trousers before I demand your shirt as well."

"The King of Sin?" The woman whispered at the man. "Sauli, do as he asks."

The color drained from Sauli's face as he unbuckled his belt and let the tan trousers fall to his ankles. Kicking off his shoes, he stepped from the fabric.

"Good boy, Sauli." Rush lifted a brow. "Hand them to me."

Sauli ground his teeth together in defiance, leaving the woman to scoop up the trousers and hold them out. "Here," she muttered.

"Thank you, madam." Rush grinned as he stepped into the scratchy fabric and caught her glancing at his length. "Where might I find your prince?"

"We haven't seen him today," Sauli spat. "The king is holding court, so perhaps he's in the throne room."

If the king was holding court, Pax wouldn't be in the room. Not when his father would be the center of attention among the lords and ladies. Rush chuckled at the idea of Pax joining and walked through the glitzy palace halls for the first time in two years. There was so much of the shining metal that he wondered whether the royal family had any left in their coffers or if they'd emptied their mines for the aesthetics. When he and Pax were children, the ornate palace had filled him with awe, but now it only made nausea churn in his stomach.

Guards eyed Rush as he passed, but none dared to interfere, only whispered to one another in recognition of him. All the more reason to stop him before he reached the bastard prince's bedchamber. However, they remained mum, too afraid to intervene.

Rush paused just outside the white door, embossed with gold filigree. Soft moans drifted from the other side. The fresh-faced guard standing on the right side of the doorframe shifted nervously, his hand going to the sword at his hip.

"Aren't you going to stop me?" Rush raised a brow. "That's your duty, isn't it?"

The young guard swallowed hard, his throat bobbing. "Are you going to hurt him?"

Rush paused at the pitiful guard's asinine question. "Only his pride."

The guard looked from him to the door and back again. Rush snorted at the pathetic excuse for a sentinel and threw a punch into the man's stomach. When he doubled over with a pained grunt, Rush slammed his knee up into his face.

"If anyone asks, you tried," he mocked as the guard crumpled to the floor.

Inside, Pax lay on the middle of his canopied bed while a blonde woman bounced on his cock. She flung herself off him with a screech as the prince jolted upward. "What the fuck?" Pax bellowed.

The woman gathered her clothing—a maid's outfit judging by the neutral-colored linen—and fled the room. Rush watched her race down the hallway, bare-assed.

"You can't just walk in here," Pax snapped. His eyes narrowed in anger, but surprise shimmered there. "Rush…"

"Obviously, I *can*." The last time he'd been here, there was a different girl in Pax's bed. There was *always* a different girl. Not that Rush lacked partners, but they knew what they were getting into. Pax, on the other hand, made the women he fucked think they were somehow special. Rush had always wondered about the girl Pax was betrothed to, had even thought once to warn her of the prince's activities. But Rush hadn't known her, and even then Pax had yet to meet her.

The prince swept his brown locks back from his face and glared. "Just like you can steal my bride?"

Rush stalked around the room, holding back the urge to unleash his dragon to sink his teeth into the prince's throat. "You clearly miss her terribly."

Pax snatched up the sheet and wrapped it around his waist. "Of course I miss her. This is just how I'm coping since it can't be Aura in my bed."

*Yes, by having another blonde to easily replace her.* Rush released a harsh laugh. "But *would* it be?"

If Pax hadn't been fucking someone against the stable, the wedding wouldn't have been delayed and Rush might not have had time to take Aura. He couldn't say that though—not without admitting the accusation was true.

"Let's not pretend you're capable of being faithful," Rush added.

Pax narrowed his eyes. "Says the King of *Sin.* I've heard about the parties you've been hosting the last few years."

"Then you've also noticed my lack of a wife or *betrothed.*" He shrugged. "But I didn't fly all the way here and steal someone's trousers just to discuss your ... *sorrows.*"

"I know you took her, you fool!" Pax growled.

"What an assumption. That I would care enough to steal your bride away. I wonder what motive you think I have?" Rush *dared* him to say it. To say exactly what tore their long friendship apart. Brought together as children, pulled apart by the prince's heinous actions. "And if you truly believe I have her, then why haven't you come for her?"

Pax merely sauntered over to where his rumpled clothing lay in a heap and pulled them on with a tight expression.

"Well, now that you're decent, the court is safe from being scandalized further today."

147

"Fuck you, Rush. Give Aura back to me."

The blood in Rush's veins boiled, his dragon begging to come out and rip this fucker apart. "Your father is holding court." Rush strode from the room as if the sight of Pax's face didn't affect him at all. "Let's have a chat in front of everyone, shall we?"

Rush retraced his steps through the palace with Pax yapping at his heels.

"This is outrageous," he almost shouted. "You're a *king*. Is this how you should behave?" When Rush ignored the comments, the prince huffed. "You couldn't let me be happy, could you? The past is controlling you."

*The audacity.*

The taste of ash flooded his mouth and smoke filled his nostrils. His dragon dug his claws into Rush, preparing to release himself. Rush shoved the beast down. If he could simply kill Pax right here in his own palace, he would—but he had something *much* sweeter in store for the prince.

"This is a political nightmare," Pax continued. "You can't take a member of the royal family and not expect consequences."

The true *nightmare* for him would be when Rush completed the spell. Then Pax could come to Moonstone and see if he could find Aura himself, albeit in a deep sleep. "She's not a royal though, is she? The wedding didn't take place."

"Because of *you*."

"Oh?" He smirked knowingly. "I heard a rumor that the entire event was delayed because you were fucking someone."

"You prick! What I do and with whom is none of your

damn business."

Rush shrugged. It really wasn't—but Aura was none of Pax's business now that she'd called off the engagement.

"You forced her to write that letter, didn't you?" he seethed.

Rush quirked a brow. "What letter?"

Red flooded into Pax's cheeks and he muttered under his breath. Something about Rush being a liar, but it was too hard to make out every word. Poor, pathetic Pax. Too embarrassed to admit his fiancée left him at the altar.

They passed guards and nameless nobles in the gilded halls. Rush ignored them all until he came to a halt outside the throne room. "After you, Your Highness."

"Absolutely absurd," Pax muttered. "My father will not take kindly to your actions today."

Rush flicked a hand through the air, wishing he could stab the prince in the throat instead. But he was patient. He could wait for his revenge. "If I gave a fuck, I wouldn't be here today."

Pax rolled his eyes and pushed into the throne room. People stood in small groups, all wearing their finest silks and velvets, chatting amongst themselves. The king perched on his circular throne. A gold back arched up over him with stars carved into the curves. Rush hadn't seen Quinton in a while, but he looked just the same except for a few grays streaking his dark hair. It seemed Pax would be waiting a long time to rule Starnight if his father was as healthy as he appeared.

Once the king spotted his son, he smiled, a few fine wrinkles deepening. Then his gaze fastened on Rush and King Quinton shot to his feet. "I heard you made *quite*

149

the entrance."

"Is that any way to greet a fellow monarch?" Rush knocked into Pax's shoulder as he sauntered into the room. "After receiving your letter, I thought it important to visit."

"My chambers," the king demanded, stepping down from his throne. "*Now.*"

"No need." Rush grinned at the nobility, their gazes pinned to him. Some in shock or fear. Some with lust in their eyes as they took in his bare torso. "I've only come to give my response in person, then I'll be on my merry way."

"Your Majesty," Quinton warned. "This is highly inappropriate."

"*No.*" Rush prowled halfway to the throne before halting. "It's inappropriate to threaten a sovereign with war when it was *your* fault for failing to protect the would-be princess of Starnight."

"A black dragon flew off with her!" Quinton snapped. "What were we to do against that? And what *other* dragon would you have us suspect?"

Rush shrugged. "Any of them."

"It was you," the king nearly shouted, his voice quaking with anger.

"Hear me, King Quinton." Rush allowed a few scales to appear over his face, chest, and arms. "I have stolen no one's fiancée. Keep slandering me and you will discover what it means to go to war with a dragon king."

It wasn't a lie—Aura wasn't betrothed any longer after she sent her letter. And Starnight would fall within days against Rush's army.

"Do you expect us to take you at your word?" Pax

150

asked.

Rush smirked as the image of him snapping the prince's neck flashed through his mind. He couldn't bring up that he knew what was in Aura's letter to Pax without admitting she was at his palace, but it hadn't implicated Moonstone. In fact, she'd made it come off as if she'd *chosen* to leave. But the king nor Pax would *ever* admit that so publicly. "I can't force you to believe what I say, yet I can promise that Starnight will burn with dragon fire if you don't cease your lies."

With that, Rush clenched his teeth and turned on his heel before sauntering from the palace. He squeezed his fists, nails digging into his palms. Quinton and Pax might not believe him, but they would think twice about bringing the conflict to Moonstone's doorstep. They might poke around, try verifying their concerns. To gather proof. But they would never find Aura.

Rush's dragon dove through the clouds, wings pressed firmly against his sides as he descended, the wind whistling in his ears. The design of his palace's lush hedges came into view and his wings cracked open. The force of the motion jerked his upper body back so his rear feet were poised to land first.

He touched ground and his scales receded, his body shifting. The dragon took most of the sun's heat with him and Rush shivered as the air skimmed his bare form. His anger simmered and faded the longer he flew—now he

151

was simply *tired*. Gathering up the trousers he'd left at the edge of the clearing, he slipped them on.

"Have a good time?" an overly-sweet voice asked. *Aura*.

Rush spun around to face her with his trousers still untied. When her gaze dipped to his chest, his dragon preened. "Are you spying on me, kitten?" he purred. "If you want to see me bare, you need only ask."

She huffed. "You're the one who told *me* to meet you out in the gardens. And with no specific time at that. So why did you want me here?" Her hair hung loosely over her shoulders and she wore a simple pink gown. The high neck and an ankle-length skirt showed none of her assets, but still, he knew what hid beneath the fabric now as he thought about her in the sheer garment from the party. He swallowed hard and snatched his tunic off the ground. Grass tickled the soles of his feet as he prowled toward her.

"Did you wait out here all day?" he asked, ignoring the question. There hadn't been a *reason* he'd wanted to meet with her other than the growing desire to fuck her—there was also a *need* to get to know her a little. He traced a fingertip over the delicate skin of her forehead, where the glass scales had decorated her brow at the party.

Her eyes widened and Rush drew his hand back. "Does it matter?" she asked, her voice dripping sarcasm. "Does that mean the dragon is feeling cooped up here? I wonder what that might feel like."

"Retract your claws." Rush smirked, shoving his white tunic over his head. "Play nice and maybe I'll take you with me next time."

"Is that possible?" She perked up. "Does the spell not

work up there?"

*Ah, fuck.* He hadn't been thinking when he said that. "The spell would still work," he admitted, but that didn't stop him from wanting to take her into the sky. They could soar over the gardens perhaps, as long as they didn't pass the perimeter. What would have happened if he and Astor had failed to stop Vikram and Dzmitry from doing just that? She would've fallen asleep in their carriage, unable to wake, while they— His dragon growled at the thought of them using her unconscious body in that way.

"Are you ever going to tell me about this curse?" She crossed her arms over her chest and bit her lip in anticipation. "Is that why you wanted me to meet you here?"

"Not yet." He paused. If he didn't give her *something*, she would never stop asking. Normally he would enjoy taunting her with vague answers, but he was exhausted. And for some foolish reason, part of him wanted to tell her everything. He couldn't, of course. "I had someone special in my life once," he told her in a strained voice. "She was a thorn in my side, just like you. And she fell in love with someone unworthy. Just like you."

"I'm *not* in love with Pax," she snapped.

Rush closed his eyes for a moment, pushing back the burn in his chest until he forced a chuckle. "Not anymore."

Aura opened her mouth to refute his claim but clamped it shut again. A wicked grin curled his lips. She couldn't deny that she'd thought she loved the Prince of Starnight at one point. That she had been delighted to marry him. Just because it all turned out to be a lie didn't make the feelings she had any less real. And, because of that, Pax still thought he owned her.

Which was exactly why she was perfect for Rush's needs.

# AURA

**O**nce Rush slipped on his boots, Aura walked beside him in silence through the lush labyrinth of green until he came to a halt. He hadn't given Aura a specific time to meet him in the gardens which hadn't surprised her. However, she'd spent the day outdoors, taking in the fresh air, the sweet smell of the flowers as she waited for him, more curious than she should've been to see what he'd wanted since he'd been mostly gone from the palace after the party. Even though deaths had occurred not far from this very spot recently, the gardens still somehow made her feel safe. It was strange, and she wasn't certain how to feel about that.

As she peered at Rush near a blossoming bush, his demeanor was the same, sure of himself as always. Yet his gaze flickered, seeming as though something bothered him.

"So, here we are..." Aura blew out a breath, averting her stare from him, who moments ago she'd just witnessed bare. *Again*. But she couldn't deny his body was made perfectly, the strong and lean muscles, the sun-kissed skin. Even his dragon was. As he flew through the sky, it was somehow both elegant and intimidating. It was beautiful. She shrugged the thoughts she shouldn't be having away.

"Yes, here we are, kitten." He smirked, playfulness seeping into his eyes, taking away whatever hidden emotion she thought she'd seen.

She tilted her head and crossed her arms. "Well? Why did you want me to meet you here?"

Rush strolled toward her and wrapped a loose lock of hair around his fingertip. "I had planned to get to know you a little more. Find out what's beneath those claws of yours. But I've had enough fresh air for the day, so let's take our conversation into the library." He slipped his finger from her hair and lifted her chin as a devious grin spread across his cheeks. "As long as you promise not to burn another one of my books."

She rolled her eyes. "That depends on your attitude." Her heart pounded while she studied that smile, how it made his face even more handsome. A handsome face on a man who could easily murder, who might have taken the life of the girl from her dreams...

With a deep chuckle, he motioned her to follow him, and her curiosity only intensified to see if she could uncover something from him. Perhaps maybe something else about her family, if Astor was still slinking about her home.

As they entered the palace, the guards and servants bowed their heads when they passed them. Rush drew to a stop just outside his room instead of the library and opened the door.

She grasped his arm, then dropped it as if it had burned her. "Why are we going inside your room?" Her pulse spiked, remembering the last time she'd been there. How he'd stroked his long length until he came. She could still hear the sounds he made, the way his eyebrows pulled seductively together.

"We're going to a different library," he purred and pressed a hand to her lower back, leading her toward one of the two doors at the back of his room. Even though she'd been inside his space before, she hadn't taken the time to look at the décor. Unsurprising, everything was mostly black. The wardrobe, the desk, the chaise, the walls, the bed, the floor, the chandelier. It was as though Rush wanted to prove that his heart could be black if he so wished.

Rush opened one of the two doors, and when she stepped inside the room after him, she gasped. It was one of the largest libraries she'd ever seen, even more so than the exquisite one at the Starnight Palace. Shelves lined the walls, filled with tomes of all colors and sizes, except for one area which held wine bottles and glasses. Two chairs rested in the center, an obsidian table between them, and a dark fur rug beneath.

The scent of leather and smoke surrounded her as she skimmed her fingers across the spines. Not a single layer of dust in sight. She glanced over her shoulder at the king. "You like to read?"

Rush's lips curled up at the edges. "The King of Sin can do more than fuck. Although, some of these are great for *inspiration*." His silver irises held hers and they became slitted as he drew out a bottle of wine, along with two clear glasses, from the rack. "Thirsty?"

Aura swallowed, her throat dry, and she nodded.

He popped the cork and poured them each a glass of red liquid. She drank a long sip of the wine after he handed it to her. The taste was sweet and velvety on her tongue.

"So, tell me your secrets," he said, swirling the liquid in his glass before he drank from it.

Aura scowled. "Why the interest all of a sudden? You didn't want to know anything about me before."

"That's not true, kitten. You were the one being difficult," he drawled.

She clenched her teeth, her fist tightening around the glass. "Me? *I'm* the difficult one? I won't remind you again how you stole me from my home and have me trapped here."

"You just did." He chuckled and took a sip of his drink.

An unintelligible sound escaped her until she thought about how he'd saved her from her wedding. At least, in a sense. And then there'd been the party… "Even though you're nothing but a pompous ass, I should've thanked you for saving me the other night. So thank you," she whispered, then added, "But you're still the one who forced me to attend the party."

His jaw clenched, the vein feathering along his jaw. "Astor and I were too easy on them."

"I'm glad we agree on that." She smiled softly.

They drank in comfortable silence while Aura read over each of the titles on the spines. She hadn't glanced back at Rush, but she could feel his eyes on her, especially when she went up the ladder to pore over a few more of the titles. These ones about journeys and battles, others of shifters.

As she climbed back down, she looked at the lower shelf, her gaze landing on a pastry tome and she inhaled a sharp breath. "You have recipe books?" She tore it from the shelf, then straightened quickly.

"They were my mother's," Rush said, his warm breath tickling her ear as he took the book from her hand. "She used to bake with Marion or help her cook meals when there was no one to entertain. It didn't matter that she was queen—she enjoyed helping around the palace."

"My mother is the same way. I mean, we didn't grow up in a palace, but she likes helping the servants with the chores and taking care of us herself." Aura smiled, then ran her finger across the worn leather cover of the tome still in Rush's hand. "My twin sister is practically married to baking. She collects any recipe book she can find."

Rush's gaze held Aura's, a line deepening between his brows as if he was trying to peel back her layers. "It's hers then."

Aura blinked, taken aback by his generosity before she narrowed her eyes. "What do I owe you for this?"

"Nothing." Rush shrugged. "Consider it my apology for putting you in harm's way at the party, even if it was unintentional. Astor can sneak it into her belongings."

Aura bit the inside of her cheek to keep from spewing venomous curses at him when she thought about Astor talking to Hana while doing it. But then she thought about how he was giving a book that had belonged to his deceased mother. Her chest tightened as she wondered about Rush, the line of royal portraits inside the palace, the past kings and queens. Was there anyone who he had left alive? "What about your family? After your father, mother, and sister... Do you have any other relatives?"

"No," Rush said through a tight jaw. His demeanor changed, hardened, and she knew at once she'd said something wrong. Perhaps he was thinking about how his parents and sister had died. With lips set in a tight line, he placed the book on the table beside his empty wine glass. As if she weren't there, he pulled out another book from the shelf and flipped a few pages before asking, "Since we're getting to know each other more thoroughly, how far did you go with the asshole prince if you two didn't fuck?"

Flames ignited beneath her flesh and heat crept up her neck before she folded her arms across her chest. "I don't think that's any of your business."

"Did you watch him fuck his hand the way you watched me?" Rush looked at her then, his eyes hooded as he smirked.

"I think we've gotten to know one another enough for the day." Aura turned on her heel and marched away when Rush's hand clasped her wrist to draw her back. She ripped her arm away and shoved his chest. "If I'm to stay here, then you need to stop bringing up Pax. You need to stop punishing *me* just because you hate him. I'm not a toy you can wind up and do with as you want."

Rush peered down at her, his hulking frame casting a shadow over her beneath the candlelight. "You're mine."

Her nostrils flared. "Stop talking."

Rush leaned in closer, his warm smoky breath mingling with hers. "Make me," he rasped. And then it was there again, a slip of an emotion. Pain?

Aura didn't know what she was even doing as she grasped Rush's silky hair, tugging it hard as she brought his face to hers. She knew she should've slapped him again, but for some reason she'd chosen this. A part of her, a deep treacherous part, wanted to see if the smoky scent of him tasted just as heavenly as it smelled. There was no hesitation as he kissed her in return, his lips slanting across hers, punishing, demanding, taunting her in a way that made her want more when he slid his hot tongue inside her mouth.

Rush flipped them both around, pressing her against the bookshelf, and she didn't even mind how the wood dug sharply into her back.

"Let me make you feel good, kitten," Rush panted in between hard kisses, his cock stiffening against her stomach. "Use me the way you were going to use Brix. Forget about Pax. Fuck me. Give me what he was meant to have."

"I told you to stop talking about him, and I told you I would never touch your filthy cock," she breathed, pulling away from him, guilt storming through her at what she'd just done.

"Oh, but you'll kiss my *filthy* mouth." He smirked, running a finger gently across her now-swollen lips.

"You—" An invisible pierce to her finger halted her, and she gasped for breath as a fierce tug yanked at her heart. She stumbled sideways, knocking a few books from the shelf while trying to clutch onto them for support.

Rush grabbed her by the shoulders and turned her to

face him. "Aura?"

Her eyelids fluttered, unable to see his expression when her knees buckled. His hold on her didn't relinquish as the world darkened—his voice repeating her name drifted farther away.

The darkness diminished, turning into daylight. Aura found herself standing near the familiar lake she'd dreamt about before and she took a shaky step back. The last time she was here a hand made from water had dragged her beneath the lake's depths. But then movement atop the water captured her attention, a body wearing a light blue dress floating on the glistening liquid.

It was *her*. The girl. "Hello! Are you all right?" Aura shouted as she hurried toward the lake. She didn't hesitate to dip her feet into the cool liquid and rush toward the still form.

Just as Aura reached her, the girl's eyes flew open, her sapphire irises blazing. She thrust forward, water splashing and her chest heaving when she faced Aura.

"You're back!" the girl shouted as Aura's heart pounded furiously. "I've been waiting for you to return. Follow me." She waved her out from the lake.

"I don't choose when I come here. I'm under some sort of spell courtesy of the King of Moonstone. Rush," Aura said while wringing out the sopping wet skirts of her dress before lowering herself on the grass beside the girl.

The girl's face paled, her bottom lip wobbling. "Rush?

He would never do anything of that nature! Unless you hurt him…"

"I never met him before he stole me away from my court!" Aura hissed, then realization struck her. "You remember more about your life?"

The girl nodded. "Not everything, but some of my memories have been staying, not seeping in and out. I remember my name. Sorcha."

Aura hadn't heard that name before, but she didn't know much about Moonstone besides the stories her mother had told her that were passed down when her family were royals. Once she was wed to Prince Pax, she was to learn everything about the courts outside of Starnight. "What else do you remember about Rush then? Last time, you said there was pain around his name. He didn't hurt you?"

Sorcha shook her head, pulling her wet hair over one shoulder. "Rush loves me and would never hurt me. But my beloved didn't want me or this child. He no longer wanted to see me. There was another that he'd chosen… I later went out to the lake and—" Her brows scrunched together. "And I… I remember the water closing around me. My lungs unable to drink in the air."

Aura gasped, pressing a hand to cup her mouth as she waited for Sorcha to continue.

"I can't remember." Sorcha gritted her teeth, tightening her fists. "But Rush was always my protector. Always."

Aura thought about how Rush had said there'd been someone special. Who was a thorn in his side and had fallen in love with someone else. Was that what twisted him? Rush had loved this girl, but she'd been in love with

163

someone else, then drowned? Marion hadn't seemed to know about a beloved, and perhaps there wasn't since this girl was never truly his…

"Wait, there's something else!" Sorcha shrieked. "I remember! He—" But when she opened her mouth to speak again, water gurgled out, spilling down her chin. Her face and lips turned corpse blue as she choked. A rack of coughs escaped Sorcha and Aura grasped the girl's shoulders.

Shock swarmed through her when her hands didn't pass through Sorcha. The girl was cold, so cold, like snow and ice, like the darkest days of winter. Sorcha's eyes rolled back in her head and Aura pleaded with her. "I want to help you. Just come back. Try and breathe." Before Aura could say another word, Sorcha vanished from her sight as she had in every other dream, leaving her alone with her arms outstretched and gripping the thin air.

Lightning cracked in the sky, and she knew something vile was going to happen like before. The ground shook beneath her feet, a long line spreading across, splitting it in half. Water seeped up from its depths, slow at first, then faster. Aura stumbled back as another line formed, zigzagging through the dirt. Around her, the trees fell, smashing against the earth, the sound ringing in her ears. Just as a large trunk was about to crash on top of her, pain drove through her finger, spreading up her hand, and she jerked forward.

Aura sucked in a sharp breath of air, the air that Sorcha had needed for herself. Her hands trembled, even when she found herself back in the palace. No longer was she in the library with Rush, but in a bed covered in black silk sheets. *His* bed.

"You're finally awake," Rush said, peering up from the desk on the opposite side of the room. Books and stacks of paper cluttered it.

"Why am I here?" Aura asked as she ran a hand through her tangled hair.

He set down the quill, then stood from his chair and sauntered toward her. "Because if I took you back to your room, you would sleep on the floor to avoid the bed I've fucked in."

Anger coursed through her and she tightened her fists, ripping the covers off her as she stood to her feet. "So you put me in *your* bed instead?"

A deep chuckle escaped his throat, the sound sending heat low in her belly. "I don't fuck anything but my hand in here. Find solace that you're the first woman to sleep between my sheets."

She scoffed. "So you tumble everywhere else in the palace besides your own room? And you expect me to be grateful? How long have I been asleep?"

"Just through the rest of yesterday and overnight."

"And where did *you* sleep?"

"Where are you hoping I slept?" he cooed, inching closer to her. When she rolled her eyes, he gestured at the velvet chaise opposite the carved wardrobe etched in glistening dragon scales. "Relax, I slept there."

"Why am I fainting? What is this spell doing to me?" Aura studied Rush, trying to see beneath his layers once more. But his neutral expression concealed all his secrets. Rush couldn't have always been known as the King of Sin. Was it because of Sorcha's death? That she hadn't returned his affections in the way he'd wanted, then died?

The Rush that Sorcha seemed to know was gone. Or maybe not fully. There had been the tiniest of glimpses. Possibly…

He didn't answer her question of course, only said, "Astor delivered the book to your twin sister while you were settling into my pillow."

Aura gritted her teeth and was about to ask what book when she remembered the recipe tome from the library. She wanted desperately to inquire about Sorcha, but she couldn't, not yet, not when she was discovering more, not when she knew Rush would make sure she never found out if she asked questions about her. He might even find a way to tweak the spell so she never found Sorcha at all in her dreams. Or even forget about her all together, the way Hana was made to not remember Rush and Astor. Rush might not have another vial, but he would find a way to gain a second from a sorcerer. Perhaps Sorcha might even know how to break the spell somehow since she knew Rush. If there were clues about Sorcha, they might possibly be in this room, but how would she ever find herself alone here? There had to be a way…

And then she remembered the shared kiss with Rush, the seductive way his lips had felt against hers… An answer rumbled within her, one that she was privier to than she wanted to accept. There was more to Rush, more to his story, and if she was going to spend the rest of her life in this palace, then she would find out precisely what was happening to her. Maybe even break the spell herself while still being able to keep her family safe. And the only way to uncover it was to give in to temptation.

Aura's eyes fastened to the King of Sin's and she bit her lip. "I want you to meet me in the ballroom for a dance. We never got to have one at the party."

He cocked his head, his gaze latched onto hers. "You danced, kitten."

She batted her eyelashes. "But not with you."

Rush arched a brow, watching her as though she were mad. "Are you going to ask me to court you next?"

Her lips curled up at the edges. "Perhaps your cock isn't as filthy as I thought."

He snorted. "Why the change of heart? I already told you I won't break the spell."

"I like that you chose to give the book to my sister." She brushed past him, taking in his smoky scent. "If you decide to meet me in the ballroom, then I'll be there after I clean up. And if not, I'll dance alone, I suppose. I do know how to pleasure myself anyhow." With that, she left his room, unable to hide her smile.

# RUSH

A soft melody poured from the piano as Rush's fingers flew over the keys. The sound was muted with the lid down and he was rusty from not having played in years, though he was never very good. His mother had insisted he take lessons when he was a child. Music never failed to put a smile on her face and he had always loved to be the one to make her happy.

Rush slowed his fingers, hitting the wrong keys as the song slowly drifted into silence. Sorcha could play well, but she had loathed it. Hated being proper and learning all the things wealthy ladies needed to learn. He missed her... So fucking much. His chest tightened and he placed her memory away, back into the depths of his mind as he always did. *Soon...*

"I didn't know you played," Aura said from behind him.

Rush jerked his hands from the keys and slammed the cover down. He clenched his jaw to take away any lingering emotion he'd let slip through the cracks. "What can I say?"

With a forced smirk, he swung one leg over the bench to look up at her. Her hair was still damp and pinned back in a braided twist. She wore a deep green dress with an embroidered bodice, the neckline swooping down to expose the swell of her breasts. He allowed his gaze to linger there as he thought about their kiss in the library and how he wanted to taste more than just her lips. She'd asked to meet here—implied she wanted more than kisses. It was something he'd been waiting for her to want.

"I know how to use my fingers for more than pleasuring women," he said softly.

"If your playing is any indication of skill, it seems your partners are protecting your ego," Aura drawled.

His gaze snapped up to meet hers. She lifted a brow at him and his lips spread into a grin. "Even a king can't be an expert at *everything*." He rose from the bench to stand close to her, his nose a breath from hers, inhaling her starlight scent. "But no one is faking their moans in my bed."

"Because you don't pleasure anyone in your bed." She stepped back and put her hands on her hips. "You fuck them in the bed you gave *me*."

A true laugh rumbled from his chest. "Touché, kitten."

"So...?" she asked coyly.

"You want me to prove it?" He inched toward her, reaching out to take her waist, but she whirled away from him with a playful smile. A smile that beckoned him to follow. A tease. A promise for more. He thought about the curse, his revenge, but in that moment, he could wait, he could prolong. It wasn't as though it was coming to fruition right then anyway.

"Weren't we supposed to dance?" Aura motioned him toward her with a delicate finger.

*Dance.* Yes, that was why she'd asked him to meet her in the ballroom. And, like a fool, he'd come straight here to wait. He remembered how she danced at the party. How she moved. And he was *just* irrational enough to let his desire for her control him.

"I have to touch you to dance," he said in a low voice.

"Touché, Your Majesty," she sang, repeating his earlier word.

Rush chuckled as he slipped a hand around her waist and tugged her firmly against his chest. She released a silent gasp. Warmth from her body radiated into his and he dragged in a deep breath. "You need to touch me too. That's how you dance," he cooed.

She rolled her eyes and one of her hands wrapped around his shoulder. Rush gently pressed his fingers into her lower back, holding her close, and lifted their free hands together. Without music, there was no melody to dance to, so Rush simply *moved*. And she followed. He led her through the ballroom with slow, lingering steps that forced their bodies together. Pulse thrumming, he sank into the feel of her. Let it warm him. The dragon purred in contentment as she studied Rush's face with desire. He wanted her closer. Wanted to be inside her, pulling moans

170

from her lips. Aura's cheeks flushed as if she were reading his thoughts, and gave no indication of wanting space.

Around and around the room they went. Lost to the rhythm of their breaths. Rush's heart pounded in his chest. Had he ever wanted a woman this badly? He'd been with many, but none had ever affected him like this. And she'd slept in his bed. Surrounded by his scent, leaving hers behind. If anyone else were in his private space like that, they wouldn't make it out unscathed, but he *liked* her being there.

Rush wasn't sure how to feel about that. She was meant for his revenge against Pax—not this. Not to seduce him or make him *feel*. He'd closed his heart away after Sorcha's death. Vowed to never care about another person again because it always brought pain. But… But he couldn't fucking help himself.

And he didn't have the strength to fight it at the moment.

Silence cocooned them. It felt as if they were in their own world where nothing else mattered. Nothing but the arousal burning inside him. His dragon preened, sensing her attraction to him, her desire.

On the fourth turn of the room, Rush couldn't take it any longer and lifted her by the waist before sitting her atop the edge of the piano.

"Rush," she murmured. Her cheeks were flushed, her breaths ragged.

"Yes?" he purred, slowly spreading her legs so he could settle between them. Her arms never left their spot around his neck. She leaned in closer, her violet eyes locked on his mouth. Rush's lips ghosted over hers as he spoke, "What is it?"

171

"I want you to…" Her body stiffened in his grip and he drew back. The pink coloring her cheeks a moment ago had drained away, leaving her skin bone-white. Her hands slipped from around his neck to hang limply at her sides.

"Kitten?" Rush took her from the piano and cradled her against his chest. "Aura, what's wrong?"

"I'm tired," she whispered, her eyelids fluttering.

Then her soft body collapsed against him.

"Fuck," he growled. The spell was absorbing her energy too fast—she'd *just* woken. Was there a trigger he wasn't aware of? Trying to leave the palace grounds, he knew, but she was well within the boundary. The fortune teller had told him the spell was working, but this wasn't what he'd asked for. For her to be tortured.

He held her tighter and carried her back to his room. The beast inside him went silent and still. His dragon would have to get used to Aura being asleep once the spell was complete, but now, there was something quite unsettling … Rush was bothered by the idea too.

Rush stared at the spinning wheel in his laboratory. The rusting pieces, the dusty wood. The spell still wasn't complete, and the spinning wheel remained untouchable. Damn the sorceress for hiding so effectively from him. If the magic continued to affect Aura this way, and if something happened to her….

"Are you making any progress?" he snapped at Astor

over his shoulder.

Glass clinked against glass. Astor held a vial up to eye level and gently swirled the liquid until it turned blue. "It's finished. I used a strand of her hair, so it should connect you to her dream, but you'll be fully aware of what's real. You can wake up whenever you choose."

Rush threw the curtain back in place to shield the spinning wheel from sight and snatched the small vial from Astor's outstretched hand.

"It works fast, so make sure you're laying down before you drink it," the hawk shifter warned. Astor had been into dreams before when he spied on people for Rush, so he trusted that it would work. Perhaps it was something he should've tried with her sooner, but he hadn't expected the process to be so drawn out. Or for him to *want* to check on her...

Rush nodded once.

"Good luck," Astor said.

As blood coursed through Rush's veins, he stormed back through the palace to his room, sending servants fleeing from his path. A panicked scream echoed down the halls and Rush broke into a run while his dragon bolted upright. Aura had made noise in her sleep before, but never so loud. Never so panicked.

Bursting into the room, he found Aura covered in sweat atop his satin sheets. He tapped on her cheeks to wake her despite knowing that was impossible. Until the spell released her, she would sleep. "Fuck," he growled. Sparing a moment to slam the door shut and lock it, he threw himself down beside her on the bed. Just as he lifted the potion to his lips, her screams halted.

A bitter taste crawled over his tongue as Astor's

173

concoction fizzled down his throat. There was little time to focus on it because the next moment, a flicker of darkness swept him away.

He now stood in the middle of his office. Or, not *exactly* his office. The room was the same, but the décor was different. Old. His father's bulky desk still took up the entire center of the room, and the rug was a hideous yellow weave. The large stained-glass window held a black dragon with blue eyes. After his father passed, craftsmen had replaced the dragon's eye color with silver, because it felt too much like the old king was watching Rush. Even now it was just the same—judgmental and heavy. If the old king were alive, he would find Rush's plans to exact revenge reprehensible.

The piece of Rush's childhood buried deep, *deep* down cringed at the disappointment, but he snuffed it out. His father was dead and his approval no longer mattered. The only important thing at the moment was Aura—who was absent from the room. Yet this was *her* dream...

"Kitten?" he called, spinning around. Why would Aura dream of this room? And where was she? Perhaps she only watched her dreams as an observer. She could be watching him now, wondering what the fuck he was doing here, cursing him up and down for doing this to her. "Kitten, can you hear me?"

His father's chair shifted on the other side of the desk. He darted around the furniture to find Aura lying face up on the floor. Soaking wet, her dress clinging to her body. Her violet eyes peered at him and narrowed. Then a cough wracked her body and water gushed from the corners of her mouth. Rush took a step closer with the intent to help her sit up, but she dragged in a ragged

174

breath and waved him away with her hand.

"What the fuck happened to you?" he asked, his voice rising in surprise, and he perched on the edge of the desk. This was only a dream, after all. She wasn't in any real danger of death. Permanent sleep was another issue…

She groaned as she sat up, her chest heaving. "I fancied a swim."

Rush arched a brow. "In my office?" All of which was perfectly dry.

Aura scowled up at him. "I'm dreaming, aren't I? Or no, maybe not…" She peered around the room. "If I am, what are you doing here?"

"You are. I came to make certain you were all right." He looked her up and down, assessing. She seemed fine enough, and yet… "You'd only just woken so it was worrisome that you fell asleep so soon."

"I shouldn't be falling asleep *at all*," Aura snapped. She gripped the arm of the chair and hoisted herself to her feet. "How terrible that your mysterious spell isn't going according to plan. Your *secret* plan."

He glowered at her. What happened in her dreams had never occurred to him before—the spell only said she would sleep and never wake when things were completed. "Is this always what happens? You come to my office for a … swim?"

"No. Occasionally, I visit other places for a swim and—" She slammed her mouth shut. "And it's terrible."

"Only if you don't like getting wet, it seems." He looked around the room and sighed. "Otherwise, it's all rather dull."

She frowned. "Yet you're the one who put me in this oh-so *dull* predicament, Your Majesty. Although, I would rather choose dancing in the ballroom over nearly drowning, wouldn't you?"

Rush pushed off the desk, every muscle in his body tight. Memories threatened to break through. Memories he refused to face. Water had left the perfect outline of her body on the yellow rug. His dragon curled in on himself and Rush wished he could do the same, demanded it. Sorcha... Drowning... A death she'd bestowed on herself...

Instead, he rolled his shoulders to loosen the muscles and smirked. "I knew I was making you wet while we danced, then while I was settled between those pretty thighs of yours, but I didn't realize you wanted my cock this much."

"Excuse me?" she hissed, her eyes widening into full moons.

"It's nothing to be embarrassed about. Dreams use our emotions, though this is rather literal." He reached for her, and she moved from his touch. "We could continue where we left off."

"You ass." Aura stared at him, radiating silent fury, before she stormed from the room. Only to appear back at Rush's side again. "What...?" She glanced at him as if it were his fault.

Rush chuckled. "Sorry, kitten. It seems your dream has you trapped here."

Her hand soared toward his face, but he only laughed as he woke himself up. He lay on the bed beside Aura for a moment, not moving. Each breath was labored and harsh. Something in his chest ached. An old, unhealed wound that he'd been ignoring for two years.

Turning his head on the pillow, he watched Aura

sleep. She seemed peaceful now that the screaming had stopped, but he knew she was raging inside her head. At him, for being a complete prick. At the spell. He ran a hand over his face. He always did this—retreated to being a bastard when confronted with reminders of his pain.

Did Aura nearly drown every time the spell made her sleep? He knew in his bones why this was happening…

*Fuck.*

It couldn't be helped.

It didn't matter if he was starting to feel something for her. He could fuck his way through Moonstone if he chose, but *damn it,* she lingered in his mind. Shoving the fickle emotion away, Rush would wait for the spell to work.

# AURA

**R**ush had slithered his way into Aura's dream, then vanished as though he hadn't been there at all. Of course he had—he liked to invade her personal space when possible. Hot and cold over and over again. Somewhat nice and concerned, then letting filthy words fly out from his shapely lips. The ballroom dancing hadn't gone as planned either. She was only able to lure the king so far, barely touch him at all, before she fell under another spell. *His* spell.

The taste of brackish water still coated her tongue, no matter how many times she tried to swallow it away. This time she didn't slip into her dream easily—it had begun with her dangling in darkness before choking on water, the same way Sorcha had when she'd seen her last. But

Aura's lungs were now clear as she stood alone in Rush's office. Only it wasn't his office per se…

Aura had passed it almost every day when walking down the halls. The stained-glass window held another dragon's eye color, and instead of black cloaking every aspect, the room's hues resembled a forest. A mixture of emeralds, deep browns, and golds. Vibrant paintings covered almost every inch of the walls, but she didn't bother to look at each one.

Where was Sorcha? The few times she'd dreamt, or at least remembered her dreams, the girl had made an appearance. She grasped the handle of a door near the back of the room, only, when she opened it, a stone wall blocked her entrance. With a frown, she opened the curtained balcony door, and a matching stone wall was visible. She tried the one out of the room, just as she had before, but another wall of stones lingered.

Aura made an unintelligible sound between clenched teeth. "Sorcha!" she called out. "Sorcha, are you here?" The girl had to be there … somewhere? Or maybe not… Perhaps when Sorcha was choking last, her flesh turning blue, death had taken her from whatever place she was trapped in.

The only sound breaking up the silence was Aura's heavy breath. Until a muffled feminine voice broke throughout the room, coming from inside the chestnut wardrobe. Aura gasped and her gaze fell to the golden handles. She rushed toward them, then threw the door wide.

Soft groans rumbled inside the large space as Aura rummaged through silk, fur, and velvet cloaks. The wardrobe was deeper than she thought when she stepped into its depths. Near the very back, a body spilled out from a cluster of dresses and toppled to the side.

Aura hurried forward, then knelt beside Sorcha to wrap her arms around the girl's trembling form. Her dress and hair were sopping wet while beads of water dotted her pale skin.

"Sorcha, wake up," Aura whispered, lightly tapping the girl's cool cheek. She could feel her again, the same as in the last dream, and she wasn't certain what that meant in the slightest.

"Aura?" Sorcha rasped, her eyelids opening to bright sapphire irises. "This is getting a bit tedious for us both, isn't it?" She laughed softly before releasing a few coughs.

Aura patted Sorcha on her back until the coughing seized. "It seems fate enjoys having us meet like this." Aura smiled. Or perhaps it wasn't fate at all... The spell... Whatever it was doing. Again, she'd hoped to get something more from Rush in the ballroom, but all she'd gotten were his hands on her waist, her thighs, and she tamped down the thought of how she'd wanted them in other places. However, she needed to focus now. Rush had loved this girl, and even though Aura couldn't decide if she liked the king even a smidge, she wanted to help Sorcha. Find a way to aid the girl and herself.

"Fate can be a tricky little thing." Sorcha blew out a breath and stood on shaky legs. Aura led her out from the cloaks and into a high-backed leather chair in front of a round wooden table lined with gold and emeralds.

"How long were you in the wardrobe?" Aura asked, pulling the other chair beside Sorcha's to sit next to her. Sorcha only shrugged so Aura went on, "Rush was just in this room. I was afraid he would find us here together

180

before I got a chance to figure out anything."

"Rush was here?" Sorcha jolted upward, her eyes no longer heavy-lidded but beaming as a bright smile spread across her cheeks. "How? Does he have a spell cast on him too?"

"If someone did to him what he has to me, let's just say he would deserve it. But no—he somehow waltzed his way into my dreams with what I'm assuming was a sorcerer's concoction."

"It doesn't sound like Rush to dabble with spells like that... Unless he found... Oh no!" She cupped her mouth, straightening. "He *knows*."

Aura furrowed her brow, waiting for Sorcha to continue. "Knows what?" she nudged.

"Hold on. It'll come back to me." Sorcha stood from the chair, pacing back and forth across the marble floor as she massaged her temples. She came to a halt, her gaze drifting across the spacious room. "When I was younger, I used to come in here and play all the time," she said with a gentle smile. "Dolls, board games, writing in my journal, reading. Sometimes Father would be working at his desk while Rush and I hid and played games in the wardrobe or out on the balcony. Father always spent so much time in his office with us and Mother. They were wonderful parents."

Sorcha ran toward the balcony door, discovering the entrance barred. She trailed her fingers over the stones, then pushed as if she could make them collapse. But they didn't budge. "Why are stones here?"

Aura's lips parted like a fish several times as she thought over what Sorcha had said. But bewilderment continued to swirl within her. "This isn't your father's desk? It's Rush's."

Sorcha gave a knowing nod as if she understood Aura's confusion. "You've heard of Princess Constance?"

She remembered briefly hearing about the deaths of the royals while in Starnight. The queen, then the king two years later, and a year after that, the princess. "I have, but you know how the courts are, they don't hear much, too concerned with their own."

"That is certainly true." Sorcha sighed and pointed to a spot behind Aura. "Walk closer to that painting on the wall. The one just above the leather settee."

Slowly, Aura turned around and squinted at a large portrait of four royals wearing crowns and fancy attire. As she crept closer, the details became clearer, sharper. The first person she noticed on the right was Rush, who was maybe fifteen at the time. His long obsidian hair brushed his shoulders, and he was dressed in his finest black shirt. Even though he didn't hold a smile, there was life in him within that picture, his eyes bright ... and happy. Behind him were who had to be his mother and father. Rush inherited the eyes and skin coloring of his mother while most of his features came from his father—the strong jaw, the high cheekbones, the long lashes. Then, beside Rush, stood a young girl with dark hair in long curls cascading to her waist, a yellow bow atop her head. Her bright blue eyes shone like sapphires, the same as her father's, the same as the dragon's within the stained-glass of this room. Aura's heart thrummed, slamming against her sternum. Sorcha was indeed a girl who Rush loved, but he hadn't been *in* love with her.

"That's you! Only younger," Aura shouted, whirling around to find Sorcha studying the painting with tears glistening in her eyes. "You're Rush's sister! Princess Constance. The one who—"

"Died," Sorcha finished, wiping away a lone tear trailing down her cheek.

Aura furrowed her brow. "But why did you tell me your name is Sorcha?"

"It was what Rush called me." She shrugged. "He told me when I was born, I never looked like a Constance, but a Sorcha, the name of the sun from one of the stories Mama had always read to him. I shine like the sun and draw the darkness out of everyone, he would say. My brother is more caring than anyone I know."

Aura's knees wobbled and she almost collapsed to the floor right there at those last words. "*Caring?*" she hissed. "Even though Rush has done a few good deeds for me, your brother stole me away from Starnight on my wedding day and is holding me prisoner in his palace. Oh wait, a *guest* of sorts." She rolled her eyes. "I can go anywhere I want except outside the palace gates because of the blasted spell he's cast." But then a thought struck her and she straightened, hope filling her. "Do you know what this spell is for? It drains me a little each day or hits me hard and pulls me into these dreams. There has to be a reason you're here too. I never heard how you died, but if this is anything to go by, I now know you drowned yourself." Until recently, Aura and her family had lived secluded from the palace and gossip.

Sorcha sucked in a sharp breath, then shouted, "I remember what I was going to say earlier! Rush must have found my journal that held *everything* in there... I wasn't ever supposed to be with him, but I fell in love." Her face paled. "No, there's more. There's a truth hidden and Rush needs to know. When I went out to the lake that day—" Water gurgled up from her mouth and took away her words. That only made Sorcha try harder as Aura held onto her shoulders. None of the things escaping her mouth were decipherable.

"Come on, Sorcha. Stay. Concentrate," Aura said with determination, but when she spoke the last word, her hands passed through water. Sorcha's skin was now a light blue, all of her was, and a dull glaze covered her eyes. The water crashed to the floor, the sound echoing off the walls, before turning into small puddles.

Aura screamed when everything else inside the room mirrored what had happened to Sorcha. The furniture, the paintings on the walls—all of it turned to liquid and collided with the marble floor. Like one of her dreams before, the water rose, the cold liquid seeping over her feet, but before it could reach her sternum, a sharp sting pierced her finger, the agonizing pain spreading up her arm and tearing another scream from her throat as she closed her eyes.

When she reopened them, no longer was she in a murderous dream but in a bedroom surrounded by black. Comforting. The darkness in this palace was somehow becoming just that. Only, Rush wasn't staring at her this time—Astor was. He sat on the chaise, twisting a wooden puzzle box around and around when he glanced up.

"Finally." He sighed. "Have a good nap?"

Aura thought about Sorcha … Rush's dead sister. Princess Constance. She jerked forward, her brows sliding together in concentration. What had Sorcha wanted to tell her? Was there a different reason she'd decided to drown herself other than being abandoned by a lover?

"Damn it!" she shouted and slapped the mattress.

"I'm not sure what that bed ever did to you." Astor chuckled softly, continuing to twist the puzzle box.

"Why are you here? Where's Rush?" she snapped.

Astor lifted a pristine chestnut brow. "The king had business to attend to. He does have a territory to run and all."

Aura narrowed her eyes. "When will he be back?"

"When he decides to come back."

"Rush's *lovely* personality seems to be rubbing off on you today."

Astor let out a breath. "Do you want to get something to eat and drink downstairs? You've been asleep for two days."

It hadn't felt that long again, but dreams never do. Aura opened her mouth to ask Astor about Rush's sister, demand answers to find out what he knew. But he was the one person here who she could trust the least. She needed to discuss Princess Constance with Rush, dig about his family in a way that didn't seem suspicious. When she arrived at the Moonstone Palace, there were two places she was told not to venture: Rush's bedroom when he was gone and the cellar. Which she assumed was why Rush had left someone in here to make sure she didn't riffle through his things.

She was certain that the journal was possibly in this room, maybe in Rush's desk drawer... But she couldn't search now. Not with Astor hovering. However, her gut instinct told her that everything she wanted to know about Sorcha would be in the cellar.

"I think I *will* have something to eat and drink," Aura

said. "I also wanted to thank you for delivering the book to my sister."

Astor studied her for a long moment before finally speaking, "Any chance for me to get to see Hana is worthy. Even if she doesn't remember me." His voice cracked on the last word, and she could've sworn a glassy sheen shone in his eyes. It was the first break she'd ever seen in his demeanor.

She blinked, biting her lip. "You're truly in love with Hana, aren't you? Not just using her to get to me."

He didn't say anything, but he didn't have to.

Aura pushed up from the bed, then glanced over her shoulder as she padded toward the door. "Chrysanthemums are Hana's favorite flower. Purple ones."

Astor pursed his lips while studying her. "Why are you telling me this?"

"You helped me by killing Dzmitry at the party. You also spoke up for Hana to bring her home when you could've selfishly kept her here with you. But if you're going to continue pursuing her, be honest with her. No lies this time." He would pursue her regardless of what Aura wished, yet maybe this time he would be fair with her.

After bathing away the past few days and putting on a silky blue dress, Aura made her way downstairs toward the kitchens. Pots clinking reverberated through the air and she found Marion speckled with flour, a few spots of grape jam smearing her apron.

Marion heaved a sigh of relief when she spotted Aura. "I heard you've been feeling under the weather, but you look well now." She placed two buttered biscuits on a plate and passed them to her, then poured a tall glass of orange juice.

"Under the weather indeed," Aura muttered under her breath. "Thank you for this." She took a sip of the juice. As she ate the biscuits, Marion taught her how to make cinnamon muffins with a special glaze. Another recipe her twin sister would die for. She hoped one day she would get to show her, but perhaps she could write them all down and have Astor deliver them to her as he had the book.

Once Marion placed the pan in the oven, Aura decided to try and ask a few simple questions as she had before. "I haven't seen any portraits of Rush's sister around the palace and would love to know what she looked like." Now that she knew Sorcha was Princess Constance, none of the paintings of the past royals held her image.

A crestfallen expression seeped into Marion's face as she brushed flour from her apron. "After Princess Constance drowned herself, His Majesty took down any portrait that had his sister in it. The princess was kind and sweet with the most beautiful blue eyes that she inherited from her father. She was a beacon of light and would sometimes help me in the kitchens with the queen, even though neither had to. But we don't speak of them—especially not where the king might hear."

"Did the princess find love the way her parents had?

Or maybe she hadn't yet. In Starnight we didn't hear much. I don't even know how old she was."

Marion eyed her for a moment, seeming to debate with herself if she should say more. "She was still very young, sixteen. Just between you and me, I believe she was in love, but she remained mum about it. I always knew when she saw her secret stranger because she lit up like a candle. Sometimes the happiest people are the saddest inside though."

If Rush knew, if he'd found a journal, he wouldn't have told anyone in the palace except for Astor. "I'm so sorry you lost them," Aura whispered. "I think I'll go to the gardens for a little while."

"Come by later and I'll show you how to make a cream puff."

Aura nodded and left the kitchens, but instead of following the hallway leading to the front of the palace, she ventured toward the back to see if she could find the cellar.

As she turned the corner, she slipped into the shadows when she caught a glimpse of Astor farther down. In his hands, he carried a wooden box. Keeping silent, she followed him down the hallway toward a door. He seemed focused on something, not paying attention as he usually did to his surroundings. Shifting the box under one arm, Astor dug a key from his pocket. The lock clicked when he inserted it, twisting, and he flung the door open wide. Aura waited as he descended a dark staircase, then sprinted forward and caught the door just as it was about to close.

Pulse racing, Aura tiptoed down the curving staircase in the dim light, her bare feet silent against the cold stone.

A mixture of spicy herbs accompanied the musky air. Her heart pounded even harder with each step she took, her tightened fists trembling. When she reached the final one, she wondered if Astor would be waiting there to tell her he knew she'd been following him all along.

The sound of another loud lock clicked and she peered around the corner, spotting Astor drawing open a wooden door. He checked over his shoulder and she yanked her head back just in time. Still trembling, she held her breath, then inched forward when his feet echoed on the stone, walking into the room. Before the door closed, she caught a glimpse of a curtain and a table cluttered with tinctures and glass vials. The bolt locked into place from inside, preventing her from entering.

It would be simple to get down there with no one guarding the area, but she still needed a key. The only other person she believed would have one would be Rush. Which meant she had to get closer to him... And there was one way that she knew how to do that with certainty.

Give him pleasure.

# 16

# RUSH

Leaving Aura while the spell had her in its grip didn't sit right with Rush. She was vulnerable when she slept, and anything could happen while he was away. He *needed* her to complete his plan, but deep down, somewhere in his hardened heart, another reason rested. A reason he ignored. Astor was watching over her in his room, the one person left alive who he trusted with his life, who would protect her at all costs as a favor to Rush.

There was no avoiding his departure though. Another urgent message had come, this time from the border town of Uleis. The letter begged for assistance as a small company of Starnight soldiers were gathering near the boundary and their lord was missing. Rush smirked, reminded of how he'd murdered the bastard along with his nephew—not that anyone was aware of that just yet.

Rush sighed as he pulled on a pair of tight trousers that he borrowed off a clothesline. His muscles rippled, on the verge of tearing the fabric as he shifted. The farm house, a few yards away, was made of unweathered wood and fresh thatching. Yellow flowers bloomed in window boxes, and the fields were full with neatly-planted rows of wheat poking through the soil.

Pride filled him. *This* was what his family had done for Moonstone and its people. What they'd accomplished since taking the throne. *A thriving court.* Not a fucking waste that had been killing its people. Now the fucking Starnight Prince was threatening the peace without being certain that Aura was there. Even though she was, but Aura was no longer the prince's—she was *his*. If she was awake when he returned, he would take her back to that piano, spread her legs once more, and let them finish what they'd started.

"Can I help you?" A young man with thinning hair stepped out of the house and lifted an axe that rested beside the door.

"No." Rush ripped a red tunic from the clothesline. He slipped it on as he walked toward the man. "On second thought, do you have an extra pair of boots?"

Recognition lit up the man's face, his brows lifting. "Your Majesty?"

"Yes, yes…" Rush paused.

"Grigor," he supplied.

"Grigor," Rush repeated. "Let's skip the formalities and move straight to the footwear, shall we?"

"Of course." The axe dropped to the ground with a thud and he disappeared into the house.

Rich, savory scents wafted from their kitchen—stew or something with meat gravy. Rush's stomach grumbled, but there wasn't time for that now.

"The *king* is here?" a woman shouted.

The next moment, a girl, no older than thirteen, stepped into the doorway, a gleeful gasp escaping her. "Your Majesty." She dropped into a low curtsy, and her dress dwarfed her small frame. "I'm Margie."

"Hello, Margie," he said, a hint of humor in his voice as he studied her.

"My papa is getting you boots." She perked up when she noticed his bare feet. "You'll need socks too!"

Then she turned on her heel and hurried inside, her footfalls racing through the house. Rush found himself chuckling, something he hadn't done in a while. But she reminded him of Sorcha. Excited about everything, happy. Until…

Grigor returned with a pair of shiny black boots. "Forgive my daughter's manners, Your Majesty. It's not every day we speak with royalty."

Rush took the boots silently and would send the man gold for the borrowed things.

"Here," Margie chirped as she reappeared, waving a pair of poorly knitted socks. "I made them myself."

"A fine job," he told her, fighting a grin. It was what he would've told his sister. His chest panged with grief as it always did when thinking about her. "Thank you both."

"Would you like to stay for supper?" Grigor offered.

"My dragon has another meal in mind," he said over his shoulder as he walked away. *Starnight soldiers.* If they stepped foot into Moonstone first, he'd save their heads to send them back to King Quinton. He wouldn't be

192

accused of abducting *and* drawing first blood in a war.

Rush trekked down the dirt road, past sprawling fields, and into the heart of Uleis. The lord's manor rested along the bank of a river, but it seemed the nobility had congregated in the square. The cobbled streets led Rush to a stone fountain with a large carved fish spilling water from its mouth. Around it stood three men wearing feathered hats, their shoulders rigid.

Rush arched his brow at the sight of them. The ostentatious ensembles—more popular in Starnight than Moonstone—told him what he needed to know about Lord Vikram's relatives: pompous assholes. But the others milling about smiled and waved to each other, chatted. Generally going about their daily tasks with good humor ... as if nothing were amiss.

"Starting without me?" Rush called to them. "Rather rude considering you *asked me* to come save you."

The men jerked up at the commanding boom of Rush's voice. "Your Majesty," they said in unison.

"Have the assholes stepped into Moonstone yet?" Rush inquired.

"N—no," a man in dark blue stuttered. "Starnight is advancing as we speak, but they're sneaking through the woods."

"Mmm. And who are you?" Rush purred, eyeing him.

"Lord Erril." He pointed to the man with the white feather. "This is my brother, Lord Narun. And my cousin, Lord Terog."

Terog, with his brown speckled feather, gave a slight bow, his features tight. "We weren't sure you would come."

Rush narrowed his eyes at the pathetic man and his

thin mustache. It was good to know how little he thought of his king. "Oh? And where is Lord Vikram? Is he not in charge of protecting this town?"

"He is," Narun answered in a stiff voice. "He and his nephew, Dzmitry, never returned from visiting the palace."

"That's because I killed them for treason." Rush lifted a brow, daring anyone to criticize him. "Who did Vikram leave in charge while he was gone?"

Erril's eyes widened before he cleared his throat. "We were sorting that out."

"Sorting it out?" Rush's voice rose. "He must've left *someone*—"

"He left me in charge," a female voice interrupted. The men parted to reveal a middle-aged woman sitting on the edge of the fountain, an ivory satin gown hugging her buxom form. "They just don't want to accept it."

"*I'm* the next in line after Dzmitry," Terog snarled.

Rush *tsked*. However little he knew about this woman, he knew enough about the men that it made no difference. "Since Vikram and Dzmitry won't be returning, the lady will continue to run the estate. Don't bother petitioning the decision, or I'll strip you of your titles." He held up a hand to silence any potential outcries from the stunned group. "Now, what have you done to prepare for a potential attack? By the looks of it, you've done nothing except wait to get yourselves slaughtered."

"We didn't want to create a panic," Terog said.

"And what do you think being blindsided with an attack will do?" Rush's upper lip curled into a sneer. He didn't have time for this. If anything happened to Astor, Aura would be left defenseless as she slept. And ... for some reason, he wanted to be there if, or when, she woke.

Throwing a disdainful look at the men, he trudged toward the forest to take care of his territory while the fools stood around. The solution was simple—he would smoke the bastards out of the forest. Half of those trees were on Moonstone soil and if his own land caught fire, spreading into Starnight, he could hardly be blamed for a natural disaster. The soldiers would be forced from their hiding places while avoiding an act of war.

Rush called to his dragon—the beast stirred, then burst forth in a single breath. Scales broke through his skin, bones shifting and expanding, and his vision sharpened. Villagers cried out in surprise, but he ignored them and leapt into the air. The forest wasn't far, only a few thunderous cracks of his wings. Just enough time for fire to course inside him. Smoke trailed from his nostrils as he dove for the edge of the forest. He opened his mouth, exposing sharp rows of teeth, and released a blistering stream of fire.

Rippling waves of heat followed the bright orange flames with precision. It slammed into the ground, leaving a shallow crater in its path. Rush turned his head so the fire traced the edge of the forest. It took mere moments before enough trees crackled, smoke billowing into the sky, that Rush was certain the entire forest would turn to ash.

Slamming his mouth shut, Rush swallowed the remaining flames. A bitter taste coated his tongue as he licked the sulfur from his scaled lips. He circled the area twice before landing at the edge of the blaze. Rush then called his dragon back inside himself, his bare human form absorbing the heat, relishing it. Fire snapped, cracked, and raged, but no screams came from any of the people. Were they far enough out that they had time to run? Rush narrowed his eyes, hoping to make out even the smallest hint that Starnight was deterred.

Pain pierced his shoulder and he clenched his teeth.

Rush spun around just as a second arrow whizzed past his ear.

*Fuck.*

Three men in blue Starnight uniforms, a silver star over their hearts, nocked another round of arrows. There was no time to figure out where they'd come from or if there were more. They'd shot at him. *Him.* A ruling sovereign. He would tear their spines from their flesh, rip them apart, then burn them to ash.

His dragon shifted and came out to play again before Rush could attempt to attack on his own. With no weapon, it was the sure way to defeat the enemy. The beast screeched, high and full of fury. And still, the soldiers ran *toward* him. Arrows sailed at Rush, striking his scales with a sharp sting, but the damage was minimal. Unlike the arrow still lodged in his shoulder joint where his wing had sprung from his back.

Rush clamped his jaw down over the first man to enter his space, not caring who the fuck it was but wishing it could've been Pax. Hot blood gushed between his teeth, and he flung the body into the blazing fire. The scent of scorched flesh filled the air alongside the smoke, but it didn't deter the others.

Dozens of Starnight soldiers raced toward him with axes, swords, and bows. Rush blasted another breath of fire at the enemy, only missing a few. A blonde woman lodged her battle axe into his front leg. Rush roared, pain exploding up his limb, but he didn't hesitate to rip her head off and swallow it.

Turning, he slammed the rest of the attackers away with the swipe of his tail. Straight into the forest fire where screams rose above the crackling blaze.

He sucked in rapid breaths as his dragon's vision sharpened. The beast shifted his hearing to focus on individual noises, one right after another, until he was certain no humans were left. Only burning woodland, trees toppling, the beat of bird wings as they escaped. He shook his head from side to side to rid himself of the piercing pain in his body.

*Fuck.*

With a glance back at the town to ensure their safety, Rush launched himself into the sky once more. The town held enough forces to handle any stragglers he may have missed. He wasn't going to wait around in this condition to see if he had—not when his body would force the shift back when the pain became too much to bear, effectively stranding him there until he healed enough for travel.

Each pump of his wings tugged at the arrowhead lodged in his shoulder, intensifying the torment. A pained screech tore from his throat as he disappeared into the clouds.

Rush stumbled into the palace kitchens through the back door. Clothing had been left for him in the garden clearing, but he'd only managed to pull on the trousers given the arrow still protruding from his shoulder. He'd waved off the night guards who had flocked to help him and ordered them to fetch a healer instead. That no one was allowed in the kitchens until he was stitched up. And not to create an uproar.

But while he waited, swaying, he needed a damn drink. A huge fucking slab of meat too. His body trembled with the pain radiating through him. It pulsed outward from where the arrowhead scraped against his shoulder blade. However, the axe wound was just as much a problem. If it weren't for his dragon form, the blow would've been much worse, but his scales buffered the impact. Still, a gaping wound on his left forearm exposed muscle.

"Fuck," he groaned.

Half collapsing onto the counter where Aura had been baking with Marion time to time, he inched toward the jug of water. The liquid sloshed everywhere as he attempted to pour it into one of the cups sitting beside it. He clenched his jaw and let the jug tumble from his hand. As he gulped down the water, a few trails of it slid down his chin.

"Rush?" Aura's voice filled the darkened kitchen. "Is that you?"

His head whipped up to find her silhouetted in the doorway, a lantern glowing in her hand. The quick movement sent sharp sparks down his spine and he winced. "You're awake."

"It appears so." She stepped into the room and used the lantern to light one of the torches on the wall.

"As you can see, I'm back," he growled. Not wanting her to see him in need of a healer, he added, "Now leave."

"And in a fine mood," she mumbled. "But I believe I

will stay."

He gripped the countertop to steady himself. She couldn't see him weak—he was the damn King of Sin. Ruthless. Fearsome. Though, for whatever reason, she didn't seem to be afraid of him.

"What are you doing down here so late?" he snapped.

Instead of answering, she lit another torch on the wall, then set the lantern on the tabletop. Her gaze lifted to him and her eyes widened. "Stars above! Is that an *arrow?*"

"Is it that obvious?" Rush said sarcastically.

"What happened?" She darted around the counter, her hands lightly touching him.

"Out of the way," a gravelly voice demanded. The old woman hurried into the kitchen and set a healer's bag on the counter. Rush's knees gave out at the sight of her, the blood loss finally hitting him, and he lowered himself to the floor. Her brown eyes scanned Rush's body. "Let's take care of the arm first."

"What can I do to help?" Aura asked.

"Nothing." The healer nudged her out of the way to kneel at the king's side. He hissed as she prodded at the wound on his arm, then doused it with a liquid that fizzed on contact.

"I've pulled out thorns from my sisters' bare feet," Aura insisted. "I can help."

Rush arched a brow. "Are you saying a thorn is the same as an arrow, kitten? Because, I must say, I disagree."

"I want to help," she insisted.

The healer set a needle to his skin and pressed it through. The thread tugged at his flesh while she stitched and he squeezed his eyes shut as the room spun.

"If you want to help," the healer said, "get a roll of

bandages."

Rush forced his eyes open in time to see Aura dig into the leather bag. What the fuck was she doing? He paid the healer *very* handsomely to take care of injuries—the woman didn't need help. It was only Rush that required tending at the moment, not a large group of soldiers. And he sure as fuck didn't want Aura to see him like this.

Still, he said nothing to stop her. The concern in her eyes was ... different. As if she might care. As if his health mattered for more than political reasons. A king's health affected the entire court, but Rush was still a man. And he ... wanted to matter to someone.

"There." The healer tied off the stitches in his arm with a final, almost harsh, tug. "Wrap the wound, girl. We need to keep it from becoming infected."

Aura knelt beside Rush and offered a nervous smile. "Are you doing all right? You're pale."

"That's the blood loss," he mumbled.

"Hold steady now," the healer ordered. Then, in one sharp movement, she ripped the arrow from his shoulder.

Rush released a muffled roar, his vision fading in and out of darkness. "Fuck." He squeezed his hand, finding something in it. Peering down, he saw that his hand gripped Aura's arm. He released it even though she seemed unbothered by it.

He scowled up at the healer. "I should lock you in the dungeon for that."

Aura scoffed. "Kings shouldn't make idle threats."

"Mmm, what should I make then?" Rush swayed where he sat and she wrapped an arm around his waist.

"My job easier." Aura sat back on her heels and gently began wrapping his arm.

She worked carefully while the healer dug her needle into the cleaned wound on his shoulder. His gaze latched onto Aura's face. The way she bit her lip in concentration and only touched his arm when necessary, he assumed, to avoid hurting him further. Until she finally tucked the end of the bandage into the folds, tying it off.

Aura was part of the reason for all his sorrows. She just didn't know it. It was why she was needed, why she was necessary for his plan against Pax. If the spell had worked properly, then—

"Finished," the healer said. "Don't shift for a few days or you risk tearing the stitches. Try not to exert yourself." She wiped her hands on her skirt and turned to Aura, tossing her a larger set of bandages. "Wrap this one now."

"Lean forward," Aura whispered as the healer packed up her tools.

Rush did as he was told with a grunt of pain. She carefully started wrapping around his abdomen, her fingers skimming his bare skin as she moved diagonally up his back to cover the wound, then down again. Her fingers were attentive, tender. He softened to her care, though he couldn't. *Shouldn't.* Aura was a means to an end. His tool for vengeance.

"Who did this to you?" she asked, her breath skating up the back of his neck, causing him to shiver.

Rush snorted. "Starnight."

"Starnight?" She paused, putting a little too much pressure on the wrapping, causing him to hiss. "I don't understand. Moonstone and Starnight are allies."

"*Were* allies, it seems. They accused me of stealing you away."

"Well..." She lifted one brow as if to say *you did do*

201

*that.*

"They have no proof. Suspicion alone is not enough to invade my court. Besides, you wrote to the prick and called off the wedding," Rush reminded her.

Aura sighed. "Even though I meant every word I wrote to Pax, there's no reason he shouldn't think I was forced to write that."

Rush scowled. She was right, of course, but his plan was falling apart. This wasn't how the spell was meant to go. Rush watched her in silence then. He did deserve the pain he received today, but it wasn't as if he didn't have a good reason for his actions with Aura. Wrongs to set right. Through everything, through two years of hatred, he now realized he wished the price wasn't Aura, yet there was nothing he could do to change it.

"I can't undo the spell," he whispered. "If it means anything, I never meant for it to torture you like this." Everything was meant to be finished when she'd first arrived. Though, he wasn't sure the dreams wouldn't have tortured her regardless. He wasn't aware of that before casting the spell, but it wouldn't have made any difference. Not at the time. "I'm willing to apologize for that bit."

"Just that bit?" Aura asked, her head tilted to the side. "At least tell me more of what it will do to me."

"Ah, kitten. I'll need a drink first for that."

She tied off the end of the bandage and rose without another word. Her work was good, the wrapping tight without being restrictive. He tested his shoulder, rolling it slightly, and winced. A moment later, Aura held out a bottle of alcohol to him.

He grinned, accepted it from her, and took three deep

swallows. It wasn't the finest he'd had, but it was strong which mattered more given the situation.

"So?" Aura nudged and adjusted the layers of his bandage to lay smoother.

Rush sighed, the pain seeming to have loosened his lips. The alcohol didn't help matters. But it was only fair Aura knew more, even if it was only a little. "It's to help someone I love dearly."

Aura's hand stilled and she watched him, her expression softening toward him.

He didn't deserve that expression, but he was a selfish bastard. "Distract me, kitten."

"Distract you how?"

"From the pain in my shoulder." He trailed a fingertip along her jawline.

The edges of her lips curled up. "You need to *rest*."

Rush opened his mouth—uncertain what was about to come out of it—when a pair of boots pounded into the room.

"Rush?" Astor called.

"In here," he answered in a low voice. Then, he whispered to Aura, "You owe me a distraction."

"I'll be in my room if you need me." A blush rose in her cheeks and she leapt to her feet. She straightened her skirts while she backed away, giving Astor space.

Rush's pulse sped up as he watched her disappear from the kitchens. He wanted her to stay—and for no true purpose at all. Just to have her there. To see her and know she was real. *Safe.*

# 17

# AURA

Aura stood at the bars of her bedroom window, gazing out toward the night sky. The stars shone brightly around a crescent moon and she wondered what her family was doing at that precise moment. Worrying, she knew.

She couldn't stop herself from thinking about what would become of them. What would the King of Starnight do if his guards discovered her in this palace and she still refused to marry his son? They would likely haul her back, threaten to take her family's titles away at the least, kill them at the worst, if she didn't follow through with the wedding. But even if they took her away from here, she would only fall into a deep sleep.

Rush had taken her, but he hadn't forced her to become his bride. And now, royals were sending guards to Moonstone to seek her out. People could get hurt because of her. *Rush* was hurt because of her.

Gripping the iron bars, Aura pressed her forehead against their coolness. When she'd gone to the kitchens, she hadn't truly been hungry at all—she'd heard the crack of Rush's wings as soon as he'd entered the gardens. She'd waited to hear him come down the hall, but when he didn't, she went searching for him. That need had coursed through her to talk to Rush, to start slyly questioning him. Instead of discovering him with his usual cocky manner, she'd found him wounded, weak— a side of him she'd never envisioned. For a brief moment, part of her believed he'd deserved it, the piece of her that remembered how she felt when she was first brought to the palace. But now, after hearing more from Sorcha in her last dream, she didn't wish him dead. Especially not after he'd confessed a tiny hint about the spell. It was to help someone who he loved.

*Sorcha.*

Rush hadn't admitted the name, but Aura knew it was his sister without a doubt. Releasing the bars, she sank down to the freezing floor, pulling her knees to her chest. There was more to this spell, the dreams, with Sorcha coming to her...

A thought crossed her mind and she gasped. There was a possibility that Sorcha's spirit was trapped not only in Grimm, or the Moonstone Court, but in this very palace. The spell Rush cast upon Aura could be to help Sorcha pass on to the gods.

"But why does he need me? Why would that require me to live in this palace forever?" Aura whispered. Couldn't a sorcerer help if that was the case? She didn't

205

even know if Rush was aware of his sister's lingering spirit, so the spell could be something else entirely. The necessary pieces were missing, but the answer was there, pecking away at the inside of her skull. She needed to find out more.

Exhaustion pulled its blanket over her and she released a tired yawn. Rush wasn't coming to her room, even though she'd said she would be there. Her eyelids fluttered shut, and she hadn't realized she'd slipped into sleep until two strong arms lifted her from the floor. She caught a glimpse of Rush, still shirtless and bandaged, before her eyes fell shut again.

"Why are you carrying me?" she murmured into his chest. "You're injured."

"I've been through worse, kitten. From now on, you sleep with me," Rush said, cradling her close.

"So demanding." Her lips curled up at the edges. "And what are we doing once we get into bed?"

"We sleep," he purred. "But tomorrow we can discuss fucking."

She was too tired to even roll her eyes, his chest too comforting against her body, the rhythm of his heart too soothing. As they entered his room, and he gently rested her on his soft mattress, she barely registered the blankets being drawn over her before she slipped into a deep, dreamless sleep.

Sunlight spilled through the window, tugging Aura from

sleep. The silk sheets draped her body and she found herself alone in Rush's room. It was the perfect opportunity to search for Sorcha's journal and Rush's cellar key. She stood from the bed and took a stealthy step forward when the library door opened, making her still. Wearing only trousers, Rush sauntered out with a book while eating a raspberry tart.

"Well, hello, kitten," Rush cooed. "You slept through the servant bringing tarts."

"My family always told me that I sleep like the dead," she said, perking up as she studied the dessert in his hand. "Are you going to offer me one?"

"That depends." Rush smirked, slowly walking to her as though she were his prey. "What are you going to offer me? These just so happen to be my favorite dessert."

Her gaze trailed up his muscular chest to the bandage on his shoulder. "I did patch you up last night, so I think you owe me."

"Mmm, the healer patched me up. *You* put a bandage on me."

"You're such an ass."

"Yes, but honest." His grin grew wide while handing her the tart. "If you want more, the tray is on my desk along with a pitcher of water."

"Thank you." She bit into the tart and moaned at its sweetness.

Once she finished eating, he leaned in close. "You missed some." He slowly swiped his tongue over her lips and licked the spot clean. "There, that's better."

A warming sensation fluttered in her belly instead of her reaching to slap him. She couldn't control herself from wanting his tongue to do other things, wicked and delicious things. Their breaths mingled, the air thick with desire. Would he kiss her? Just as she tilted her chin up, he stepped back to grab a shirt from his wardrobe. She took in a deep breath, shaking herself out of whatever *that* was she was feeling.

Rush looked at her over his shoulder. "I have to speak with the guards about Starnight, but I'll meet you in the ballroom after."

"I would like that." She bit her lip, focusing on what mattered—hoping this was her chance to be left alone inside his room to search it.

"Good. A servant is waiting in the bathing chamber for you."

*Damn it.* That was Aura's queue to leave. But Rush had said she would be sleeping in his room going forward, which meant she would have another opportunity. She just couldn't fall asleep first...

As Aura stepped into the hallway and closed the door behind her, Astor came around the corner, his hair disheveled.

"Did you bring those flowers to Hana?" she asked.

He furrowed his brow and studied her as if he didn't understand why she was talking to him. "Not yet."

"Would you mind delivering something else to my twin? Recipes from Marion. You don't have to say they're from me. Just make sure she gets them."

"I can do that." Before Aura walked away, Astor added, "I can deliver anything you need me to. I don't mind at all."

Aura blinked, surprised by his kindness. "Thank you, Astor. And remember, stay honest with Hana."

But really, could he be completely honest with Hana

when Aura was living in this palace just under Astor's nose?

The door opened and Astor turned to face Rush, who now wore a black tunic. As Aura padded down the hallway to leave them alone, she caught wind of Astor asking the king in a heated tone, "I didn't realize this was a permanent sleeping arrangement." Why did it matter to him anyway?

Aura collected a silver dress from her wardrobe, then rinsed off in a warm bath filled with scarlet rose petals and oils. As she studied the pretty redheaded servant— Janee—Aura wondered if she'd ever pleasured Rush, if she'd been the one who he'd brought to bliss just outside her room. A bit of envy crawled through her, but Janee was nice and talked about several of her lovers while Aura listened.

Before going to the ballroom, Aura ate one of Marion's meat pies in the kitchens while the woman instructed two other servants on how to bake proper miniature cakes. The ballroom was empty so Aura took a seat at the piano and brushed her fingers across the smooth ivory keys, playing one short note after another.

"I wasn't sure it was possible to play worse than Astor." Rush smirked as he settled beside her at the piano, his smoky scent consuming her senses. She hadn't even heard him come into the room.

Aura rolled her eyes. "I never learned to play the piano."

"Ah, so you need a lesson then." His large hands fell atop hers, warm, so deliciously warm. "We start slow. I may not be the greatest, but I can teach a simple melody." He gently pressed their fingers against the keys before playing, and she clumsily followed. "That's not too terrible."

"Continue being honest. *Please.*" She laughed softly. "Growing up, I never had an interest in playing an instrument."

Rush raked a hand through his hair. "Oh? A young woman meant to become a royal of Starnight? I'm surprised you weren't forced to be accomplished in all things."

"I was *encouraged.*"

"What did you have an interest in?"

Aura opened her mouth to answer, but there was nothing... She thought about it, really thought about it, wishing she could say something like swordplay or archery. *Something.* "I don't know... I honestly don't. I lived with my family away from the palace, secluded past the mountains. My life was so focused on marrying the prince that I don't even know what *I* like. No matter that I've helped Marion bake, I don't like it any more than I did. Maybe gardening? After spending time in yours, I quite like plants."

Rush snorted. "I think there is a difference between observing a pretty garden and working in one."

She folded her arms. "I won't know until I find out."

"Then, by all means, go outside and work in mine. Get those pretty little hands of yours dirty. I don't mind watching." The King of Sin's eyes grew hooded as his gaze slowly traveled up her form to lock on hers.

"You're ridiculous. Besides, don't you have Starnight matters to think about?"

Rush grew serious. "Starnight will grow bolder. According to Astor, Pax is demanding to wed you immediately after you're found."

"Immediately?" she hissed. "Why does it matter? He can wed any of his other conquests if he so chooses."

Rush shrugged. "You wounded his poor little pride. He isn't going to let you go so easily."

*Says the king who won't let me outside his royal gardens...* "Hmm, sometimes I want to show you a mirror when you're discussing someone. What about my family? Are they safe?"

"They are. Astor is making certain of it."

But if they found Aura, that could change... "How do you know what Pax is like anyway?"

Rush inhaled sharply through clenched teeth. "Our fathers held meetings since our courts are so close to one another. I thought Pax was a friend once, yet he proved I was a fool."

Aura wanted to dig more, but she had to switch to something else before he closed himself off. "Why did you come into my dream the other day? You can do that anytime you want?"

"If Astor makes a potion I can." A grin spread his lips. "Why? Do you want me to come again?"

"If you play nice, then we'll see."

"Oh, I can play however you want me to play, kitten," he purred.

Aura's heart thudded in her chest as her gaze fell to his full lips, the way his index finger slowly skimmed the lower one. She needed to continue fishing about the dream while she had him in this moment. "There's something I noticed in my dream that I wanted to ask you about," she prodded. "A painting was there. Of your family. You don't have a single one hanging in the palace that I've seen though."

Rush pursed his lips into a tight line, his hands balling into fists. "I still have them. They just aren't hung up."

"Your sister looked like you. She was very pretty."

"Stop talking," Rush whispered, his nostrils flaring.

"If something happened to one of my sisters—"

"Sisters." Rush slammed his fist against the piano keys, the dramatic sound echoing, adding to the current mood between them. "You have four. I had *one*. She's dead. Sorcha was the most caring person in all of Grimm. But that was all taken away because of..." He stood from the bench. "This was a mistake. All of this is a mistake."

Aura had to keep going, not wilt into herself from his anger. She pushed up from the seat and took a deep breath as she looked up at him. "It's all right, Rush. I may have four, but even if I lost one of them, a piece of me would be forever gone. My sisters may still be breathing, yet I understand the pain, the grief. You haven't only lost Princess Constance but both your parents. And I understand why you lose yourself in so many women to forget."

"Is that what I do, kitten?" he snapped. "Fuck any woman who wants to ride my cock so I can forget? Even before that I've always enjoyed a good fuck. I'm the King of Sin, am I not?"

Aura swallowed, believing he was hiding his emotions behind his words. "Have you touched anyone since the night of the party?" she finally asked. "Have you had your daily orgies? Has anyone stroked or tasted your cock?"

"No," he rasped, his chest heaving. His pupils dilated as he continued to watch her.

She tilted her head to the side. "And why is that, Your

Majesty?"

Rush moved swiftly, backing her into the piano before setting her atop it. He spread her legs, his strong body nestling between them until they were in the same position they'd been in last, his mouth oh-so close to touching hers. "Perhaps there is only one person I have my sights set on tasting, touching, *fucking*."

"I suppose there is only one foolish man I want to kiss," she said, her voice breathy.

And before she could utter another word, his mouth was on hers, the kisses hard, wild, and frantic. His tongue slipped inside her mouth as his hands cupped her buttocks and brought her nearer.

Aura prayed the pleasure would bring him closer, so she could find a way to help both the princess and herself. But she couldn't deny she relished the smoky taste of his kisses, the feel of him. She'd told herself she hadn't wanted him, but that was all a lie. However, this would only be temporary—it had to be. As the kisses grew even more heated, her fingers digging into his lower back, she wrapped her legs around his waist, letting his hard length press into her softness. A euphoric thrill coursed through her at the contact, and she wanted the layers gone, wanted to know how that large cock of his would feel sliding inside her.

Rush's mouth left hers to trail kisses along her jaw, down her neck, to speak in her ear, his voice lowered, "Did the prince ever lick your sweet cunt until you quaked beneath him?"

"I never came from his tongue," she breathed.

He smirked as he drew back. "You will from mine."

And she wanted to, desperately. She nodded and Rush

hiked up her dress, then drew her undergarments down her legs. "Lay down," he demanded.

Heart pounding in anticipation, she did as told and he brought her legs over his shoulders. With one swift sweep of the tongue, he slowly licked up her center and she gasped in pleasure. Not once had Pax done something like this to her first. It had always been his needs met, then barely any time for her. Not once had there been attention given to her in this manner.

Rush's tongue continued to work her, stroked and glided before plunging into her depths to drink her nectar. And then his fingers replaced his tongue so he could use it to circle her pearl. She craved this moment, craved for him to never cease.

"Fucking moan for me, kitten. Be as loud as you want." The vibrations from his words against her only made everything more pleasurable.

With Pax, he always wanted her quiet, but here and now, she could do what she desired. And so she listened to Rush, releasing whimpers every time he fucked her core with his mouth. She didn't care if anyone walked in on her at the moment and saw the King of Sin between her legs. Let the whole staff see how he was making her feel—it wasn't as if it wasn't something they hadn't glimpsed before.

And then a blissful wave of pleasure crashed through her and she quaked beneath his impish tongue, his wicked fingers, leaving her gasping for breath.

"I've been waiting to hear you come apart," Rush said, a satisfied grin lighting up his face.

Once she sat up, his mouth captured hers again. She reached for the button of his trousers and he grasped her wrist to stop her. "From now on, the only one who you kneel before is me."

"Oh, is that so?" she drawled.

Rush lifted her from the piano, pulling a squeak from her as her legs tightened around his torso. He then carried her out of the room and ascended the stairs, his mouth never leaving hers. Somehow he managed to not trip up the steps or crash into the walls. Laird opened the door for him, and Rush kicked it shut behind them.

He sat her on the bed against the headboard, then settled in front of her. Aura peered up at his ravenous gaze, her pulse erratic with anticipation as he lifted his shirt over his head. Lips pulling back into a smile, she unfastened his trousers and drew them off him. She took in his length, the glistening tip, and her own arousal pooled between her thighs. "I thought you only fuck your hand in here."

"Not anymore," he said, his voice gruff while he gripped the headboard.

Aura grasped his length, stroking a few times as Rush groaned, loud and deep. It sent another wave of heat through her.

She licked up his velvety skin from base to tip before wrapping her mouth around his cock. Her hands traveled to his buttocks and she dug her fingernails in, urging him to go at the pace he desired.

"Fuck, kitten, your mouth feels so good," he ground out as he slowly rolled his hips.

Aura continued her movements, enjoying the salty and smoky taste of him. He slid back and forth, his teeth digging in to his lower lip as she watched him. And then his cock jerked. She gripped his buttocks harder as he spilled his seed inside her mouth. A lusty growl poured out from between his lips. "Aura." Rush snaked an arm around her waist and pulled her down until she was beneath him. "How much more do you want?"

"So much more." It wasn't a lie, not in the least.

"I give it rough." He flicked his tongue across her lips. "Can you handle that?"

"Show me what else the King of Sin has to offer," she said, trailing a finger down his bare chest.

A knock pounded on the door and Rush jerked before yelling, "Go the fuck away."

"I need to speak with you. *Now*," Astor called.

"Fuck!" Rush's jaw tightened as he slipped from the bed. "Give me a minute." He didn't bother to fasten his trousers after yanking them up. In a few long strides, he whipped the door open and stepped from the room. The door shut behind him, their voices too low for her to hear.

Aura had just been ready to take things with Rush even further, yet this was what she'd been waiting for. She didn't know how much time she had before he returned, but she could work until she heard the door open, then make up a lie if needed.

Tamping down any remaining lust, she hurried to the desk and riffled through each drawer. Most were filled with blank sheets of paper, some empty, others held books that weren't a journal. And no key.

Aura checked under the settee, the bed, inside the wardrobe. She squeezed the clothing, searching for anything hard. Her heart hammered in her chest, knowing Rush could come back in at any moment.

Just as she shut the wardrobe door, the knob turned

and she bolted for the bed, resting herself in an upright position as though she'd been waiting for him.

Rush slipped into view, his gaze raking over her. "You look good in my bed, kitten. But we have duties to attend to for now."

She arched a brow and leaned forward. "What duties?"

"Things a king must do." He held a hand out to help her from the bed. "And it looks like you get to try your hand at gardening while I'm occupied."

# RUSH

Rush paced from the onyx fireplace to the liquor cabinet and back again, the taste of Aura's starlight flavor still on his tongue. He ran a finger over his bottom lip in memory of her sweet center. Astor sat in a velvet wingback chair in the middle of his office, scowling at him. Starnight was likely offended that he'd slaughtered their guards. He'd *only* eaten one's head and obliterated the rest. If they tried hard enough, Rush was certain they could find all the pieces scattered over Uleis.

"The guards I sent to the border will keep them at bay," he mused, mostly to himself. There wasn't time for a war at the moment—it would take him away from Aura, away from his plan. Even if Pax found Aura, attempted to lay claim to her, he couldn't take her unless he wanted a bride that never woke. Besides, Aura would remain *his*.

"Yes," Astor agreed in a solemn voice.

Rush paused his pacing and turned toward the window. The gardens spread out below the second-story room and a particularly nice patch of fragrant flowers circled an iron bench. Aura was there now, dressed in a simple bronze gown covered in a long white apron as she knelt beside the bench. The head gardener leaned over the bushes beside her and pointed at the leaves with her weathered hand. Cracking the window, he strained to hear their conversation.

"These grow best in this part of the garden because they get at least six hours of sunlight," the gardener explained. "And you see three inches of mulch here as well."

Aura nodded and, though her back was to him, she seemed to be paying rapt attention as she used a spade to dig a small hole in the soil. The stable hand passed by them on the other side of the hedge with a quick nod, but he didn't stop to chat or offer a smile. *Smart man.* If he'd tried to flirt with Aura again, Rush would've had to make good on the threat to cut off his hand.

"Rush," Astor spat.

He shut the window before his loud tone drew Aura's attention away from her lesson. "What is it?"

"She might not be awake long enough to find a pastime," Astor said, his gaze narrowed in disapproval. "You spelled her, remember? Her life force is being drained away, and soon, she'll never open her eyes again. I know you like a good fuck, but this is low, even for you."

"Shut your fucking mouth," Rush hissed.

"Why?" Astor leaned back in the chair and crossed his

219

arms. "Is the truth too much for you, Your Majesty?"

Rush balled his hands into fists. "We may be close Astor, but I warn you—"

Astor released a mirthless laugh. "As long as you understand that your feelings for Aura *can't* stop you now that the spell is underway."

Something tightened in his chest. Squeezed like a vise. He ... *couldn't* have feelings for Aura. It wasn't possible. He'd closed himself off to anything more than fucking when he became the last living member of his family. It was easier to go through life alone. Keeping people at arm's length helped avoid the pain of losing them.

"I don't have feelings for her," he lied. It had nothing to do with how she sucked his cock or how sweet her cunt tasted either. Somehow, he would be troubled if anything happened to her, and not just because of the spell.

Astor shrugged, his expression knowing. "Then why is she sleeping in your room? Why are you watching her every move? Don't tell me it's because you want to protect her. She's perfectly safe here and you know it."

"I'm not willing to risk her security," he snarled.

Rush turned his back on Astor to watch Aura through the window. She set a small shrub into the hole she'd dug, then gently brushed the small pile of soil over the roots and tucked it around the stem. A bright smile crossed her face when she turned her head toward the gardener.

Soon, there would be no more smiles. Soon, there would be no more Aura. She would be asleep, trapped in a dream. He would be forced to carry her down to the cellar and place her on a stone slab. Slide a large stone over the entrance to her tomb. Then leave her there so no one discovered what he'd done and use it to start a war.

He watched Aura in the garden. Watched as she stood, brushed the dirt from her long apron, and lifted a basket of cut flowers. She followed the gardener toward the orchard until he could no longer see them between fruit trees.

What would Sorcha think of him for this? His sister had always been kind and caring, willing to go without if it benefited someone else. She would loathe him for what he was doing to Aura, would've told him to give up on revenge.

*Fuck.*

He took a handful of heavy breaths. Indecision warred within him, tearing his thoughts in different directions. Astor's chair creaked behind him.

"What the fuck are you doing, Rush?" Astor said, his voice weary. "Do you even know anymore?"

Rush bared his teeth and stormed around the hawk shifter. No, he didn't know. Because if his plan succeeded, he still might lose everything. There had to be a way out of this. The sorceress hadn't told him how to break the spell, nor had he asked, but there had to be a way. *Just in case.* He wouldn't use it—not unless he absolutely had to. Things were already not going as planned when Aura didn't fall into a permanent slumber upon arrival, so if anything else went wrong… There was no point in Aura suffering without a tradeoff.

*Just in case,* he told himself.

"Where are you going?" Astor asked from behind him.

Rush hadn't even realized he was being followed.

221

"Nowhere you're allowed," he snapped. "Why don't you go pine over Hana?"

The sound of Astor's footsteps halted as Rush descended a staircase. Within moments, he made his way into the dungeons. It was dark and cold, water clinging to the stone walls. This wasn't where Hana had been kept, but the *old* dungeons. The ones fortified by his great-great grandfather with illegal blood magic.

At the bottom of the staircase, Rush took a dagger from his belt and pricked his thumb. One of the illegal spells his great-great grandfather acquired from a sorceress was for sealing—unless a dragon shifter placed his blood on the wall, the door would remain part of the stone. He wiped the crimson droplet over the harsh sigils carved into the stone door and it groaned open.

As he stepped inside, he lit the torches. The light glinted off his hoard of gold, silver, and precious stones. Piles of coins. Necklaces, bracelets, earrings. A glass case of rings. Broaches. Crowns and tiaras. Raw stones. Amulets. Gilded frames and crystal vases. Rush's dragon purred, begging to come out and play, at the sight of all the treasure.

He took a deep, calming breath, and sauntered down the center of the room. Over the years, he'd collected precious artifacts with magical properties. He approached a wall decorated in vases and candlesticks, figurines and gem-encrusted boxes. Inside one such box, on a bed of green velvet, rested a pocket watch, dozens of small rubies adorning the gold cover.

Rush lifted it by the chain. Losing such a finely crafted object... His dragon hissed and sent flames coursing through him as he realized what Rush was about to do.

*I'll replace it,* he assured the beast.

Besides, he'd been searching for the sorceress that gave him the spell since it was cast, so what made him think he could find her now?

Rush flew to the mountain range he'd given to the sorceress, clutching the pocket watch in his talons. After circling for most of the afternoon, he spotted something ... new.

A small house built at the end of the edge of a cliff. The thatched roof sat upon stone walls and a path was worn into the grass, leading to a square patch of a garden.

Rush touched down on a rocky overhang above it and dragged in a deep breath. The scent of freshly chopped evergreens permeated the air along with the hint of a dying fire. He leapt from his perch into the clearing around the home, shifting to land on his human feet.

Rush strode toward the cabin, slipping into a pair of trousers that were just his size and rather *conveniently* left at the edge of the property. He peered into one of the windows—inside, a variety of dried herbs hung from the ceiling. In the center of the room, containers of powders and jars filled with teeth rested on a long table. Embers burned in the fireplace at the back, and in one corner, a mossy green curtain was pulled away to reveal a bed covered with bearskin. More containers lingered on shelves lining the walls, the contents unclear from where he stood. Papers and books were heaped into random piles throughout the entire space.

It certainly appeared to be the home of a magic user. But was it the same sorceress? He never stipulated what she needed to use the mountain range for when he gave it to her. There was no telling if this was the *right* sorceress. Rush clutched the pocket watch in his hand. A soft creak drew his attention toward the door. It pushed inward slowly, gently, but with no one present to move it.

Rush stepped boldly over the threshold and the door slammed behind him. "Sorceress?" he called.

"My name is Aradia," came a scratchy female voice. "As you well know, Your Majesty."

Rush's gaze narrowed as he scanned the interior. On the opposite side of the table, a shape formed, ever so slowly. Wispy, then a shadow. The vague outline of a human shimmered into a woman. An extravagant blue dress hugged the sorceress's curves and gray streaked her long dark hair. Rush held his breath for a moment, uncertain if, after all this time of searching for her, she would vanish as she had before.

"Don't look so surprised, King of Sin. I've seen you circling the mountains for weeks." She scanned him up and down. "I see you found the trousers I left out for you."

Rush's lips parted in surprise, but he quickly wiped the expression from his face. *Weeks?* If he didn't need her help at the moment, he would remind her exactly who's court she lived in.

She chuckled as she opened a glass jar and extracted a dried leaf. "Your dragon isn't subtle."

"You knew I was searching for you?" he ground out.

She shrugged. "A trick of the light kept you from

seeing my new abode as easily as it kept you from seeing me a moment ago. I prefer not to be disturbed."

Rush snarled. "And I don't like being lied to."

"I did not lie." Her gaze lifted to his and it danced with secrets. She crumbled the leaf into a small glass bowl, not a speck left on her fingers. "The spell I gave you is working. The fortune teller spoke true."

"Aura's still awake," Rush growled. "It took two years to find every single ingredient to cast the spell, and when I did, you said it would be immediate." Anger thrummed within him, not because Aura wasn't falling into the spell but because he had been forced to get to know her, to second-guess his actions. Neither would fight the other— the sorceress needed Rush alive to keep her claim of the mountains while he needed information. And yet, she was the only one who could make him feel uncomfortable.

"It won't be much longer now." Aradia pulled a glass jar across the wooden table toward herself, the sound of it echoing through the room.

"And if I wanted to ... slow the progression down?" Rush asked.

Aradia laughed. "There is no delaying the effects of a spell. You either break it or you do not."

The muscle in his jaw ticked. If the spell was broken, Aura would be free of the curse, but... But he would lose his last thread of hope. Still, he needed the option. "I want to know how to break it then."

Aradia paused in scooping gray dust from her jar to stare at him. "After all you've done to cast it, I'm surprised you would even ask."

Rush sneered. "Answer me."

"I do not fear you, King of Sin." Her piercing brown

eyes flashed in defiance as she shoved the spoon back into the dust and set it aside. "I *did* warn you against this kind of dark magic. I would need a *favor* in the future to do so."

"I have something you might want more." He grasped her wrist, slipping the pocket watch into her palm. "I will not owe you a favor, sorceress."

"This is … ancient," she mused. If she thought he was unaware that it held magic, she was wrong. Not that he cared what the watch did—just that the shine made it perfect for the hoard. But giving this in exchange was better than Aradia showing up at his palace, demanding something that he was unwilling to give in return.

"Do we have a deal?" Rush narrowed his eyes, his dragon anxiously awaiting her answer.

Without a word, she stepped away from her concoction, then tore the corner from a sheet of paper and used a bit of charcoal to scribble letters across it. When she finished, she folded the paper and held it toward him. "This is for *their* sake. Not yours."

Rush snatched the cure from her and scanned the words. *Break the spindle on the spinning wheel.* He jerked his head up, his nostrils flaring. "What the fuck is this? I can't *touch* the spindle."

The corners of her lips tilted up at the edges as she tucked the watch into her skirt pocket. "Figure it out. You've overstayed your welcome." The door flung open, a gust of wind rattling the herbs above. "Goodbye, King of Sin."

# AURA

Aura placed two more red roses into the wicker basket the gardener, Farah, had given her. She brushed the lingering dirt from her palms against her apron, adding to the stains after planting flowers, removing weeds, and pruning the bushes. Gardening was more work than Aura had thought, and yet, she found it relaxing and a distraction from everything that was happening. Rush had gifted her this opportunity when he knew how much she wanted to try it, even when he could've demanded her to await his return inside the palace…

"Do you need help with anything else?" Aura asked, handing the basket of roses to Farah, but the gardener nudged it back toward her.

"You keep them. You did well today. Tomorrow I'll

teach you more if the king allows it." Farah looked as though she wanted to say more yet held her tongue. Aura had been there for weeks now, and no one dared to ask what her name was, most likely waiting for her to introduce herself. But she still wouldn't risk that. And if anyone had discovered her true identity, possibly through court gossip about the Starnight Prince's betrothed being taken on her wedding day, they remained mum on the subject. Loyal to their king.

"Oh, he most certainly will allow it," Aura said, matter-of-factly. "I'll see you tomorrow." She turned on her heel and went inside the palace. Her throat was dry, even though she'd drank several glasses of water while working beneath the blazing sun. A while ago, Rush had taken off in dragon form which meant she wouldn't be allowed into his room until he returned. *Blasted.*

If she had a chance to search his space again, the key could be anywhere. Astor always maintained a wide distance between them, so she wouldn't be able to sneak his key from him either. What she needed was to ask Sorcha, to see if she would know. Perhaps the chance would arise soon…

Wiping the perspiration from her brow, Aura stopped in the kitchens and placed the basket of roses on the counter. Marion knelt in front of the cabinets and took out a large silver pot.

"I brought you something," Aura said with a smile.

"You did?" Marion glanced at her, a horrified expression on her face when her gaze swept up Aura's filthy form. "Stay right where you are! I don't need dirt in the king's meal."

"You could tell him it was a gift from me," she teased.

228

"I only wanted to bring you these roses. I figured you taught me recipes and I never really had anything to offer in return."

Marion blinked, then pushed up from the floor. She lifted a red rose from the basket and ran a finger across its velvety petals. "They're beautiful. Thank you." Her eyes glistened. "These were the princess's favorite. Always the red ones."

"Oh! I didn't know. I'm so sorry." But she should've known—in several of her dreams, there'd been red roses.

"No, no. Memories are good to have," Marion said hurriedly. She then cocked her head and placed a hand on her hip. "You haven't eaten properly today, have you?"

Aura shook her head. Besides some water, she only had a small slice of jerky and a piece of fruit.

"Let me grab you something to eat while you take a seat here." She drew up a stool for Aura to sit on and handed her a glass of water. As Aura drank the cool liquid, Marion made her a chopped lamb sandwich, then cut her a slice of peach cobbler.

As Aura took the last bite of the heavenly dessert, Marion studied her while fighting a smile.

Aura furrowed her brow, watching her curiously. "What is it? Do I have crumbs on my face?"

"Nothing," Marion sang. "You've just been here longer than I expected... Not that it's any of my business, but you're good for the king. Even though the circumstances are rather unusual with your poor sleeping habits."

Rather unusual indeed. Her, his prisoner. And just because she could be good for the king, did that make him good for her? They may have elicited pleasure from one another, but he held secrets, ones that he would have to confess to her eventually. Why couldn't he have told her precisely what the spell was and what it would do? It wasn't as though she could leave his palace grounds anyway.

"I suppose I should bathe. Thank you for the meal. It was lovely," Aura said, choosing not to respond to Marion's comment about the king. He would have to let her step outside his palace gates without falling asleep before she would even consider that he could be good for her.

As she ventured down the hall to her room, Tanix stood outside Rush's door and Laird opposite him against the wall. She gave them a polite nod before entering the bathing chamber to prepare the water, but, instead, Janee was already doing it for her.

"Hello, my lady. The king told me to draw your bath once you came in from the gardens. It's still a bit hot though." Janee smiled as she placed a handful of white petals into the water, then added a few drops of chamomile oil.

That was kind of him... "This is perfect. The hotter the better." Her muscles needed it after the constant crouching and bending over in the garden.

"Do you need my assistance with anything else?" Janee asked, wiping her hands on a towel.

"No, but thank you. I'm going to rest in here a while."

Janee nodded and left Aura alone in the room, the wonderful floral scent clinging to the air calling to her. Aura peeled off the dirt-stained attire and moaned as she lowered herself into the warm bath. Before washing herself clean with a neroli soap bar, she took the time to catch her breath, to not think about Rush, his tongue and fingers on her.

Setting the soap bar down, Aura leaned her head against the back of the tub and closed her eyes. It was only meant to be a brief rest, but then an invisible prick slid into her finger and hope filled her—this was the moment she'd been begging for since searching Rush's room.

She flicked open her eyes to find herself in complete darkness and her body still in water. Only, she wasn't in the tub—she sank below the surface of cold, dark water, falling deeper into a blackened oblivion. Heart hammering, she thrashed her arms and swam upward.

"Hello!" Aura gasped, spitting out brackish water when she broke through the barrier. "Sorcha! Are you here?"

"I'm here," the princess whispered so close that it sounded as if she were floating a hair's breadth above her.

Aura passed her arm through the air and connected with nothing solid. "I can't feel you, and I can't see a thing."

"Neither can I," Sorcha said, her teeth chattering.

"Before we finish where we left off, this is important. Do you know where Rush keeps the key to the cellar? I want to see if your journal is there and to possibly find a way to break my curse."

Sorcha blew out a breath. "Rush will hate me, but I do owe you, Aura. You can't continue to meet me in these dreams. Father always kept it in between the pages of his book on piano keys in the library of my parents' bedroom. The book is located on the first shelf, third row from the bottom. Once the room and library were Rush's, the key

231

remained there. He might still keep it in that location, but I'm not certain. There's something else I need to speak to you about. So much more you must hear. I remember you from when I was alive, and I want to tell you I'm sorry, so very sorry. I was a fool. When he—"

Before she could hear the rest of Sorcha's words, Aura was yanked below the water. Fingers didn't crawl up her ankles, and hands didn't grasp her flesh—it was the water itself. She writhed and twisted, whipping her arms forward to break the surface. Yet she remained in the same position, the water trapping her there, preventing her from moving anywhere.

Aura's lungs pleaded for air as they clenched, but then that abrupt pain struck her digit, driving up her arm to her heart before she jolted forward, her eyes flying open. No longer was she residing in watery darkness but in the bath, the liquid now cold and brown from washing herself.

Sorcha remembered her… But Aura didn't remember her, only hearing about the princess briefly when she'd died. It made sense that she knew who Aura was though… Sorcha would've known Aura was betrothed to Pax since Rush had been friends with him. A lot of people had heard Aura's name even if they'd never met. For now, she needed to focus on the information she received. The key, if Rush kept it in the same place still, was in his personal library. And tonight she would find a way to get in there.

A black silk robe atop a fluffy towel rested on the chair beside the bathtub. Aura quickly dried her body, then slipped on the robe. As soon as she went out into the hallway to get dressed inside her room, footsteps

232

echoed. Footsteps she recognized. She remained where she was and watched as Rush entered the corridor. His molten gaze met hers, and his lips curled up at the edges. He didn't stop at his door—no, he sauntered toward her, ignoring the two guards as they bowed their heads.

Aura's traitorous body heated at the way he was looking at her. She awaited him, his touch, the way to get that key. Rush backed her into the wall, then snaked an arm around her waist and lifted her chin with his callused fingertips. "How was your time in the gardens, kitten?" he drawled.

"Lovely," she said, her voice breathy.

"So, you got dirty?"

"*Very.*"

He ran a hand through her hair and purred, "You're wet." The King of Sin's fingers trailed down her neck, her collarbone, between the valley of her breasts, to her mound. The place where she needed his touch the most. "How about here?"

"*Very* much so. You can see for yourself if you wish."

A deep growl escaped Rush's throat and he drew open her robe, her nipples pebbling at the cool air. His gaze swept up her body, a ravenous hunger shining there. He leaned in and whispered in her ear, "Do you want me to fuck you right here in front of the guards?"

She shook her head, and even though thoughts of the key vanished the more he touched her, she managed to get out, "Your bed."

Rush stilled, seeming to mull something over before he hoisted her up, pulling a yelp from her. He held her against his chest as he carried her into his room. Night shone through the slit in the curtain concealing his

233

balcony doors, and a lit lantern illuminated his desk.

"You don't have to always carry me." Aura grinned. And she hated to admit it, but she *liked* it, liked the way his strong arms felt around her.

"Of course not—I'm the king. But I want to." Rush set her on her feet in front of the bed. His fingers brushed the edges of her robe, and she arched forward. He slowly pushed back the fabric, letting the robe pool on the floor. His eyes grew hooded as he raked her over. "Fuck, kitten, I need to be inside you." And then his lips were on hers, gentle in a way she never expected from him. His tongue slipped between her lips, deliciously massaging hers. They only broke the kiss so she could lift his shirt over his head.

As their mouths locked once more, she stroked him over his trousers before unfastening the button. He shoved the fabric down and entangled his hands in her hair as he kissed her with furor. The way he kissed, the way he touched, she wanted every moment of it.

Aura grasped his thick length and he groaned, low and guttural, while she stroked him thoroughly.

"Enough," Rush commanded, then lifted and brought her into his lap as he sat on the bed. Her bare flesh was pressed to his hard cock, her body yearning for more. She moaned when he gripped her hips, urging her to move atop him. She'd never wanted Pax like this, so desperately, so needy, so *raw*.

When Rush's hot mouth closed around her taut nipple, circling it with his tongue, she couldn't handle it anymore. "Take me. Make me yours." It was meant to be a lie—however, it tasted of truth. If the King of Sin kept doing what he was, she would be forever his, regardless if she was bound to his home or not.

"You're already mine," Rush purred, nipping her lower lip, then rolling them so her back hit the mattress. "Even though this is your first time, I promise you this— you'll fucking come."

Aura's eyes widened, anticipation stirring in her lower belly while he ventured down her body until his alluring face was at her center. His wicked eyes never left hers as he ran his tongue ever so slowly up her core, teasing her before trailing heated kisses up her stomach to her breast.

Circling her clit with his deft fingers, Rush's lips found her neck. He kissed and sucked, and she craned her neck further to give him more access. His length replaced his hand, brushing her soaked entrance. Biting her lip, she arched back with a loud gasp as he buried himself inside her. The ache stung and she opened her mouth to curse him, but then his hips gingerly moved, and another feeling blossomed there. Small at first, a closed flower bud opening a bit of bliss with each roll of his hips.

"Claw me all you want, kitten," he said in a gruff voice. "I don't give a fuck how much damage you do to me."

In answer, Aura gripped his hair as he continued his delicious pace, as the friction picked up, harder and *harder*. Her hands skimmed down his back, holding onto him. There wasn't an ounce of nervousness or discomfort within her at having him be the one to take something she'd saved her whole life to give to someone else.

Rush lifted one of her legs over his shoulder, bringing himself in deeper, hitting her bud over and over again. Building and building. Until a small flame flickered, growing and pulsing within her before it fully ignited, euphoria rolling through her, unleashing inside her veins.

"Rush!" she screamed, yanking on his hair once more as her body vibrated in gratification.

"I like hearing you scream." He smirked and slipped out of her. "Now, grip the headboard."

Catching her breath, she nodded and turned, kneeling, to grasp it. He was only gone a moment before he thrust into her from behind. Another moan slipped out of her. Especially when his hands were on her breasts, kneading, then trailing one between her legs. Her eyes fluttered as he moved inside her and a second bout of ecstasy graced her. Rush released a roar at her back, his body quaking against hers when he came.

"Fuck," he rasped, then echoed it again, "*Fuck.*" He didn't pull out of her and toss her aside as she expected. Instead, he remained above her, his arms circling her for a few more moments before he brought her with him to lay on the bed. "Damn, kitten. The next time, let me see what else you can do with those claws of yours."

Aura's chest heaved as she rested her head against his chest. The next time… Would there be one if she found the key tonight? She didn't know. But what she *did* know was she wanted him to pleasure her more times than the number of stars filling the sky.

As the silence stretched between them, she finally broke it by asking, "So … how come you've never had anyone in your bed? Curiosity has gotten the best of me."

Rush glanced down at her, his lips pursed. "It never felt right to bring anyone here. The royal bedchamber is meant for a king and his queen, not for conquests."

"But I'm not your queen," she stuttered, wondering why he would choose to allow her in his bed then.

"No." He furrowed his brow, seemingly lost in

thought.

"What will you offer her then?" she asked. Envy churned within her chest and she swatted it away.

"I have nothing left to give."

"I think you have plenty. Perhaps you can tell her your secrets. Be honest, truthful."

"Truthful?" His silver eyes studied her face, thoughts swirling in their depths.

"Yes! It's what people should do when they care about someone."

"Oh, kitten, how facetious of you to think I would care about anyone." His face then softened, or, perhaps, she imagined it. "*Honestly*, I hated you when I shouldn't have. I've treated you dishonorably by stealing you away and forcing you to stay. You're not what I expected, and things ... haven't gone as planned." Before she could think on what he said, Rush changed the subject, speaking in a low voice, "Tell me what you would do to see your sisters again."

Her eyes widened in surprise at his question, wondering why he would ask such a thing. Or was he thinking about Sorcha in that moment? But she mulled over his question, truly thought about what she would do for that chance. "As long as they're safe, even if I never see them again, I have comfort in that."

"My sister would've liked you." Rush smiled then. "She got along with everyone, but the two of you would've been friends. Even though she..." he trailed off. "Did you find working in the gardens pleasing?"

Aura's chest tightened, but she went along with another change in matters. "Perhaps tomorrow you can come out there and get *your* hands dirty with me and find out."

He arched a brow and smirked. "I'll watch."

Aura laughed softly, then went into the importance of the types of soils that she learned from Farah until Rush's eyelids fluttered. She lulled her tone to make it softer, more soothing, waiting for his breaths to come out deep and steady.

When she was certain Rush was asleep, Aura lifted off him and froze as he rolled to face her, his lids still closed. With one fragile movement after another, she slipped from the bed before she put on her robe. Aura tiptoed to the library door, taking the lantern from his desk, and carefully drew it open. She shut the door behind her, then hurried over to the first bookshelf. Hunching over, she skimmed her fingers across the books until she found the title she was looking for: *A World of Piano Keys*.

Aura held her breath as she opened the large tome, the light scent of vanilla from the old pages caressing her senses. Her heart raced when she flipped through the pages, thinking she wouldn't find what she was looking for, until finally, near the center, there it was. The key, gold and slender. As quickly and quietly as she could, she put the book back on the shelf.

Praying to the gods that Rush wasn't awake, she placed the key into her robe pocket and snuck into the bedroom to his heavy breaths echoing off the walls. *Thank the gods.*

Aura placed the lantern back on his desk, then neared the bed when Rush rose on his elbows, patting the mattress in search of her. She halted, her hands coming to the tie of her robe. "I'm over here," she said, managing to keep her voice even.

238

"And where do you think you're sneaking off to, kitten?" he asked in a groggy voice.

"But for a dessert, of course." She paused. "I'll be back in a bit."

"Mmm," he purred. "Bring me back something sweet, and I'll give you something even more sweet in return."

"I can't deny that trade." Aura smiled, guilt crawling through her and her hand shaking as she took the lantern from his desk before leaving the room.

Rush might try to join her in the kitchens if she took too long, but she couldn't wait until tomorrow and have the opportunity be ruined. If he decided to go to the cellar in the morning, he would certainly notice the key gone unless she was able to sneak it back into the book. She had to take her chances now.

Pulse thumping, Aura passed the kitchens and went down the hall leading to the first locked door. She hurried inside, then descended the staircase, the air damp. As she reached the next door, she prayed Astor wouldn't be in there, but when she opened it, she found the room blissfully empty. Letting out a relieved breath, she locked the bolt behind her.

Mint combined with lemongrass permeated the air of the large room. Besides glass vials cluttering a table and the curtain she'd seen briefly, shelves lined the walls. Jars and metal devices were scattered across them. Opposite a worn, leather chaise, a desk, beautifully handcrafted, rested in one corner, books stacked atop it. She darted to the desk first, setting down the lantern to shuffle through the tomes. All of them were about sorcery. She yanked open a drawer, finding spare quills and ink. In the one below that was another stack of books. She drew them out. More tomes on sorcery, except for one near the bottom—her hand stilled on the leather cover. A *journal*.

Aura opened it and scanned over the first few entries. This certainly belonged to Sorcha as the princess discussed her parents continuing to make her practice the piano even though she wanted to learn more about how to help the court, things that mattered. Then Aura became lost in the pages as the content grew deeper. Sorcha spoke of a boy who was several years older than her and how she yearned for him to notice her. How her heart grew more and more in love with him each time they spoke. And then the day came when he finally noticed her after grieving the deaths of her mother from the sweating sickness and her father from a hunting accident.

Page after page, the man's name was never explicitly revealed, however, in the last entry, Aura knew precisely who it was and her stomach sank, the room seeming to topple over.

*I loved him more than anything, and foolish me, I knew he was betrothed to another. Her name is Aura and he chose her over me. Yet they have never once met! He promised me we could be together, even if his father disowned him for calling off the engagement. Then he betrayed me and crushed my heart by breaking his promise. He claimed he never wanted the marriage, that he loved me, and I believed his venomous lies. I thought he would care for me and our child. I cried tears and tears for him, yet now I only loathe him. I'll make it so he never sees me or our child ever again. As for Aura, she'll get the life I had always dreamt of.*

Aura's hands shook as she clenched the journal. Sorcha had known her because she was in love with the Prince of Starnight, and Aura had been betrothed to him.

The princess's beloved was Pax all along. The *bastard*. That was why Rush hated him so much, hated Aura since Pax had chosen her over his sister. But had he really? Pax still tumbled women behind Aura's back. The relationship between Sorcha and Pax must've been kept a secret from everyone, including Rush. Yet Rush held his sister's secrets now—he knew everything.

Aura set down the journal and went toward the red velvet curtain, drawing it to the side. Before her rested an old spinning wheel, its wood split in a few areas. Behind it hung another curtain. "Strange..." she murmured, studying the spindle, its sharp point. A pit formed in her stomach as she thought about all the times her finger had stung before and at the end of her dreams. She reached out to touch the spindle, and it was as though a wall was blocking her from doing so. *Magic...*

Biting the inside of her cheek, she yanked her hand back, then pushed the next curtain aside. Aura gasped and stumbled back in horror. As she clenched the thick fabric, her hand trembled at what lingered before her. A girl lying on a bed, pink silk blankets beneath her. She wore a pretty blue dress with gold stitching, and her hair was as wild as when she first saw the girl in her dream. The small bump on her stomach unnoticeable beneath her dry garments, but Aura knew it was there.

*Sorcha.*

She was beautiful and serene. No rot. No sickly scent of decay. Only the princess whole, her eyes shut as if she slept. Perhaps she wasn't dead at all... She rushed forward to check on her, pressing her fingers to the princess's neck. No pulse and cold to the touch. She wasn't alive. Up close she wasn't as perfect as Aura had

241

thought, her skin too pale and her lips slightly blue. But still, she'd been dead for several years and looked like this? *How?*

Footsteps echoed behind her and Aura whirled around as the curtain lifted. Her gaze met Astor's worried stare, then, over his shoulder, Rush's stony one.

"What is *this?*" she hissed, her voice shaky. "Why do you have your sister's body down here preserved as if she were a *trinket?*"

Rush's response was muffled when the sharp prick to her finger came and sleep pulled her away from this nightmare.

# RUSH

*What is this?* Aura had asked, horror etched into her
heart-shaped face, a look Rush wished he could unsee.
But rage boiled within him—she had snuck into his
private space, a place she knew was forbidden. For *daring*
to touch Sorcha's journal with all his sister's secrets that
included Aura's fiancé. And then she'd discovered
Sorcha's body... A twinge of shame washed over him.

How had she found his key? She had just been in his
bed, the one he allowed no one in, letting him take her
virginity. Had she fucked him to gain access to the library?
But that didn't explain how she knew where the key
was...

Aura's eyes fluttered shut, then she swayed and
stumbled forward.

"Fuck." Rush shoved Astor aside and bolted for her. He swept her into his arms just before she collapsed to the stone floor, asleep. The fucking spell had pulled her into its clutches at the worst possible moment.

"That's one way to avoid your wrath," Astor drawled.

*Fuck.* He tightened his grip around Aura, torn between attempting to shake her awake and tucking her carefully into his bed. Of course the first was pointless and the latter only made him want to shout at her more. This was a betrayal of his trust. Of *him*. But... But he couldn't blame her for her curiosity either. It wasn't as if he'd been forthcoming.

"Astor," he growled. Since the spell wasn't complete, it could be days before she woke again and he would be damned if he waited that long to confront her. Beneath his anger grew a numbness that would only fester if he didn't speak to her. He knew it well—the *pain* his mind hid from him. *No.* This conversation needed to happen now, regardless of her slumber. "Do you have any more of the potion to visit Aura's dreams?"

"Enough for a single use," Astor replied.

With one apologetic look toward his beloved dead sister, Rush turned on his heel. "Bring it to my room," he ordered while carrying Aura from the cellar.

He took the most direct passageways to reach his room as quickly as possible. Once there, he kicked the door shut behind him, the *bang* echoing off the walls. The bed was still rumpled from their rigorous fucking.

After setting Aura carefully on one side of the bed, he tucked the blanket over her. Her soft lips were parted, even breaths escaping, and he brushed a loose lock of golden hair from her forehead. This was his folly. Letting her get to him. Allowing emotions to overcome sense. He was supposed to hate her, just as he had for the past couple of years, when he'd read her name in Sorcha's journal. After he found his sister dead, he went to her room, searching for a letter as to why she'd drowned herself. And instead, he'd found the journal that not only answered his question but so much more. The reason his sister was dead had been because fucking Prince Pax had chosen Aura over his sister. If the damn spell had worked the day she arrived, then—

Someone rapped on the door, pulling him from his thoughts. "Astor?"

"Yes," he called through the walls.

Rush hurried to crack it open just enough to snatch the potion from him. "Remain there. Be sure that no one comes in until I'm awake again."

"Of course," he agreed.

Rush slammed and locked the door. He popped the top off the vial as he made his way to the bed. The bitter liquid slid down his throat before his head hit the pillow.

Darkness enveloped him, twisting and turning his mind until he stumbled to his feet inside Aura's dream. His head cleared as gray light filtered into the blackened space, and he realized where he stood.

*The lake.*

Panic crawled up his spine, his fingers flexing. Why was he *here* and not in the office like last time? *Fuck the stars.*

"Aura?" he called, his voice rough with anger and disgrace.

He averted his gaze from the still water, the muddy shore, searching for her. A flash of green caught his

245

attention near a small overturned boat on the grass. He raced toward it, finding Aura laying on her back, just like last time. She wasn't in the dark robe she'd been wearing, but a pale green dress with a square collar.

Only now, she was dry and ... still asleep.

He knelt beside her and gently shook her shoulders. She felt just as real as when they were awake—warm, soft. "Aura, wake up. We need to talk." She didn't so much as stir. "*Now*, Aura."

"She's asleep," came a soft voice. A *familiar* voice.

Rush froze. His heartbeat thundered in his ears. No— it couldn't be. This was Aura's dream. It was just the lake playing tricks with his head. Playing tricks on him. Spirits. His past haunting him.

"Brother?"

Taking a deep swallow, Rush rose to his feet, his back to the spirit. He could hardly breathe as the word repeated in his mind.

*Brother.*

*Brother.*

*Brother.*

"It's ... me," she said.

Rush squeezed his eyes shut, willing the lie away. His sister was still *dead* at the moment. Her body was in his damn cellar, right behind the spinning wheel she loved so much. She'd adored creating tapestries, weaving her own threads. Dead but not decaying because of the spell. The same one that was siphoning Aura's energy was keeping Sorcha *exactly* how she was before. It was the first part of the spell set two years ago—Aura was the second. And Rush wasn't ready in this moment to be reunited.

Memories flooded through him. Their unbreakable

sibling bond. Him gifting her rare threads for her spinning wheel to see her smile. Her comforting him after their parents' deaths even though she was his younger sister. Then him finding her limp body in the lake. Flashes of fear and shock and rage. Grief. Betrayal when he'd found the journal. Replaced, finally, with the determination to get revenge. Sorcha had killed herself because of Pax. Because Pax had chosen Aura over her and their child. He needed to pay for that, for using Sorcha.

"Rush?"

He held his breath as he turned to face his sister. It fell, heavy, from his chest at the sight of Sorcha standing in front of him. A boat's length away. Porcelain skin, dark hair matching his, wide sapphire eyes. Her wet brocade dress clung to her, highlighting her stomach, where a small bump rested that he and no one else had noticed before pulling her body from the lake.

"Sorcha," he rasped.

His younger sister gave him a hesitant smile. "I remember everything now. Seeing you... It all came back."

"How are you *here*?" He stepped toward his sister, leaving Aura on the grass. When his hands rose to pull her into an embrace, he halted. What if she wasn't real? What if touching her made her disappear?

"I'm not sure." She bit her lip. "Aura's been coming to visit lately, but I'm uncertain where *here* is. She thinks it's a simple dream."

"It *is* a dream," he insisted. Otherwise, Sorcha wouldn't be moving, speaking, breathing.

Sorcha threw her arms around his neck. "Oh, brother.

If that's true, it's a nightmare. But this place is more than that. It's been my home—*my purgatory.* The lake, the palace, all the places I frequented while I was alive, yet all tainted with my death."

Rush clung to her, holding her to him, crushing her in the embrace. His sister was always the one who'd hugged him, and once she died, he continued to regret not returning them in the way he should've. She no longer smelled of sweet spices but mud. The cold water from her clothing soaked through his. But none of that mattered. She was real.

"I've missed you so much," he said into her damp hair. Once their parents died, she was all he'd had left. The one who'd kept him in check.

"I've missed you too." She pulled away and looked him over. "You seem different."

"Is it the hair?" he asked, though it was the same length.

"You're harder," she mused. "There's no joy in your eyes."

His chest tightened at her words. "It's been hard since you…"

"I'm sorry." She tugged on his sleeve, leading him to the overturned boat. But, while Rush's gaze never left his sister—too ashamed to look at the girl he was sacrificing on her behalf—Sorcha's eyes were fixed on Aura. "I know I was a disappointment—"

"Sorcha, no." He gripped her hand, squeezing tightly. "I couldn't have asked for a better sister. Caring, sympathetic, and kind. Moonstone loved you nearly as much as I did. Nothing about you was disappointing. You were never that, do you hear me?"

"Except this." She pressed a hand to her stomach, the one she'd concealed with ill-fitted dresses.

The child would've been walking by now if they had lived. Rush would never get over what Pax had done to his sister. If he'd genuinely loved Sorcha, given up his betrothal and fucking other women for her, he would've allowed them to be together in his court. It was torturous to learn about everything from her journal, to confirm that she was indeed carrying a child. Not only had he grieved his sister, but also the loss of his unborn niece or nephew.

"Is that what you think?" His voice came out hoarse with regret. It was true his initial reaction to the pregnancy would've been appalling if he'd found out while she was alive. He glanced at the lake behind them.

She released a heavy sigh and sat down on the boat, then patted the seat beside her. "This beautiful lake no longer holds wonderful memories for me."

Rush lowered himself next to her on the boat. "It doesn't for me either." Since her death, he could never stop imagining his distraught sister walking into the lake. "Aura discovered your journal and read it."

Sorcha shifted uncomfortably beside him. "I didn't know that Aura was Pax's fiancée when we first started meeting in her dreams. I couldn't recall anyone's names or anything else for the longest time. She's very pretty and very kind."

"He doesn't give a fuck about her, Sorcha. The marriage was arranged. He wasn't going to stop fucking other women because he is incapable of love." Rush clenched his jaw. *Like I was.* As much as he hated to admit it, things were different now. Somehow, he found himself wanting Aura—and for more than a good fuck. He'd believed himself unable to fall for anyone. Especially *her*. "You knew he was betrothed, Sorcha. Why would you be with him? *Anyone* else at court would've treated you right."

"He lied," she whispered.

Rush knew that. He'd read about them in her journal. All about how Pax claimed that he'd choose her over anyone else, how he would defy his father if he had to.

"The bastard didn't deserve you or Aura," Rush spat.

Sorcha stared at him for a long moment. "You seem to care about her… And yet, she told me you cast a curse upon her. Tell me that's a lie. That it isn't true. But it is, isn't it? Because of me… Because of that journal…

Rush's heart thumped painfully in his chest. Aura, who slept so peacefully on the damp grass, was the only reason Sorcha had a chance at returning. And when Sorcha was alive again, Pax would be fucked.

"It's true. I cast it," Rush admitted and held his breath. One person he was always honest with was his sister, even if she'd hid secrets from him.

Her bright blue eyes found his. Searching. Almost pleading that she would find a lie somewhere in his expression. When it was clear she would find none, she turned to fully face him. "Why would you do that?"

He ran a hand through his hair and inhaled. She would like the answer even less. In all the time he'd planned his revenge, he'd always avoided thinking about what her reaction to the spell would be. How she would feel about what he'd done. That was the reason he was hedging around the truth now. "I chose her because I needed a woman for the spell. I believed it was only fair that I use

250

the one who Pax chose over you."

"But she's innocent!" Sorcha snapped. "Why would you do something so heinous? That's not you, Rush."

"I'm not the same, Sorcha. The only thing good I've continued to do is take care of my court. I know you and our parents wouldn't want it to return to the way it was when Aura's ancestors ruled it. As for the spell, it's meant to give you life so you can come back." His eyes shifted to her stomach. "But … it will only work for you. A life for a life, not two."

"Come back?" She leapt off the boat and paced in front of him, cradling her stomach. "*Come back?* And without my child?"

*Fuck.* He knew she wouldn't like it, but if he could fix the situation, how could he *not* cast the spell? There was nothing to be done about the baby, but saving one of them was better than neither. "I did it for you, Sorcha. So you could get your revenge against Pax for lying and deceiving you. You left because of what he did!"

"Why are you saying I *left*?" She whirled on him, her eyes narrowed. "Do you think I *wanted* this? I had a small child growing inside of me and would have loved them the way our parents had us, regardless if Pax wanted no part of the child's life."

Rush scowled, holding back the rage igniting in his blood. "Then why did you do it? Why would you go to the lake you love so much and drown yourself?"

Sorcha's eyes went wide. "So everyone truly thinks that?" she whispered.

Rush rose to his feet. What everyone *thinks*? What was that supposed to mean? She had gone for a walk that morning, refusing any company. Three different servants

251

and a visiting lord had seen her making her way toward the lake just outside the palace walls, then later, a fisherman witnessed her standing at the water's edge as he was leaving with his daily catch.

"Rush!" she shouted, breathing rapidly. "Does everyone believe I drowned myself?"

"What else would they think? What else would I think? I read your journal, Sorcha." He grabbed her upper arms and she gasped for air. "Breathe, sister. Tell me what's wrong. What can I do?"

Her shaky hands clasped onto his cheeks as if she were willing him to look at her. To *see* her. "I went to the lake as I did every morning. Pax knew my routine—we'd met there secretly countless times." Tears filled her eyes. "He wanted to get rid of the child. I told him that I expected nothing from him, that I would never tell who the father was, but that wasn't good enough for him." Rush's heart thundered in his chest as she continued, "Pax dragged me into the lake after shoving a liquid down my throat that prevented my dragon from coming out. He put his hands around my throat to hold me under the water until I died."

Rush felt the blood drain from his face and his dragon stirred inside him, rage clawing at his flesh. "You're telling me the prince murdered you, and I've let him live these past two years?"

"Yes." She stepped out of his grip and peered down at Aura. "But that's not the point! You can't use this woman to bring me back. I'm *dead*, Rush. I've been dead for a long time now. And you're saying the reason I'm trapped here, reliving it over and over, is because you think I want to wake up and fulfill some sort of revenge

252

plan you conjured up?"

Each breath heaved from his lungs. Pax killed his sister. *Murdered her.* Strangled her. Drowned her. Stole away his only remaining family because… Because his sister carried a Starnight heir. The fucking prince deserved everything he had coming to him. *Everything.*

When he didn't say anything, Sorcha's bottom lip trembled. "I don't care what you do as long as you break the spell. Let Aura go. Let *me* go."

He backed away from Sorcha, his gaze flicking between the two women. It was never Aura's fault, even if he'd blamed her like the prick he was. And all this time, Aura and Sorcha were meeting while she dreamt. Soon, Aura wouldn't wake but Sorcha *would.* How could he deny his sister her life? A second chance? Sorcha deserved to avenge herself against Pax more than ever.

"He needs to pay for what he's done," he whispered.

"So make him pay." She advanced, her arms outstretched as if to cling to him, beg him, but Rush backed away from her. "Let the truth be known. Destroy him. Let your dragon burn the entire Starnight palace for all I care, but don't let Aura pay the price for it. One tragedy is enough, Rush. You're better than this."

Nerves tingling, hands quaking in anger, thoughts swimming with indecision, Rush shook his head. He *wasn't* better than this. Since Sorcha died, he'd done everything in his power to bring her back. Killed. Imprisoned. Cursed. And he wasn't sorry.

Or was he?

"I'm not." Rush moved forward, folding his arm around his sister and kissing her forehead. He couldn't stand under her scrutiny a moment longer, not after

253

hearing the truth. "I love you."

"I love you too, brother, but—"

He held her tightly, not wanting her to disappear. Looking down at Aura over his sister's head, his heart clenched. *Fuck!* He had to leave now before he thought too much on it.

The next moment, Rush woke himself, lurching up in his own bed. Pulse thundering, his eyes darted wildly around the room. He glanced down at Aura who still slept peacefully beside him. The sorceress had told him how to end this, how to break the curse. *Break the spindle on the spinning wheel,* the bitch had wrote. He was surprised he'd gotten that out of her though. But if he figured out a way to touch it, could he let his sister disappear forever? And if he didn't try, could he let Aura be forever trapped in a hellish nightmare?

At the moment, there was something else important to deal with. Rush leapt from the bed and tore open his door to find Astor standing across the hall. The hawk shifter took one look at the king's face and stiffened.

"What's wrong?" he asked.

Rush's upper lip twisted into a sneer. "I'm going to tear that bastard apart."

Astor lowered his brow in confusion. "Who?"

"Pax!" he seethed. "He needs to come here—to Moonstone. *Now.* Send him an invitation for a peace talk in our old meeting spot."

"*Peace* talk?"

Rush bared his teeth. "Slaughtering him will bring me peace."

# 21

## AURA

"**Y**ou need to wake up," a soft feminine voice pleaded. "Wake up and save my brother. I know you read my journal. Rush told me while he was here in your dream. You now know what I did, and I'm sorry. So very sorry. I can't have a life, Aura. Not anymore. I want to pass on, and I want you to live yours."

Aura tried to wake yet couldn't. She wanted to see outside of this darkness, ask Sorcha so many things, but then a sharp prick struck her finger. When Aura could finally open her eyes, an obsidian canopy rested above her. No longer was she inside of a dream or lingering in a horrific room down in the cellar, but laying on Rush's bed.

Shouting from the hallway reverberated through the walls, and *everything* came back to her.

The body. *Sorcha's* body resting like a pristine doll in a beautiful bed...

Sorcha had spoken to her, mentioning Rush had come to the dream, yet Aura didn't remember any of it, couldn't remember him there, only darkness before his sister had spoken to her. She clutched the side of her head as she threw off the blankets, thinking that, perhaps, she'd heard voices around her but no clear words.

She was going to find out precisely what sort of sick game Rush was playing with her and his sister. Heart pounding, she clenched her fists and stormed out into the hallway.

Two sets of eyes turned to her. Rush's jaw was hard, his gaze blazing with fury while Astor seemed to hold pity, guilt. No guards stood in the corridor as if they'd all been sent away.

"You're awake," Rush said through gritted teeth.

Aura narrowed her eyes. "I suppose we need to have a conversation."

Rush waved a hand in the air toward Astor, his nostrils flaring. "Leave us. Deliver a letter to Starnight *now.*"

Astor looked as though he wanted to say something else, but he bowed his head and left at a brisk pace.

"You were in my dream again," Aura said, breaking the silence.

"What did you hear?" His tone was more rigid than it had ever been.

Aura squeezed her eyes shut, attempting to remember anything, but she couldn't. "I don't know."

"But I know some things. You've been speaking to my sister. You snuck a key from my library after *fucking* me, and then you went to the cellar that you knew was forbidden."

"What other choice was I left with?" Aura asked, incredulous. "You're the pretentious ass who put me in this predicament! Regardless, *you* are going to tell me precisely what you're doing to me! *You* are going to tell me why you have your sister's dead body in the cellar! *You* are going to tell me why you chose to bring me here! I demand to know everything!" With each sentence, she shoved at his chest, backing him farther down the hall until they'd reached her room, her original prison in this villain's palace.

"I don't have to tell you a damn thing," he seethed.

She pushed her way into her bedroom and flung open the wardrobe, wrapping her fist around the blade she'd taken from the kitchens. Whirling around, she held the knife to her throat just as Rush stepped into the room.

"Tell me," she bit out. "Or I'll slit my throat right here and thwart whatever wicked plan you've been hatching."

For a moment, only a brief one, she thought she caught his throat bobbing before he spoke, "I could easily take one of your sisters, or perhaps, your mother, and try again from the beginning."

Aura dug the blade in harder, the sting biting into her flesh. Hot tears pricked her eyes. "Stop the threats. Confess everything to me. *Please.*"

Rush shut the door behind him, slowly walking toward her as though he might frighten her away. "You read the journal, kitten. I think you know why you were the one chosen. Now, put the knife away." His hand brushed hers, drawing the blade from her throat. He took the knife from her hand and tossed it across the room

257

before leaning into her, his smoky scent caressing her senses. "That was foolish of you. Incredibly foolish."

Even in her fury, she hated herself for liking his closeness, especially in a moment like this. A moment where she hated him and wanted to shred him to pieces.

"Don't act as though you're the one who should be angry," Aura hissed. "I started to feel sorry for you and your loss. I didn't learn who the girl from my dreams was until recently. Even then, I believed she was a spirit. But I wanted to help her move on. And yes, free myself too."

"She *is* a spirit, kitten. That's the problem you're here to solve," he murmured, his eyes boring into hers. "You in exchange for her. I wanted revenge against Pax, wanted to see his face when she came back from the grave to confront him. I wanted him *ruined*."

Aura blinked, a pit forming in her stomach. "What do you mean in *exchange?*" When he didn't speak, she shouted, "Answer me, Rush!"

He pursed his lips, his knuckles turning white as they tightened. "I wasn't going to end your life, Aura. That was always the truth. You would still be alive in a permanent sleep. Pricking your finger with the spindle ensured that."

Aura couldn't believe her ears, couldn't find air to breathe. "You fucking bastard!" she screeched, darting around him to grab the knife once more. But he was too fast. He crowded into her space until she was backed into the window bars. "That's why I couldn't touch the spinning wheel. Break the curse. Now!"

"No," Rush said simply as she writhed.

"You are not my king. You are not my anything!" Aura spat in his face, and he didn't bother to wipe it away.

"Is that so?" he purred. "Then why did you let me

258

slide my cock into your sweet cunt so willingly? Why did you so easily quake beneath my touch? Was it only to get the key?" One of his hands left her arm to trail a finger across her jawline and down her neck to her collarbone. Her traitorous body heated, her eyelids fluttering.

"It was for the key," she said, her voice breathy.

"Liar." He took that perfect finger of his and drifted it lower, to just below her navel. "If I touched you now, would you be wet for me?"

"You're heartless."

"Am I? Seems my heart is beating just fine." Rush smirked and took a step away from her as though taunting her to feel it.

Nostrils flaring, she slapped him across the face, not even a flinch in his expression.

"Again," he cooed. "I told you I like it rough."

"Break the curse!" she shouted, bringing her hand to his cheek once more.

He caught her wrist as she went to slap him a third time. "Enough," he growled. And then his mouth was on hers, his body pressing her into the bars. She didn't hesitate to kiss him back, to punish him with her mouth.

Rush broke the kiss, his chest heaving. "You're mine. You may hate me, but I've hated you longer. Now, say you want me to fuck you hard, that you want to take out your aggression on me."

Aura couldn't say no, hated herself more than him at this moment because she couldn't deny the pleasure that could be had. She needed to take her aggression out on something, someone. Then she could think clearly, remember that she wanted to hurt him.

"Fuck me hard," she whispered.

Grinning wickedly, Rush spun her around and she gripped the iron bars. He unfastened his trousers, then hiked up her robe. With one hard thrust, his delicious cock was inside her, one arm draped around her waist, the other on her mound. Aura squeezed the bars harder as she moaned.

His fingers moved in perfect clockwork circles for a few moments before both hands came to her hips and he slammed into her. Her eyelids fluttered at the euphoria of it all until her raging emotions came back and she wanted to be the one in control.

"The bed," she demanded. The place where she hadn't wanted to sleep, hadn't wanted to touch, but now she would show him that she would fuck him on it. She would fuck him anywhere she damn well wished.

"Mmm, I like this side of you, kitten." Rush pulled out of her so she could face him, his mouth catching hers as he walked her backward to the bed. He only left her lips to remove his shirt and trousers. "Ride me hard. Make me regret every damn thing. Punish me until I'm the one on my knees before you."

"You deserve it," Aura said, peeling the robe from her body as he brought them onto the mattress. She then cradled his thighs with her legs and sank down on his hard cock.

Rush groaned and caught one of her nipples between his teeth, sucking and flicking it with his tongue. His hand cupped her other breast, kneading it with expertise that made her even more aroused.

As she rolled her hips forward, she yanked his head back by the hair, showing him that she could end him if she decided to, could destroy him in the way he had her.

"Kiss me," he rasped. "Kiss me like you're fucking me. Make it hard. Make me bleed."

Aura's mouth caught his to shut him up, to make him hers as his fingers dug into her hips, urging her to move faster. The hate swelled within her heart because she was liking this too much, wanting it to never end, wanting him to make her come again and again. She'd felt pity for him and all the while he'd planned to put her into a permanent *sleep*. Her pace grew faster, their teeth clacking as she kissed him harder. One of her hands came to his shoulder, digging her nails in until he bled. Rush's growls became deeper, their fucking more desperate.

And then a wave of pleasure crashed through her entire being. She left his mouth, biting down on his shoulder while she screamed his name. The mini quakes continuing to wreck her body in the best possible way.

"Harder, kitten," Rush ground out. She ran her tongue up his neck, then dug her teeth into his salty flesh, her hips rolling furiously into his. His body jerked and he growled her name as he spilled himself inside her.

Aura's chest heaved against his, his arms wrapping around her and holding her tight as though she was his anchor. Finally, she gathered enough strength to straighten her spine and tug his hair back once more so his molten eyes locked on hers.

"End the spell," she demanded.

"I can't," he rasped.

"Why? Is it because you need the sorceress's help who gave you the spell? Then find her," she begged.

"I did find her, but you don't understand... There's something Sorcha told me in your dream." The pleasureful expression he held before turned into something darker.

"No secrets. It's not as if I can leave anyway. Be truthful now."

Rush's jaw clenched. "Sorcha didn't drown herself in the lake. Pax did it—he murdered her. All to keep the baby a secret because she wouldn't rid herself of it. My sister didn't deserve death, but he does. He'll pay in blood."

Aura stilled. Pax murdered Sorcha... He murdered her to keep the proof of their affair a secret... A horrific thought crossed her mind—had he done that to others if they'd become pregnant? It was very much possible.

She released Rush and stumbled off him to collect her robe from the floor. "In my dreams, Sorcha couldn't remember everything, but that was what she must've been trying to tell me all along..."

"I know Pax, and I know he did it so he wouldn't be forced to marry my sister, so he wouldn't create scandal within the courts. But what he doesn't know is that Sorcha held a journal where she kept her thoughts. I didn't know he was the one my sister was in love with until she mentioned your name in it." Rush snatched his trousers and shirt from the floor, then put them on as she drew on the robe.

Aura took a deep swallow. "Even when you thought Sorcha drowned herself out of despair, why didn't you tell Starnight?"

"Because it wasn't my secret to tell—it was Sorcha's. That's why I planned to bring her back. For the time being, I only told Pax that I knew he'd fucked my sister, that she killed herself because they couldn't be together, and why I didn't want to see his face again."

Blood boiled inside her once more, igniting heated flames that spread through her veins. "And so you held all of this against *me*? A woman betrothed to a man who didn't know he fucked all of Starnight and, apparently, any of the other courts he wished."

Rush inhaled a sharp breath. "Watch your tongue."

"You watch *yours*," she bit back.

He furrowed his brow, his gaze fastened to hers. "For you, I found out how to break the spell because I..."

Aura folded her arms. "Your actions prove enough. You found out how to break the spell and haven't done it. I like your sister. I do. But does *she* want this? Or is this something *you* want? In my dream she told me she wanted to move on, yet revenge seems to be more important than the people, or *one* person you claim to care about. I was beginning to think there was more to you. I thought there was something good inside you, but there's nothing in that selfish heart of yours."

Not saying a word, Rush turned his back on her and took the knife from the floor. As he opened the door, he looked over his shoulder, his eyes holding an unreadable emotion. "You will remain in this room, where it's safe, until the prince is dead. This is the last time I'll ever lock you in." His gaze softened slightly. "If it makes a difference, you're the only one I want to fuck, kitten, the only one I ever want in my bed. Whether you're awake or asleep, I'll find you again. I vow it." With that, he locked the door behind him.

"If that's what you consider a love sonnet, then you're a bigger fool than I thought," Aura shouted as she bolted to the door, pounding on it until her hands were raw. "Let me out of here, you bastard!"

# RUSH

Two days had passed since Rush discovered that Pax had murdered his sister.

Rush needed to face the prince. Look Pax in the eyes and tell him that he knew what he'd done to Sorcha before the torture began. He would then burn him to a crisp. Send his unidentifiable corpse back to the King of Starnight.

The scent of ash filled his mouth as his dragon stirred, ready to destroy his enemy.

"Do you have something against that piece of parchment?" Astor asked from the other side of the cellar table. A small fire burned beneath a muddy brown concoction that the shifter was experimenting on.

Rush's fingers flexed around the paper in his palm.

264

He'd read over the sorceress's words a dozen times now. As though maybe there would be a secret riddle hidden. There wasn't. He'd thought about all the ways to break through the barrier of the spinning wheel to distract himself. From Sorcha. From Aura. From revenge.

He couldn't even release Aura from the spell that forced her to sleep when leaving the premises since Astor had linked it to the original curse. The original spell would need to be broken for her to be completely free.

Rush had locked Aura in her room, and the last time he'd seen her, she'd fucked him like he'd never been fucked before, made him feel things that he'd never felt from all the past women he'd bedded. He'd lost himself in not only her body, but *her*.

And then he'd fucked it up.

Now that he'd had time to think about his conversation with his sister, he couldn't be a selfish prick since his and Sorcha's desires with the spell didn't align. Sorcha didn't want revenge. Rush didn't want to lose Aura. And Aura didn't want any of this. He'd made her hate him when he'd confessed everything about the spell and what it would do to her.

An emotion brewed deep in the pits of his shadowed heart, and it couldn't be what he thought it was. Even though fucking her was always meant to hurt Pax— instead, it had only made Rush start to...

He studied the spinning wheel behind the tied-back curtain once more, knowing he couldn't break the spell without being able to touch the spindle.

His gaze narrowed on it as he stalked closer. The spinning wheel seemed so innocuous sitting there. Wood and metal. Common.

But that wasn't true. Sorcha had *loved* the wheel, had spent hours sitting at it.

*Fuck it.* He was going to get through the barrier.

Gritting his teeth, he reached out to grab the spindle that Aura had pricked her finger on. To rip it off. Destroy the damn thing and break the spell. But the barrier refused to open for him. So he would play harder.

Rush swung a fist at it, determined to strike the spindle. But his hand bounced off, splitting his knuckles in the process. He pursed his lips and circled it. Again and again he attacked the wheel with both fists and feet, but it was no use.

He spat at it, and his saliva bounced off too. "Fuck you," he growled.

"I don't think you can destroy it like that," Astor said.

Rush dragged in long, frustrated breaths. "It's the only way to break the spell. How can I stop it if I can't…" He balled his sore hands at his sides. There was a way to get past the barrier to the spindle—there had to be. "Aren't you supposed to be flying?" He had tasked the hawk with scouting so they would know the moment Pax approached.

Astor opened his mouth as if he were about to say something more, yet clenched his jaw and nodded.

Once Astor left the room, Rush ran his hands through his hair and released a frustrated sigh.

"Fuck."

His hands shook as he drew back the second curtain and entered Sorcha's room. She lay peacefully in the center of the bed, just as she had for the last two years. The day Sorcha died, the sorceress hadn't hidden herself, allowing him to strike a deal within hours of his sister's

266

body being returned to the palace and him finding the journal. The spell kept his sister from decaying, but it was clear she wasn't simply sleeping. Her skin was too pale, her lips slightly blue. Her chest still.

"I'll fix this," he whispered. Not before he said a final goodbye though. Astor would need to make another potion so he could visit Sorcha in Aura's dream one last time.

Rush spun on his heel and made his way to Aura's room. He held his breath and rapped his knuckles against the door. "Aura?"

Silence.

"Aura, are you awake?" he asked.

"I'm not talking to you through the door," she snapped.

Rush smirked. "Well, I'm not opening it, kitten. Not when your claws are out."

A floorboard creaked from inside the room. "What do you want?"

"To make sure you're all right." He leaned against the door frame and closed his eyes. Aura said nothing. "I'm sorry. I don't want to keep you here like this, but it's for your own safety." He wouldn't mention the torture that would ensue before he killed him just yet. And, while he'd promised Sorcha that he'd fix things a moment ago, she couldn't hear him. Promising Aura was different. But he couldn't tell her that he planned to continue to try and break the spell. Not when she would get her hopes up. Because if he couldn't... "It's only until I'm finished with the prince."

Fabric shuffled inside the room along with the soft pad of bare feet. When Aura spoke again, her voice came from directly on the other side of the door. "Can you just—"

"Rush!" Astor skidded around the corner, his eyes wild.

*He's coming.* The hawk shifter didn't need to say it out loud—it was written all over his face.

"Keep your claws out while I'm gone," he told Aura in a low tone.

Astor walked beside him through the hallways. "Pax is riding from town in the direction of the palace. He traveled with a small entourage, but they're still in the tavern. There doesn't seem to be anyone following him."

"That doesn't sound like him." The Pax he knew wasn't courageous enough to do anything on his own, let alone face the King of Sin. The letter Rush sent requested that the prince come alone, but Rush hadn't expected him to *listen.* "Stay here with Aura."

"But what if—"

"If the bastard tries to attack me, my dragon will devour him," he snarled. "Don't leave her unguarded until I return."

"Of course," Astor relented before sprinting back down the hall to Aura's room.

Rush pounded out into the gardens, ignoring the startled looks from the guards, and made straight for the side gates with dusk lighting up the sky. Vines grew over the black iron, curling around the metal design, with small red flowers only starting to bloom. The gate hadn't been used since the day Sorcha was found—she would always use it to explore the woods.

The hinges fought him as the king shoved the gates open, but it stood no chance against the adrenaline coursing in his veins. He broke apart the rust in mere moments and trudged on. It was a short walk through the thinly wooded area to reach the place where Pax and him would sneak wine when they were boys.

His heart hammered as he got closer, anxious for Pax's torture to begin. The wide trees stood tall, and as a child, Sorcha would climb the flowered one in the distance.

Rush slowed his steps as he reached the meeting spot, then leaned his back against a trunk. The ground was muddy and wet from heavy rain the day before.

When Pax had yet to make an appearance, Rush prowled around a tree, listening for the sound of approaching hoofbeats.

Inside, his dragon lifted his head. Held his breath. The way the beast hunched, still and wary, sent a prickle of awareness across Rush's shoulders. Memories of Sorcha stirred the beast's ire. And the fact that Pax was moments away from death by Rush's hand.

The King of Sin paced, cracking each knuckle in turn as he waited. And waited. Until his dragon stood. *Stop*, he chastised. He couldn't allow his dragon to take over. Rush would handle this business himself, and that required words first. He wanted Pax to know *why*—to know that the truth had been exposed.

A snarl tore from the dragon's mouth, rumbling up Rush's own throat without his permission. It was then that the prickle of watchful eyes on his back registered. He drew in a breath, preparing to turn and see the face of Sorcha's murderer. He must've dismounted his horse and approached by foot. The bastard was sneaky—he'd give him that much.

When Rush turned, it wasn't Pax who stood mere feet away, but a sorceress in onyx robes, holding a staff. Black braids hung loose over her shoulders, dark kohl rimming her deep brown eyes. She watched him, expressionless.

"Where the fuck is the prince?" he demanded.

She simply lifted her staff. A cloud of orange smoke spilled out from it and rose around Rush, coating his body in a fine dust. Rush couldn't feel his dragon. Couldn't feel his own body.

Dozens of blurred figures crashed through the woods, the sound of their footfalls deafening. Still, Rush couldn't move. Could barely *think*, let alone comprehend what was happening.

"—the chains!" a man yelled.

The clink of metal echoed as cold steel wrapped around Rush's body, the faceless figures ripping his arms behind his back until his shoulders screamed in pain. He shook his head to clear his vision. To see fucking *anything*.

As orange dust fell from his lashes, he could make out the silver star gleaming on one man's chest. *Starnight.*

That bitch… What had she done to him? A cloaking spell, perhaps, to hide herself and the fuckers who now bound him. But the smoke, the way it clung to him, he'd never seen anything like it. How did Starnight even acquire a sorceress?

Rush's knees buckled as the men thrust the hilt of a sword between his shoulders. Shoving him down until the mud soaked through his trousers. Cold and wet. Feeling flooded back into his knees, and he attempted to move again, to stand, but his muscles refused to cooperate.

"Tie his ankles," one of them said to another.

Rush tried to focus on their voices. To ground

himself. Pull himself into the present and fully assess the danger he was in. To get himself *out* of it and slaughter them all. He searched inside, digging deep, for his beast. Where he usually rested was weighted like a boulder. A dark barrier disconnecting them from one another. Was this what Sorcha felt when Pax took her dragon away before drowning her? Rush had been prepared for Pax trying something similar to him but nothing like this.

"Wh…" Rush's voice faded. Lost.

*Gods damn it!*

His knees sunk deeper into the mud, washing away more of the dust and returning the sensation to his legs. He squeezed his eyes shut and threw himself forward. Hands clutched one of his arms and the momentum of his body sent him tumbling sideways into the muck.

"Hold him," a man ordered. "The prince is coming."

*The prince.* Rush clung to that bit of information. Clawed his mind out of the fog as his pulse pounded.

Someone yanked his chains, hoisting Rush to his knees once more. Air hit the cold mud along his side, sending a shiver through him. If only the lake or a pond was here to rinse all the powder away.

*Fuck!*

The figures standing around Rush parted, allowing a lithe one to slip through. Unlike the others, no Starnight emblem shone on his chest. Instead, he was clad in the black uniform of a Moonstone guard.

"You summoned me, King of Sin." Pax's voice burned through the remaining haze of whatever spell had been cast. "It's too bad we'll have to postpone our chat for a bit. Now, if you'll excuse me, I have to collect my betrothed." Pax laughed as he sauntered away, the sorceress following at his heels, while Rush raged and writhed in his bindings.

# AURA

**A**ura went to the bars of the window and tried to pry them apart to no avail. "I wish I was a sorceress," she muttered. "Then I would turn Rush into a piece of furniture as soon as he returned."

She'd been in her room for two days. Since locking her in, Rush had come back to see her once, without opening the door she might add. Although before that, she could've sworn she'd heard his feet pacing outside her door as though controlling the urge to open it. A while ago, she'd watched him disappear out of the palace's side gates and wasn't certain how far he'd ventured.

Releasing a sigh, she looked toward the bed where she'd rode him to bliss—where both their bodies had been slick with sweat—that now smelled of his addicting smoky scent. When she'd let him fill her with his cock, she'd been angry with him, her blood on fire. But beneath those layers, sorrow had rested there too, for what he'd been through, for what had truly happened to Sorcha. Because of *Pax*. Then she'd hated him again after he locked her in this room. But did she really? It would be the last time, he'd said. If he walked through the door at this very moment to set her free, what would she do? Slap him or run into his arms?

"Perhaps both," she grunted.

The door opened and she spun around to find Astor casually walking in with a bowl of steaming soup in hand.

"Eat," he said softly when his gaze fastened on hers. "The guards said you haven't been touching your food."

Each time the guards had opened the door, she'd attempted to fling herself past them but hadn't even made it out into the hallway. On her list of things to do if she got out of this forsaken room would be to learn how to properly fight and wield a blade. Instead of marriage, she should've focused on that, but she'd believed there'd been no need. She'd been wrong. Yet she'd been wrong about a lot of things.

"I'm not hungry," Aura lied as she took the soup from him. She had wanted to eat, but her thoughts consumed her every waking moment.

"The king is doing this for your safety. He cares about you."

"Cares about me indeed." She frowned, bringing a spoonful of the tomato soup to her lips. The zesty flavor caressed her tastebuds as it slid down her dry throat.

Astor sighed. "In his own way, yes, he does. You uncovered his secrets. Surely you must understand him somewhat."

"He locked me in here. *Again.*"

"Aura, he was left with no choice. If you didn't have this spell cast on you, he wouldn't have kept you in here. Do you think he doesn't know the effects of what he's done? Believe me, he does." Astor paused, biting his lip. "I shouldn't tell you this, but he's tried to break the spell. He couldn't. Don't ask me anything further. Just take it that I owe you something after you told me Hana's favorite flower."

Her lips parted at what he revealed. Rush had tried to break the spell but couldn't... Did that change anything when he was the one who'd cast it? But somehow it did, even if it was only a sliver, a crack. A crack that could spread until it opened fully.

Aura thought about it, truly thought about how she'd been feeling the past two days. The tiredness, the exhaustion, her forcing herself not to fall asleep. "I don't have much time left. I can feel it. My body wanting to collapse, to shut down." She remembered the duke and his awful nephew, how they'd almost stuffed her inside their carriage. If she fell asleep in the gardens, it would be too easy for someone to steal her away. She shuddered at the thought. Although she wouldn't admit it aloud, perhaps it was better she stay here for a bit longer. "But as soon as the king returns, if I'm still awake, he will open the door and talk to me properly."

Astor's lips tilted up a fraction. "Yes, *Your Highness.* Now finish eating. I'm to keep you company until the king returns." He took a seat at the edge of the bed and drew out a puzzle box from inside his pocket.

Aura hated to admit it, but she didn't mind his quiet

presence. She brought the spoon to her mouth once more, practically inhaling the remainder of the soup from the bowl.

They sat in comfortable silence for a long while until a shout echoed out in the hallway. The click of the lock sounded and Astor stood from the bed in front of her, a blade in his hand. As the door opened, it was one of the guards. Only it wasn't—he wore a black Moonstone uniform, but he wasn't one of the guards. She took in his narrow jaw that she'd loved running her fingers across, his high cheekbones she used to kiss, and the deep brown eyes she would study. Now they belonged to a face she would rather not see, one that hid secrets and betrayal beneath that veil. She wanted him dead, the way he'd drowned Sorcha.

Astor charged forward, but the prince moved faster and kicked him in the chest. The shifter stumbled backward, striking his head on the edge of the night table, knocking him out.

Aura snapped out of her frozen state as Pax brought up his blade to stab him in the chest.

"Stop!" she screamed while darting in front of the prince to block him from Astor.

Pax drew the blade back, blinking, his gaze settling on hers.

"What are you doing here?" Aura growled, tightening her fists and taking a step toward him. "You shouldn't be here." He should be dead. Rush should've killed him. A pit formed in her stomach at what that could mean.

"Is that any way to treat the prince who has come to save you?" His face softened. "I've missed you, Aura."

She would rather be locked away in any other room in

this palace than have a conversation with this deceitful man. "Fuck you!" she said between clenched teeth and lunged around him. Before she reached the door, he grabbed her by the waist and yanked her to his firm chest. "Let go of me! Guards!"

"Hush now, we have much to discuss," Pax pleaded. "I received your letter and whatever the king whispered into your ear were his sinful lies. All of it. You are my betrothed. You were meant to already be my wife. Only you."

"Yes, while you pleasure everyone else! Get this bastard off me!" she screamed, waiting for Tanix and Laird to rush in with their swords. "The Prince of Starnight is here!"

"No one is going to hear you," Pax said. "What have they done to you? Why are you looking at me with such loathing? They've cast a spell on you to turn you against me."

Aura's breath caught. "What did you do to the guards?" Whirling around, she pulled back her arm and slammed her fist into Pax's face. She slipped from his grasp, fleeing out into the hallway. She stilled when she found Tanix and Laird. They lay in slumped heaps on the floor, bright crimson pooling around them.

"I have other plans for the traitorous king," Pax ground out. "He thought me a fool, that he could lure me to his court. But *he's* the fool."

Aura ran to Tanix and took the fallen sword beside his dead body, then spun to face the prince. Her arms quaked under the weight of the weapon, but she didn't drop it. "I know what you did to Princess Constance. You *murdered* her and the child she carried. *Your* child."

Pax winced and she could see the truth in his expression even if it was only briefly. "I did nothing of the sort. Why would you accuse me of something so heinous? The princess drowned herself."

Aura held the blade higher—she might not know how to wield it properly, but she would thrust it well enough to sink it into his chest, piercing his deceptive heart. "Even though you knew of our betrothal, you continued to pleasure, to ravish, to *fuck* other women. You knew Princess Constance was in love with you and you found her an easy target. She was only sixteen, and when you learned she was pregnant, she was of no use to you any longer. You demanded she get rid of your child, and when she didn't, you *murdered* her, you heartless bastard!"

Pax pursed his lips and shook his head. "More lies from the king. He was always jealous that I was betrothed to the most beautiful woman in all the courts. He wanted you for himself, Aura. His sister killed herself because she wanted away from *him*."

Aura inhaled sharply at the easy way lies fell from his lips as though he believed them himself. "I might be tempted to consider your lies if I hadn't met the princess myself. If I hadn't come across her spirit or her journal. But I did. I know everything *you* did. You even fucked someone on our wedding day, you ass!"

Pax inched toward her, but she didn't bow down. He tucked his sword into his sheath and held up his hands as if she would lower hers. "No more lies, Aura. I promise. I'll admit to you everything, but you have to listen to me. I did it for *us*. Yes, I was a fool then. But I'm a fool no longer. I swear to you this, after our wedding, it would've only ever been you. It is only you. I admit I surrendered to temptation, that I had to remove the wedge that could alter our future. It's all in the past now, and we can keep this a secret between us."

Aura's eyes widened in horror. Did he truly believe her to be the naïve girl she used to be? "I will do no such thing, and I won't pretend as though I will either. Whether that's foolish on my part or not." She barreled for him with her blade at the ready, but he easily dodged the blow. He was a trained fighter, skilled for years. However, she threw her arm forward again, this time stabbing him in the shoulder.

Ignoring the blood blooming to the surface, Pax growled and swung his uninjured arm, then knocked the sword from her hands. Before she could slip away, he wrapped his hand around her throat and slammed her against the wall. "Shut that treacherous mouth of yours or all of Starnight will believe you drowned yourself too. You will do as I say. You will obey your future king and husband."

Aura kneed him in the groin, giving her enough room to escape his grip and flee toward the stairs as she screamed for anyone to hear her. She would've easily made it down the steps, but an invisible prick came to her finger, and she knew what that meant. *Not now.* A wave of exhaustion made her sluggish, her limbs heavy, and she stumbled. Pax yanked her back by the throat and hauled her into his arms as she writhed.

His grip didn't slacken while he carried her down the steps. At the bottom of the stairs, a woman in a cloak, her dark braids swaying, stood over two other guards slumped on the floor. Orange magic poured out from a staff in her hand.

"Everyone is asleep. You don't have long before they awaken," the sorceress warned.

"Besides the two upstairs." Pax chuckled. "The treasonous king better still be where we left him?"

A sinking feeling stormed through Aura as she focused on the sorceress. "What did you do to him?" she screeched. "Prince Pax is a murderer!"

"Shut your mouth," Pax seethed. "I'll decide your fate soon enough." He turned toward the sorceress who refused to look at her. "You'll get the remainder of your payment once this is finished."

Aura thrashed harder as Pax carried her out the open door and into the gardens. "You can't take me away from here, you fool! I'll fall asleep! I have a spell on me!"

"I wanted you awake for this, but perhaps that will make my plan all the better," Pax grunted, holding her tighter. Around the garden, a few of the servants lay on the ground in their own sleeping states.

As Pax brought her through the gate, another sharp invisible prick pierced her finger. But this time also her heart, her lungs, *everywhere*. Aura struggled for breaths, to find the air she desperately needed. Never before had it been like this, to where she couldn't breathe. Her body turned limp in the prince's arms, and her eyes fell shut.

Aura was vaguely aware of her body moving, being carried, the air on her skin, but it seemed like ages before she could open her eyes. And when she did, darkness surrounded her. Water sloshed against her flesh, the prince's arms no longer confining her. She was beneath the surface, and she couldn't breathe, couldn't swim.

Her lungs tightened, the burning sensation in her chest becoming unbearable. Her eyes slowly closed once more, and she felt herself drifting away, dying. Yet she remained there, in her watery grave.

Aura finally peeled her lids open, the same scene unfolding as she struggled to breathe. Without a doubt, she knew that this was meant to be her eternity. One in which she would die over and over again so Sorcha could live.

# 24

# RUSH

The chains bit into Rush's arms, the pain dull but welcomed. It meant whatever the sorceress had done to him was wearing off. The Starnight soldiers stood around him, sneering as he laid on his side.

A blond bearded man spit on the ground beside Rush. "I don't see what's so special about him."

"He's probably got a huge cock," another said.

"I bet it's minuscule, but no one's brave enough to speak the truth," the blond soldier replied.

Rush allowed them to talk, to insult him, as he methodically worked feeling back into his limbs. While they were worried about his manhood, they wouldn't be concerned with the rest of him. His dragon hummed inside him like a second pulse. The beast tried to break free of the spell, clawing and growling, raging and waiting.

The snap of a twig sounded, the first sign of someone approaching, followed by the crashing of heavy, unconcerned boots. The soldiers around Rush straightened, their taunts silenced. Rush lifted his head, hoping they were too distracted to notice how much movement he'd regained in his body.

A shadow emerged from the trees and a thought struck him. If Astor abandoned Aura to make sure this meeting went according to plan, Rush would lock the hawk in a cage then murder him. Pax wanted Aura—she was the priority at this moment.

A figure appeared, one much too short to be the hawk shifter. Rush squinted through the darkness and froze as he made out Pax carrying Aura over his shoulder, her arms hanging limply down his back. Rush's heart thumped painfully in his chest at the sight of her. Aura in this asshole's clutches. The man who'd *murdered* Sorcha. Defenseless. Had the fucker knocked her out, or was it Rush's fault she was this way, that his spell came into effect once she was off palace grounds? It didn't matter— Pax would die, would be shredded apart, left for his dragon to consume, for touching her. And the sorceress—where the fuck was that bitch?

"Put her down, bastard!" he roared and strained against the chains holding him.

Pax's eyes danced with amusement. "You're in no position to tell me what to do with *my* betrothed."

Not yet. But *soon*. His dragon became more present by the moment, and it wouldn't be long before the spell shattered beneath his claws. Rush flexed his muscles, testing his strength.

"What do you think, men?" Pax sauntered to where Rush lay on the ground and stopped. "Should I humor the King of Sin?"

Harsh chuckles rose up from the soldiers, booming off the trees while Pax grinned down at Rush.

"Follow me," he ordered his men. "Bring him."

The men hoisted Rush by his upper arms. His feet dragged in the mud as they followed their damn prince through the woods. Rush forced himself to take steady breaths, to focus on regaining full movement of his body so he could destroy them all.

"Just up here," Pax announced.

A bolt of realization struck Rush then. He'd picked this meeting place for how close they were to the lake. So after the torture began, he could drag the prince to the lake and shove him down into the same waters that Sorcha had been murdered in. Over and over, he would've pushed him into the water before torturing him more. The trees thinned as they walked, giving way to the shore. His breathing became erratic then. His pulse thundered through him and his skin felt hot when they approached the water, stopping at the edge. The lake was still, almost glasslike. It once held an alluring appeal. Plentiful fish, picturesque mountains in the distance, fragrant blossoming trees.

But all of that was overshadowed by death.

"Fuck you," Rush seethed. The men shoved him down onto his knees. "I will tear you apart, you fucking bastard!"

"You want me to put the bitch down?" Pax cooed, seemingly unbothered by Rush's threats. "All right, then."

It took a moment too long for Rush to understand

what was amusing about the prince's request. Aura slid from Pax's shoulder straight into the lake. Water splashed onto Rush's side as her body slipped beneath the surface. Seconds passed, and Rush couldn't stop from imagining the future. *His* future. Cold, dark, and bleak. *Lifeless.*

Inside, his dragon roared louder, clawed harder to escape. To burst free and feel the prince's blood flow between his teeth. Chase down the soldiers and watch them burn. Rush would tear apart anyone his dragon left behind. This bastard brought him to the same lake where he'd murdered Sorcha, where Aura would drown if he couldn't get out of these fucking chains.

The bolt of panic ripped through the barrier imprisoning his dragon. Rush sucked in a breath as the beast emerged. Scales materialized along his skin, spreading, bones elongated, fire flooded his throat, and the chains broke. Smoke rose from his nostrils, seeped out of his lips. The Starnight soldiers shouted, but his pulse thrummed too loudly to understand their last words. And not that he gave a fuck either—they would *perish.*

Flames erupted from his mouth, lighting up the shore. Fire licked across the guards' skin, filling the air with the rancid scent of burnt flesh. Their shouts turned to screams of anguish as his dragon whirled around to face the prince. His vision narrowed on Pax and the prince pulled a sword from his belt. Rush fought the urge to rein in his dragon in order to kill the prince with his own two hands.

But there wasn't time to waste. Aura was drowning.

His dragon lunged forward, and Pax leapt away, out of his path. But he wasn't quick enough—Rush's wing clipped him, hard, sending him flying through the air to the mud. Rush would deal with him in a moment. He lifted Aura from the water in between his talons. She hung there lifeless as water dripped from her hair, her dress. He pulled her close and pressed her protectively to his chest. Against the softer scales, he could feel her heart hammering.

*Alive.*

Satisfied by that knowledge, he turned on Pax.

The prince was sprawled in the mud, his teeth chattering in terror. Pitiful. His dragon reveled in the moment, the wide eyes, gaping mouth, ragged breaths. Rush wanted the death to be slow, painful, leaving a memory behind in its wake that Rush could relish. But Aura's life was more important than giving Pax a long death.

"Rush. Y—your Majesty," Pax pleaded as he pushed up onto his elbows and scrambled backward. "I'll bow down to you. You don't know the truth about your sister. She begged me to be her lover. I felt sorry for her, and then she trapped me on purpose. Her obsession was becoming too much, her lies. I had to. We can talk about—"

Rush slammed his clawed foot down on the prince. Bones snapped and cracked beneath his weight. He felt the heat of Pax's blood, heard his body crunch. *Dead.* His vengeance at last.

Cradling Aura, Rush launched himself into the air. A mix of emotions churned within him, but he focused on her, the woman who he'd once hated but now only wanted desperately to save. He flew to the palace, his wings cracking against the wind, and shifted the moment he landed in the garden. Not a single guard hurried forward to help him as he ran to the doors, stepping over the unconscious bodies scattered about.

Inside wasn't much better with prone guards everywhere. "Astor!" he shouted. However, he didn't come down the stairs or hurry through the hallway. Where the fuck was he? Was he… *No.* He couldn't be dead. Not the one person in his court who was like a brother, who he trusted more than anyone. *Fuck!*

There wasn't time to check right now. He had to get Aura to the cellar first. "I'll fix this," he promised her, and started for the cellar. After she was situated and safe, he would search for the hawk shifter.

Pausing outside the first door, Rush growled. His key was in his torn clothing at the lake. "Damn it." He shifted Aura in his arms and kicked the door. It shuddered against the impact and he did it again, harder this time. The wood splintered around the lock and it flew open. He then charged down the stairs and repeated the motions with the second door until it gave way. As he stepped inside, his heart nearly stopped.

"Sorcha?" Her name fell from his mouth in a choked whisper.

Behind the tied-back curtain, his sister stood beside her spinning wheel, still in her blue dress, her dark hair wild like always. Her bright sapphire gaze met his, then roamed around the room. Rush could've sworn all the blood drained from his body. She was *alive.*

His chest constricted at what that meant… He held Aura tighter against his chest.

"Sorcha," he repeated.

"Rush," she said softly. Her eyes then widened.

"You're unclothed."

"Give me a moment." Thoughts spinning, he hurried into the bedchamber and rested Aura on the mattress with shaking hands. He grabbed the blanket from the end of the bed, shaking it out, and wrapped it around his waist before stepping back out.

Sorcha peered around him when he exited, her lips tilted down as her gaze landed on Aura. "You didn't listen to me."

He dragged in two deep breaths. That wasn't true— he *had* listened. It was simply too late to stop what he'd begun. "I..."

"I told you to break the spell." She rounded the wheel and approached him, her chest heaving. "What have you done?"

He looked at his sister and his confidence crumbled for the first time since he'd become king. "I tried to break it. I'm sorry—I *tried*. I killed Pax after he nearly drowned her, after he spewed lies about you. But Aura is still here." Though she wasn't awake.

Tears filled his sister's eyes. "I hate him. I hate myself for ever being captivated by him, for what he did to Aura, for what *I* did to her, knowing she was his betrothed." She paused, closing her eyes for a moment.

"The spell needs to be broken, Rush. I'm not meant to remain here. When it's time, the gods will allow us to meet again, but until then, I want to be with my child."

Rush swallowed deeply. "The sorceress said I need to break the spindle from your spinning wheel, but I can't touch it anymore. No one can."

Furrowing her brow, she turned back to her spinning wheel. She lifted her fingers and pressed them lightly against the wood, then wrapped her hand around the wheel. "That's not true," she gasped. "It seems *I* can." The line between her brows deepened once more as she released the wheel. With a shaky breath, she wrapped her arms around Rush, squeezing him tight. "I know what needs to be done. When Aura wakes, tell her I would've liked her as a friend. Tell her … that I'm sorry."

"Sorcha, I'm not good without you here. You don't know all the things I've done," he admitted, holding his sister in the way he always should've when she used to hug him.

"Then fix them, Rush. You're not like Pax. Your heart isn't consumed by darkness. Besides, we all have a vicious side." She stepped away from him and pressed a hand to his shoulder, her eyes shining with truth in her words. "Now, I'm going to see if this will work. And if it doesn't, then I'll find a sorceress myself."

"But—"

"Keep fighting your shadows and being the king our court needs, brother. I love you." A smile graced her lips as she grabbed the spindle and snapped it, the crack reverberating through the room like thunder.

"No!" Rush shouted. He needed a minute. Just one to prepare himself for it. He hadn't thought it would break like that when he'd easily removed it to spell Aura. But his sister's body crumpled. He darted forward and caught her before she hit the floor. "Fuck!" Cradling her close, he carried her to the bed and rested her beside Aura.

"Rush?" Astor's voice wavered from the cellar hallway. "Rush, are you down here?" The king brushed the curtain aside to find Astor standing in the doorway. Blood ran down the side of his neck. "Thank the gods!

289

Marion saw you carrying Aura past the kitchens as she woke. Everyone else in the palace is still—"

"Where were you?" he demanded, then held back the curtain and pointed to Aura. "You were supposed to protect her."

"Unconscious." He touched the back of his head and winced. "What happened?"

"The sorceress was right. The spindle needed to be broken off the wheel. But Sorcha was the only one who could do it," Rush said softly. "She saved Aura and herself."

Astor's lips parted in surprise. "If the spell is broken, shouldn't she be awake?"

Rush looked at Aura's heart-shaped face, her long lashes still pressed against her cheeks. Then he glanced at Sorcha, her eyes open and glazed over in the same way when he'd first discovered her dead. Dull. Lifeless. He regretted ever casting the spell—ever depriving her of a peaceful afterlife with her child. And Aura, she deserved to live a happy life.

"We need to give my sister a proper funeral without anyone seeing us." No one knew his sister's ashes weren't already in the royal tomb. It was something he should've done before. But if he had, he wouldn't have learned the truth about Pax, wouldn't have talked to his sister again, and wouldn't have met Aura… So even if he was a bastard, his only regret was Aura not waking.

"Once the guards wake, I need them to prepare a funeral pyre," Rush said. "Tell them to build it but not to burn any of the dead until I give the word."

As Rush carried Sorcha's body through the empty back halls of the palace the next morning, every inch of him was numb. His muscles, his bones, his heart. It didn't matter he had barely gotten any sleep either.

Astor had cleared the path from the cellar to the pyre, and Aura lay in his bed, sleeping. Trapped. But he tried to focus on one task at a time.

Once outside, Rush approached the stone slab surrounded by freshly chopped birch. The white bark lined the table, though with dragon fire, it wasn't necessary. It was simply needed so no one suspected it was a royal being burned.

He brought Sorcha to the table and set her at the center. As he smoothed her skirt and arranged her hair, he took every effort to avoid seeing how ... empty she looked. Before, she wasn't awake, but she was *there*. Now, it was clear she was gone.

He stepped back and rubbed at the ache in his chest. "I'm sorry I couldn't protect you."

But he could protect Aura now. If it wasn't too late...

"I'll see you in the next life, sister," he whispered, and his dragon hung his head. *Come on,* he urged the beast. This needed to be done before anyone noticed, and Astor couldn't delay them from using the pyre forever. They couldn't let word get out that it was possible to bring someone back from the dead.

The dragon stepped forward, shifting. It wasn't the grand send-off Sorcha deserved, and that was his fault.

Another thing he robbed her of. With a deep breath, Rush stirred the flames. They flowed from his scaled mouth, engulfing the Princess of Moonstone.

Rush closed his eyes as the flames reduced his sister to ash, too afraid to see any part of it. Yes, *afraid*. He'd nearly forgotten what that felt like—he'd been a child the last time he allowed himself to be frightened. His dragon kept breathing fire for a few moments before he retreated to his own sorrow. The beast needed to mourn the loss of Sorcha and her dragon too, in his own way.

"I'll have her ashes brought to you," Astor said from behind Rush.

The King of Sin nodded once, then slipped on a fresh set of clothing and strode back into the palace to see Aura before he left for the sorceress. But when he walked into his bedroom, praying she was awake, she wasn't.

And she wasn't alone.

The same bitch sorceress who had spelled Rush in the forest sat beside her.

"Don't you dare move, or I'll kill you both," she said, her voice calm as she spoke. "I got what I wanted, and I know my sister helped you with the spell to raise your loved one. Don't worry, no one knows." The sorceress's fingers spread across her staff. "I'll tell you how to wake her if you vow not to hunt me."

"I'll just get the answer from your sister," he said between gritted teeth.

"You won't. No one finds her if she doesn't want them to. You know this." She tilted her head to the side. "Now, do you want the girl to wake or not?"

Rush held back the urge to let his dragon burn the sorceress to ash. He looked from her to Aura, a desperation consuming him for her to open her eyes. "Yes. I vow not to hunt you."

A hint of a smile crossed the sorceress's lips as she cradled her staff. "Kiss her. If you truly love her, she'll wake. If not, she'll die." With that, she vanished from the room.

Rush tightened his fists, his hands trembling as he studied Aura. She still lay beneath the blankets, her golden hair haloed around her. He sank down beside her, his heart pounding faster than it had all day. Love... He'd never loved any woman that wasn't family before. But he did love her.

As he gazed at her long lashes, her beautiful lips, the lips he wished would move, would curse him for what he'd done to her. He knew with complete certainty that he was in love with the woman he'd once loathed.

"I love you, kitten. Now wake for me," he whispered and pressed his lips to hers.

# AURA

**B**eneath the surface, water sloshed against Aura, her pulse pounding in her ears. She closed her eyes—she didn't know how many times she'd died but believed it didn't matter anymore.

Then something soft brushed her mouth. A delicate caress. Her lids flew open to familiar molten silver eyes as he peered down at her with a furrow between his dark brows.

"You're safe now. The spell is broken," Rush whispered.

Aura gasped for breath and jolted forward in his bed, drinking in all the air she could, air that she hadn't known if she would ever have again. All the moments before her horrific dream stormed back through her, and she screamed.

"You left me locked in my room!" She sobbed, slapping Rush's chest, remembering Pax carrying her out the palace gates, how she was uncertain if the king was alive. "The prince, he—"

Rush's arms folded around her, keeping her from lashing out. "I killed that fucker. I made sure he would never harm you again."

The news of his death didn't stir any melancholic feelings. Not satisfaction. Not remorse. Nothing. Because he was *nothing*. But then fear crawled through her at what could come next. "Starnight will—"

"Do nothing. The prince had me bound with every intention of ending my life. He already killed my sister and no one will blame me for protecting the royal line. The King of Starnight will not touch my court unless he wants his ripped apart," Rush growled, even though his fingers gently combed through Aura's hair.

She thought about it, the guards he'd attacked. He was right—the king wouldn't be foolish enough to start a war with a dragon king after all the things Pax had done. "Is Astor alive? Tanix and Laird… And Pax wasn't alone— there was a sorceress helping him."

"Astor is fine. The guards and servants who were unconscious have woken. As for the sorceress, she and I worked out a bargain."

"I hope the bargain was worth it." She wondered what the sorceress offered for him not to have killed her.

"It was," he murmured, not taking his eyes off her. "My sister aided in breaking the spell. Sorcha wanted you to know that she's so very sorry for everything."

"You spoke to your sister again?"

He nodded. "Sorcha woke this time and was the only one who could snap off the spindle to end the curse. She didn't want to remain here, knowing her child wouldn't awaken too, nor did she want you to stay under a spell. Astor and I gave her a proper send-off for a royal, but we must keep it between us. There would be too many questions and those who would want to bring their loved ones back from death."

Aura's chest tightened. Her life wouldn't have woken the both of them, only the princess. Sorcha had a chance to live again, and she chose not to. Not only for her child but for Aura too. Aura hoped Sorcha could release any guilt she had about her relationship with Pax. A heart couldn't help who they loved, and Pax was the one who'd preyed on the princess. One day, Aura hoped to thank her when the gods decided her time in Grimm was finished.

She took Rush's hand in hers, squeezing it gently. "Your secret is safe with me. I'm so sorry you had to lose her again. Is there anything I can do?"

"I don't want to talk about her anymore. Maybe one day. But not now." His voice wasn't harsh, only exhausted.

Aura shakily shifted to the edge of the bed, her pink dress hugging her body. She was grateful that it wasn't the same color as the one she'd worn when she'd died beneath the water. "I need fresh air." Even though she could breathe now, she wanted to get the brackish taste of the water from her mouth, her tongue, and her lungs.

"I'll take you to the gardens, kitten," Rush said softly, staring at her in a way he never had before, as though she might break.

296

She stood from the bed and stumbled, her legs weak. "Hold onto me," Rush murmured, wrapping his arm around her waist as he walked her out of his room into the hallway.

Two guards she'd seen around the palace now hovered near the walls. Her heart plummeted at the sight—she'd gotten used to seeing Tanix and Laird's familiar faces, and the space seemed empty without them. Not a drop of blood lingered on the floor as if it had never been there at all.

The servants and guards walked with brisk steps or stood stiffly in their assigned places. Fear shone in a few of their faces, not a hint of their normal relaxed states.

As they went outside into daylight, a light breeze ruffled her hair. Her muscles regained their strength, and even though she enjoyed Rush's touch, his warmth, she leaned away from him to breathe a little freer.

They walked in silence to a willow tree near the large area where he would land when in dragon form. Aura rested her back against the trunk, drawing in breath after breath, promising herself she would never take something so simple for granted again. Rush studied her, his gaze intensifying by the moment.

"Remember, you swore you wouldn't lock me in a room ever again. Are you going to keep your word?" She arched a brow.

"You're free to go home, kitten." He sighed and motioned at the open fence. "It's not a trick. You can go to your family. Go back to Starnight." Before she could speak, he dropped to his knees, his head lowered with his chin to his chest. "A king never bows to anyone. A king never apologizes. But I'm sorry. I know what I've done to you should not be forgiven—however, you drew some of the shadows from my heart. You made me *feel* which is something I never expected. So Aura, I bow to you now. Forgive me. Now go."

Aura looked around, noticing the servants, the guards, Brix, and Astor stealing glances at them. Her cheeks heated. "Get up!" she hissed. "There's no need for that."

"Unless it is a different sort of kneeling, I presume?" he cooed as he stood, his chest so close to brushing hers.

Aura swallowed the desire brewing within her and focused on what he'd said about leaving. "You truly expect me to go out that gate and walk the entire way back to Starnight?"

He tilted his head as he moistened his lower lip. "Would you prefer me to fly you home? My dragon won't mind one bit."

"I see you're returning to yourself." She rolled her eyes. "But if you want to be forgiven, then you will have to do more than fly me home."

"A rightful heir of Moonstone already making demands. Go on." He smirked.

"You will not only come to Starnight with me—you will come to my home. You will have a word with my family. If you can get them to forgive you, then so do I."

"Such a simple task." He turned to Astor and gestured him toward them.

The hawk shifter hopped over a shrub, then hurried in their direction. "Yes, Your Majesty."

"Keep watch over the palace until I return."

"With my life," Astor said.

Her gaze returned to Rush, roaming him up and down. "Bring your clothing. My father won't be impressed otherwise." Even though she'd already seen him bare on several occasions, she turned around and focused on the rustle of his clothing so she didn't dwell on everything else that had happened with Pax ... her drowning.

"Now you can properly get acquainted with my dragon," Rush purred.

Aura faced him just as sharp, curving talons pierced from his fingertips and obsidian scales spread across his flesh. Within a couple of moments, the beautiful dark beast broke free, his molten silver eyes growing brighter. Not since he'd stolen her from her court had she been this close to the dragon. Smoke puffed out from his slitted nostrils, and she ran her palm over his scales which were smoother than she'd expected. A low, pleasurable growl escaped him and she smiled.

The dragon knelt and Astor helped Aura onto the beast's back.

"Hold on to the spikes along his spine," Astor called up to her.

As soon as she settled against him and grasped his spikes, the dragon didn't hesitate to leap toward the sky. This time there wasn't the ache to scream when they soared through the air, only the budding sensation to take in everything. She drank in the wonders around her—the clouds so close, the treetops below, all the things she'd never seen before—and never felt more alive.

After a long while of gliding past mountains and forests, over villages and fields, a yellow and brown cottage came into view. Rush circled the area, then descended toward the edge of the forest. As soon as his feet connected with the earth, he knelt to let her slip from his back and down his leg. The dragon shifted, his body shrinking and his scales giving way to soft tan skin. Rush's eyes danced with amusement as her gaze latched onto his perfect form and he pulled his clothing on.

"I want you to return to Moonstone after this." He paused, a flicker of uncertainty in the way he studied her. "I won't force you."

Her eyes widened. "And leave my family here?"

Rush cocked his head, seeming to mull something over. "They can come too. For Astor's sake."

"Yes, for *Astor's* sake…" Aura echoed. She was the first to break away from their stare and walk out of the woods toward the cottage. Her heart pounded as she observed not the home itself but who stood outside its door—her mother and sisters.

Her family gazed around the area before her mother's eyes fell on her.

"Aura!" she shouted and barreled toward her, lifting her skirts as she tore through the field. Her arms folded around Aura and worry filled her eyes. "I've been worried sick! You're not hurt, are you?" She sniffed, wiping away falling tears. Her sisters surrounded them, so her mother released Aura from the hug, then she narrowed her eyes at Rush. "*You!* You dragon beast! You took her from us! Who do you think you are?"

Rush's lips curled upward as he looked at each of the hostile faces, except for her two younger sisters who looked at him with curiosity. "The King of Moonstone. We have much to discuss, but know that your daughter was safer with me than she ever would've been with that bastard prince."

"He's not lying about that," Aura added. "I wanted to

stay with him after learning about the prince's secrets. Prince Pax is more horrible than you can ever imagine. *Was* horrible."

Aura's mother blinked, and her hand went to her heart as something like guilt shone on her face. Screams broke the silence when the two youngest sisters, unable to contain themselves any longer, flung their arms around Aura.

"Sister! Why did you not come see us? Mama won't tell us anything!" Fern shouted.

Saffron peered up at Rush, her nose wrinkled. "Will you teach me to turn into a dragon too?"

Fern pushed her sister aside. "You must be *born* a shifter. But he can fly us somewhere!"

"He will do no such thing." Hana frowned, lifting Saffron into her arms as though Rush would steal her away too. Aura honestly couldn't blame Hana for her fear.

Liana stepped around her sisters and nudged her arm with Aura's, never one to issue hugs.

"I sent you a recipe book," Aura said, bumping her shoulder in return.

"So that was from you! I suspected it, but I would've rather had your presence as a gift."

"Are you certain about that?" She laughed softly.

The sound of hoofbeats drifted within the forest as Aura's father tore through the trees on horseback. He leapt down from his stallion and ran toward Aura, pulling her against his chest. "You're safe. Where is it? Where's that beast you rode in on?"

"He's right here," Rush said, inching forward. "I would like to speak with you and your wife, along with Hana and Liana."

301

Her father stared at Rush, his gaze icy. "Haven't you done enough?"

Both Saffron and Fern interrupted, hugging their father's legs and pulling the edge of his tunic. "Can we come too?" they both asked.

"Not now," Hana batted them away. "Go to your room and play for a little while."

They both stuck their tongues out at Hana while releasing a fit of giggles as they ran into the house.

"Give the King of Moonstone an opportunity, Father," Aura said. "Sometimes we do things with a reason, even though others may think it's wrong. But believe me when I say marrying Prince Pax would've been worse than death for me."

Aura's father pressed his strong hands on her shoulders. "Then I will listen. For you only."

Her mother pursed her lips and motioned Liana into the house with her father behind them.

As Rush stepped inside, Hana drew Aura back by the shoulder, and said in a whisper, "Something doesn't feel right. I know him, don't I? Somehow I know I've met the king before. It's like I'm missing something. You know what it is, don't you?"

Aura took a deep breath, unable to keep this part from her sister. "You did meet Rush before, once. Also a man named Astor who works for the king. You were given a potion to forget your earlier encounters with them. However, Astor should be the one to tell you the rest. Not me. Once you talk to him, I'll be here in any way you need. I promise. You're my sister and I love you."

"Astor…" Hana inhaled a sharp breath, her hand grasping a teardrop ruby hanging from a gold chain that

302

Aura had never seen before. "I-I've talked to him a few times, and he brought me flowers. No one's ever done that before him. I'm going to hate him, aren't I?" The last few words came out hushed.

Aura bit her lip. "Maybe for a little while. That all depends on you though. I once hated them both, but now I see them differently." She lowered her head, a pit forming in her stomach. "You may even hate me since I believed it was best for you to forget at the time."

Hana's body trembled as a rack of sobs escaped her. "You deserve to hate me more. I knew what the prince was doing with other women. I just wanted you to be happy. I've always wanted that, and instead I stayed silent."

Aura circled her arms around the middle sister and tears pricked her eyes. "I know you did. *Do.* And maybe now I can be. Come on." She led Hana inside to the sweet scent of strawberries and cake, and she knew she needed to introduce her twin sister to Marion at some point. They walked down the short hallway to the sitting room where Rush sat across from her parents and Liana. When his gaze found Hana, he started his story at the beginning, admitting to his faults, how his sister had held a journal that revealed Pax to be her love, how he'd believed the princess had drowned herself, that Hana had come to save Aura and he'd given her a forgetting potion. He went into great depth about everything except how he'd gotten Astor to woo Hana and spelling Aura, saying only that he'd taken her as a way of revenge against Pax. It was more than she'd expected him to confess, but it was enough for now.

"I care for your daughter greatly, and I vow to prove

it," Rush said, casting his attention to her father. "And I know she won't come to Moonstone without her family. Therefore, if you agree to come, I'll make you a duke. Your family will have as many guards and servants as you wish, and a grand home near the city. Hana will have a shop of her choosing while Liana will have a bakery, the finest Moonstone has to offer."

Liana beamed, a bright smile on her face as she clasped her hands together. "Not just any bakery, but the finest? Please tell me I'm not dreaming."

Aura's eyes widened in surprise. Rush knew her sister would never refuse such a gift, a way to easily get her to come to Moonstone ... and forgive him. Hana remained quiet which was unusual for her, but she was most likely wanting to learn the story's entirety.

"And my girls will be taken care of? All of them?" her mother asked, perking up in her seat over the news.

"All of them," Rush promised.

"Can we have this in writing?" her mother added.

He lifted one brow. "You have my word, but if it makes you feel more secure."

"I will never agree that you taking my daughter was the right decision. However, you've proposed a fair deal." Her father rubbed his chin, then looked at Aura. "But what do you want? If the Starnight King ever finds out you were at the palace and acted against his son, things here might not go so well. Is everything the Moonstone King said true?"

Aura's father could tell when she was lying, and this was a way for him to know if Rush was being deceitful. "It's true. Prince Pax took lovers, he murdered Rush's sister, and then he was either going to force me into silence or murder me." She remembered Pax's anger toward her, his fingers digging into her flesh while carrying her writhing body from the palace. But somehow her voice remained steady as she spoke, "I don't want to stay in Starnight and be reminded of how my life revolved around the prince. I'd rather begin a new tale."

"We should go to Moonstone," her mother announced, her gaze shifting from Rush to Aura as though she were about to propose a match right there after hearing the full story.

She didn't want her mother to act like she had when Aura was betrothed to Pax. This wasn't the same—Rush was the King of Sin, dabbled with as many women as he pleased. He may have said he cared about her, but that didn't mean he loved her. "May I speak to the king alone?" Aura asked.

"Of course. Take your time," her mother said, ushering her father and sisters out of the room.

Once the door shut behind her parents, Aura whirled on Rush and pressed her hands to the chair's arms as she leaned toward him. "I'm grateful for what you are doing, but you were supposed to get genuine forgiveness. Not buy it with gifts. I know you didn't tell them every detail of what happened, and that's fine because they wouldn't understand. The issue is that you have my mother believing we will get betrothed!"

Rush grasped Aura by the waist and pulled her into his lap as she gasped. "Perhaps we will. When I saw the sorceress at the palace, she told me to completely break the spell, I had to kiss you. If I didn't love you, then you would've died instead." He tucked a lock of hair behind her ear. "So you now know my truth—I love you, kitten.

I'll prove to your family how deeply I do, if you'll allow me to court you."

Her brows rose. "*Court me?*" Love? He didn't only care about her but *loved* her. She could've died from what the sorceress had told him to do, which would've been better than being trapped beneath the water in an endless cycle of deaths, but his kiss saved her. A kiss of unexpected love.

"Yes. We can start over, properly this time," he drawled, trailing his fingers up her spine while the other gripped her waist and drew her closer. "We can pretend I had come to Starnight." His lips found hers, coasting gently across. "Saw you at one of the balls and lured you away."

"Even though I was betrothed?" she asked, her voice breathy.

"I wouldn't have given a fuck. You know that." He leaned in and lifted her chin, his smoky scent intoxicating. "You still would've been mine. Let me court you."

She couldn't stop the laughter from bubbling up her throat at the ridiculousness of it. Yet she wanted that, *absolutely* wanted that. "Yes, you may court me, but does that mean chaste kisses, keeping our hands to ourselves, and leaving our clothing on?"

Somehow he pulled her even closer, her eyelids fluttering when she felt his hardness beneath her. "Let's not get hasty now," he said in a gruff voice. "I am the King of Sin after all."

"Our first proper outing will be in your palace gardens. You on your knees and working in the dirt beside me." If he did this, she would gift him three words in return. Words that were aching to come out already. *I*

306

*love you.* She didn't know how they both came to that point after so much animosity between one another, after a spell that should've only made her hate him more. Yet the effect had been opposite, and though no one would understand it, she did. And that was what mattered most of all.

Rush ran his finger across her lower lip. "Oh, I promise you we will both be on our knees and getting filthier than you could ever imagine."

# RUSH

**R**ush wasn't far from the pristine home he'd purchased from an older couple to give to Aura's family. At first they were reluctant to sell, but Rush had made it worth their while. A dragon king always does.

He peered up at the sky as he rode his horse and gripped the reins of another mare. "Send down your prayers, sister. Today will be the first time I'll be a proper gentleman."

Before he'd left, Astor had arched his brow at seeing Rush change shirt after shirt until he settled on one that was buttoned all the way up. He couldn't remember the last time he'd done something so ridiculous. Rush wasn't the only one having a meeting today with one of the sisters—Astor was going to see Hana this evening, to confess everything, the lies, the truths, how he felt.

Rush had sent the King of Starnight a letter about what his son had done to the Moonstone Princess. And in return, what Rush had done to Pax. An eye for an eye. He didn't leave out that if the king retaliated, he would burn the entire palace down. The king only wrote back with promises of peace.

As Rush approached Aura's home, he halted his horse and slipped from its back. Aura opened the door and sprinted across the cobblestone. Rush smirked at her from beside his horse while holding the reins of her mare. Since he was courting her, he should've knocked on the door. Spoken to her father. Asked her to accompany him, despite the fact that this was a preplanned outing. But she hadn't given him the chance.

"You're late," she said, placing her hands on her hips, a smile curling the edges of her lips as she slowed her steps and walked toward him.

"I'm on time." He lifted a brow. Aura and her family had finally settled in to the new home, so the first courting had been arranged. Every moment of waiting had felt like a lifetime.

And as though she couldn't hold her eagerness any longer, she flung her arms around his neck. "I thought you might come earlier."

Rush chuckled, surprised by her affection as he drew her close. "I do have a court to run, kitten."

"Excuses." She laughed and stepped out of his embrace, then reached up to the top button of his shirt. "So proper today. I think we should undo one of these."

"Thank the gods."

She rolled her eyes and peered up at him with a smile.

"Help me on the mare?"

"I think you just want me to touch you," Rush drawled, taking her by the waist and lifting her onto the mare, his hands lingering. *Gods*, she was as beautiful as starlight, like her scent.

"Perhaps." She laughed, and when he didn't remove his hands, she added, "You promised me an orchard at the palace."

"So I did," he said. "The gardener spent over a week clearing a plot of land behind the gardens for you. You can plant whatever you wish."

"I suppose it's time for you to get your hands dirty then, Your Majesty."

"For you, I will." He chuckled again.

Kneeling in the dirt, gloved-hands covered in it, Rush feigned care with his sapling. Aura had walked the empty orchard, directing the gardener where to place each type of tree, then asked her a handful of questions before she left. It was then that Aura turned her full attention to Rush again. Instructing him with more confidence than he'd expected. He wasn't sure if what she told him was true, but he would follow each step she gave with precision.

"Then we just brush the soil back into the hole," she said, burying the roots of her fruit tree.

There was nothing she could plant that would be sweeter than the sight of her at his side. Hidden away from the prying eyes of his court, she tucked a small wisp of a tree into a hole. Her golden hair was pinned up, away from her neck, her skirt bunched up around her knees, exposing her smooth legs. He imagined caressing them, slipping between them, discovering what other garments she wore beneath the cream-colored silk.

"You have to plant the tree if you want it to grow. Not *look* at it." He caught a hint of her smile even though she didn't glance up from her work.

Rush smirked, peeling off his gloves. "Oh, I'm certainly looking at something. Very smooth stems." His fingertips danced over her ankle and trailed up her calf, pulling a soft laugh from her. When his hand slipped beneath her skirts to skate over her center, she gasped. "They lead to my favorite flower."

"We are planting fruit trees," she said, her voice breathy. "Not flowers."

Rush moved closer, shifting his body toward her, and nipped at her ear. "Would you like it if I planted myself in you, kitten? So deep and so hard that—"

"You've done a lot of things lately. Things you didn't have to do." She sucked in a breath as his fingers crept higher up her thigh.

"I didn't have to. But I did them." He kissed her neck, breathed her in. "Your father is a duke with a fine estate. Liana has her bakery, Hana her beauty shop, and the twins are designing their own tree house with my best builder. Judging by my treasury, your mother is filling her days by putting together enormous dowries for each of you."

"Yes, you've effectively bought their forgiveness." She rolled her eyes and drew him closer, his chest against hers, the sweet smell of starlight surrounding him, a scent he would never tire of. "But I'm not impressed with your riches."

"No." He swooped her off her knees, positioning her on his lap to straddle him. Another gasp escaped her as he stared into her beautiful violet eyes. So lovely, so kind, and he couldn't help but loathe himself for what he'd almost done to her, a woman that now held his heart so fully. "What are you impressed by then?" he purred.

"That when you care about someone fiercely, you would do anything to protect them, to make them happy."

"Don't tell anyone my secret," he whispered and placed a gentle kiss to her jaw. His hands slipped to her backside, drawing her closer, and she moaned as he hardened against her. "I believe this is something else you like, isn't it? My cock inside you?"

"Are you certain of that?" she teased while reaching between them to unfasten the laces of his trousers.

"Let me remind you," he drawled. "Please." For once, the King of Sin's voice came out raw, desperate. He hadn't touched her in what felt like so long, and his pulse sped, yearning to hear her moan his name as he drove them both to climax. She held his gaze, her chest rising and falling with heady breaths

"The King of Sin doesn't beg," she said with a grin. "He pleasures me without remorse and makes it so I yearn for him when he doesn't. The way I have been since we last touched." Then she pressed her mouth to his.

As Rush slipped his tongue between her lips, her sweet flavor caressed his taste buds. He groaned. *So damn good.* Like sugar. Like bliss. Rush may never have begged, but when he was with Aura, he wasn't only the King of Sin. He was just *himself*.

Her palms fell upon his chest and glided down his abs until they reached the edge of his tunic. She broke away to lift the fabric over his head. "Wreck me."

"Sinfully," he said in a gruff voice against her lips. His hands skimmed up her thighs, slipping beneath her skirts to find her undergarments already soaked for him. She rolled her hips forward, grinding against his hand. He pressed two fingers into her heat as he trailed kisses down her neck.

As she rode his hand, he needed to feel her warmth around his cock, to feel her ride him instead. He drew his hand back, and she released a needy sound, the same sound he was holding back. She watched him with a dilated stare and he licked her arousal from his fingertips.

Aura sucked in a breath and pulled his trousers down his hips so she could free his hard length. Rush smirked and grabbed her undergarments, ripping them off.

"Black," he quipped. "I was wondering."

Aura silenced him by brushing her core against the tip of his cock, driving him mad. "All these years I yearned for something that wasn't real. But you're more real than anything," she rasped. "Even when you're impossible."

Rush's lips spread into a wide grin. He would continue to be impossible—it was too entertaining to be anything else. "I'm all yours, kitten. And I want *you* to wreck *me*."

With that, Aura sank down on him with a beautiful moan. Rush tilted his head back and gave a low groan as he peeled her dress from her body. His palms skated over her skin, grazing her breasts, her sides, her thighs, until he grabbed her waist and helped her grind down on him. She rolled her hips. Taking and giving, lifting and lowering, making the King of Sin himself want to beg for more. Always. Ruining him a little more each time. It was impossible for him not to shift his hips to meet with a thrust. To bury himself deeper. Harder.

Aura's pace grew faster and she wrapped her hands around his neck, tugging him closer as she brought her mouth to his. Rush swallowed the sounds of her pleasure as she came, her body vibrating against his while she took him over the edge to wherever she damn well pleased. He would follow her anywhere, something he never thought he would do with anyone. But she'd proven him wrong.

As she relaxed against him, he flipped them both so she was on her back beneath him, the emerald hedges surrounding them.

"Destroy me again and again, Aura." He kissed the tip of her nose, her cheeks, her forehead. "Because I love you. Even if you don't ever forgive me, I vow I will always protect you."

She stared up at him with wide eyes. "The King of Sin doesn't need to vow anything to me because I already know. And I forgive him." She cradled his face and kissed his lips once more. "I love you."

Rush stilled. Even though she was here with him, even though she'd fucked him, allowed him to court her, he didn't believe she would return the sentiment. Not after the horrific things he'd done. However, he was trying to make it up to her, to be good for her in the way she deserved. "I think I need to hear those words again, kitten."

She lifted her head so she could murmur in his ear. "I love you. Now I do believe you need to finish planting

314

the tree."

Rush smirked. "I have other *seeds* I need to plant first, and then for you, I will plant as many trees as you wish." He lined himself with her as her fingers gripped his back.

"Now, destroy me, Your Majesty," she demanded.

**Did you enjoy Spindle of Sin?**

Authors always appreciate reviews, whether long or short.

**Want another series like Once Upon A Wicked Villain? Try Vampires in Wonderland, beginning with the short story prequel, Rav.**

**You think you know Wonderland. But you don't.**

Imogen, the Queen of Hearts, is known for taking the hearts of those who betray her, including her servants. Her king, Rav, ventures to the mortal world to lure in new prey to replace their dwindling help. One bite, one simple exchange of her blood is all it will take for a mortal to become one of them. And this time, Rav chooses a girl named Alice.

# ALSO FROM CANDACE ROBINSON

**Wicked Souls Duology**
Vault of Glass
Bride of Glass

**Marked by Magic**
The Bone Valley
Merciless Stars

**Cruel Curses Trilogy**
Clouded By Envy
Veiled By Desire
Shadowed By Despair

**Cursed Hearts Duology**
Lyrics & Curses
Music & Mirrors

**Immortal Letters Duology**
Dearest Clementine: Dark and Romantic Monstrous Tales
Dearest Dorin: A Romantic Ghostly Tale

**Campfire Fantasy Tales Series**
Lullaby of Flames
A Layer Hidden
The Celebration Game
Mirror, Mirror

**And Then There Was Silence**
**These Vicious Thorns: Tales of the Lovely Grim**
**Between the Quiet**

## ALSO FROM AMBER R. DUELL

**The Dark Dreamer Trilogy**
Dream Keeper
Dark Consort
Night Warden

**Forgotten Gods**
Fragile Chaos

**Faeries of Oz Series**
Lion (Short Story Prequel)
Tin
Crow
Ozma
Tik-Tok

**Darkness Series: Temptation**
Darkness Whispered

**The Prince's Wing**
**When Stars Are Bright**

**Vampires in Wonderland Series**
Rav (Short Story Prequel)
Maddie
Chess
Knave

**Once Upon A Wicked Villain Series**
Spindle of Sin

## Acknowledgments

We had such a great time creating this new world of ours that was inspired by the Grimms' Sleeping Beauty fairy tale! Going into this new series we knew we wanted to focus on villains. There is just something intriguing to know why a villain does the things they do. And for the readers that have come on this journey with us, thank you!

To our families and friends, you know how much work writing a book is so thank you for your never-ending support. To Amber H. for being the master at helping us pick out those last fixes. Jerica for finding those awkward spots. To Lindsay, Ann, Marea, Ariella, and Victoria, you guys are so incredibly amazing!

Now that our Sleeping Beauty retelling has come to a close, our next villain can be found in our upcoming Rapunzel story!

## About the Authors

Candace Robinson spends her days consumed by words and hoping to one day find her own DeLorean time machine. Her life consists of avoiding migraines, admiring Bonsai trees, watching classic movies, and living with her husband and daughter in Texas—where it can be forty degrees one day and eighty the next.

Amber R. Duell was born and raised in a small town in Central New York. While it will always be home, she's constantly moving with her husband and two sons as a military wife. She does her best writing in the middle of the night, surviving the daylight hours with massive amounts of caffeine. When not reading or writing, she enjoys snowboarding, embroidering, and snuggling with her cats.

Made in United States
North Haven, CT
25 July 2024

55450215R00198